The Journey Back

By

Conrad Jones

Author's Note.

War is not the saddest thing on the Earth. The old men who start them are much sadder, yet people still listen to them. I realise soldiers are not to question why, but to do or die but don't they still have the sense of right and wrong?

Shooting civilians and rape are personal choices, not following orders. Allowing one man to begin a conflict against a peaceful European nation and doing nothing, is the saddest thing I've seen. History teaches us the warmongers are to blame and yet we watch them and do nothing.

I hope one day, if the cause is wrong, people will refuse to fight and say, 'no more…'

Dedication

I never thought there would be a sequel to The Journey but here it is. You asked me to write it. I have.

I hope I haven't let you down…x

THE JOURNEY BACK

JUST TRYING TO GET HOME...

THE JOURNEY BACK

CONRAD JONES

CONRAD JONES

PROLOGUE

Fifteen Years Ago

Beb felt like he was being crushed. His lungs were burning, and his mouth was full of sand. He tried to move, but his limbs were trapped, and he couldn't budge. He was breathing through his nostrils. His right arm was bent across his face and had created an air pocket, but the oxygen was dwindling, making it difficult to breathe. His body was screaming for him to breathe deeper, but he knew that if he did, his lungs would be filled with burning sand. The sand was compacted around him, restricting his movements, and his muscles were cramping. He wriggled his toes and fingers, then his feet and hands, trying to make some room between him and the sand that engulfed him. The movement sent white hot pain down his spine. His neck was injured, the soft tissue bruised, and the muscles tightened like a vice around the nerves. Beb knew he was going to suffocate if he didn't move right then. He began to thrash against the crushing weight, moving a millimetre more each time, every muscle twitching and contracting. His oxygen was depleted, and his head was beginning to spin. White lights exploded in his mind like giant camera flashes and all the time his body told him to breathe. Just suck it in, deep and hard. He knew he was fading, his awareness dulling, sleep beckoning. A long dark sleep where there were no dreams, no feeling, no anything. Relax and let it happen. It would be easier to stay here.

1

He saw his mother standing over him, looking down, her face radiant.

Breathe, Beb. Fight for your life, son…

Beb gave one more mammoth jerk of his muscles and felt the sand loosen. One arm pushed upward and penetrated the surface. He could feel the cold air on his skin and her calling to him inside his head.

Come on, Beb. Do you want to live or die?

With an almighty effort, he managed to turn slightly onto his front and used his knees and arms to push upwards. He broke the tension, and the sand fell around him. Fresh air reached him, and he spat sand from his mouth before sucking in a lungful of air, deeper than he had ever breathed before. The oxygen coursed through his body as he sucked in breath after breath, driving himself upright. He crouched and coughed and spluttered for a long time, trying to regain control of his senses as the panic subsided.

Every muscle and sinew in his body ached, and he rubbed the sand from his nose and eyes, spitting into the sand each time he exhaled. The silence of the desert engulfed him, and he embraced it. It had been his home for years, but now it felt alien to him. Something had shifted in his psyche. He instinctively felt for his gold coin. It was the only thing he had from his past, and it was the only lifeline he had for his future. The coin was gone. So was his mother. He had heard her voice so clearly for the first time in years. It was crystal clear and so close to him. His heart broke, and he sobbed for the family he missed so terribly, but most of all, he sobbed for himself and his wretched life.

The memory of what happened was fractured and only fleeting images remained. He had been sleeping near to Damilola and the goats when he felt a devastating blow to his neck at the base of his skull. A blanket was thrown over his head. He remembered being dragged and then he vaguely remembered the sensation of being dropped into a hole, the sand cold around him as it was shovelled over him and then there was nothing until he woke up suffocating. How long he had been there, he didn't know. Time had warped into then and now, the measurement a mystery. Another tribe must have attacked them while they slept. There was no other explanation.

He looked around for any sign of Damilola, but it was dark and there was nothing but the endless desert. A breeze was blowing, shifting the top layer of sand, covering tracks, and destroying any evidence of what happened to him. The shifting sands of the desert gave nothing away. His throat was parched, and he began to shiver from the cold. He had been with the Tuareg long enough to know he wouldn't last long in the Sahara without water and shelter. Staying still wasn't an option. Move or die.

CHAPTER 1

Present Day

Kissie, Chernobyl

When Kissie was born, she was Beb's youngest sister, but now she was his only sister. Her two older sisters, Oke and Isime were missing, presumed drowned during their fateful crossing of the Mediterranean, along with their mother, Esse. Beb hadn't made it that far, kidnapped when their truck was stolen with him asleep inside it. The family had searched for him for days, but when the truck was found burnt out in the desert, they had to assume he was dead. Kissie had seen her mother close to breaking point, and she refused to leave but the Boko was relentless, attacking everything and everyone in their path. The war was moving closer every day, and they had to leave. Sadly, only Kissie and Kalu survived the boat sinking.

Kissie and her father, Kalu, had believed Beb was killed in the Sahara but ten years after they'd settled in London, he was miraculously returned to them. He told them he'd been taken from the truck and sold as a slave to a Tuareg tribe and had travelled around the Sahara with the nomads for ten years. The desert had become his prison, which needed no guards or bars. Leaving the caravan which fed and watered him was suicide and if he hadn't taken the chance to escape when he did, he would still be tending the goats.

His return from the dead had been earth-shatteringly good news. It had been ten long years since they'd seen him, and they felt so blessed. Neither realised Beb wasn't Beb at all. He looked so like him, spoke like him, smiled like him. Why would they think otherwise?

It had gone well at first, but as the years passed, his increasingly bizarre behaviour had caused a rift between the siblings, and they grew apart. Kissie didn't feel the bond between them that they'd had as children. It wasn't there and despite her best efforts, she couldn't rekindle it. Before his kidnap, he had been such a kind and considerate boy. Now, he was selfish, inconsiderate, and rude. He made no effort at all, and the way he looked at her sometimes made her uncomfortable. Even her friends commented on how odd he was, staring at females like a dog staring at a pork chop. Kissie put it down to the fact he hadn't seen a woman's body since being a child. He struggled to relearn English and although Kalu spent hours teaching him, he was slow to learn. Young Beb had been intelligent and quick on the uptake. Beb was lazy and seemed to have no desire to study and become educated and he was a constant drain on her father's wallet. Kalu was so riddled with guilt, he allowed Beb too much leeway, and that caused arguments between Kissie and her father.

The years ticked by and while Beb the impostor was deciding what he wanted to do with his life, Kissie had performed well at school and university, gaining a PhD in radiobiology; her dissertation was a study of the lasting effects of the Chernobyl disaster on the environment, humans, plants, and animals. She wanted to apply her degree to her working life and earned a position on a research project working in and around Chernobyl and the abandoned town of Pripyat. It was her ideal position, and she left London with high hopes and a thirst for knowledge. Leaving her father at the airport had been emotional. Their sense of the loss of Esse, Oke, and Isime was debilitating and their love for each other was what had got them through the dark times. No words needed to be spoken. Their love was unconditional. Her father had held her tightly and told her to come home safely, and she promised she would.

Kissie was eight weeks into the research project with an international team of scientists from all over the planet, when the first warnings of a military build-up across the border in Belarus began. It appeared Russia was posturing and showing the Ukrainians what they thought about them joining NATO. At first, the locals were saying they'd seen it all before and Putin was sabre rattling, but the rumours persisted and became increasingly urgent. Russia began a series of war games close to the border, which the news was describing as a cover-up for the increasing deployment of men and machines. It was too much for some of the scientists. Nine of the team had packed their bags and headed home, afraid of an invasion, but Kissie and six others remained, working as normally as they could under the circumstances. Their workload had increased to compensate for their colleagues' departure, and the atmosphere among those who stayed in the surrounding area was tinged with fear and the expectation of impending conflict. Many of the Ukrainian workers in and around the affected area had gone home to their cities to be with their families. The threat of invasion was becoming a reality. Their departure in numbers increased tensions among the remaining workers. Ukrainian troops were arriving along the border in increasing numbers, and Kissie noticed many of them were volunteers. Their uniforms were either different from the regular army or non-existent. Some wore tracksuits and trainers but donned helmets and carried weapons. It was a worrying time, and although she felt anxious, she steeled herself to hope for the best and enjoy her work while she could. False alarms had happened before. Maybe they would again.

The research team was short on numbers so Kissie was working alone in the Red Woods, collecting fungi, which were very good at absorbing Cesium-137 and poisoning the locals who ate them. The woodland floor was peat covered with a layer of decaying leaves, branches, acorns, and moss. Fungi thrived on it, but the radiation they absorbed was invisible. Even the trees absorbed it and it was engrained in every molecule of the wood. The locals who returned to the abandoned villages in the area collected the wood and burnt it as fuel, unwittingly releasing the radiation back into the air. Everything was contaminated and would be for centuries.

She used a dosimeter over a cluster of misshapen mushrooms, and it responded enthusiastically, crackling loudly. Kissie whistled at the reading.

'I can't believe people are still eating these little buggers,' she said to herself. 'These are going to give you glow-in-the-dark superpowers, but you won't be able to enjoy them for very long.'

'Kissie,' her comms buzzed.

'Hello,' Kissie said.

'Where are you, Kissie?' her team leader asked through the speaker. She was a professor from the USA called Angela.

'I'm in the Red Woods about three kilometres east of the river,' Kissie answered. She checked her watch. It was too early to be packing up. 'What's up, boss?'

'I need you to make your way to the Pripyat Road,' Angela said. Her voice was calm, but there was an edge to it. She sounded concerned about something. 'A red Toyota minibus will pick you up. Radio in when you reach the road.'

'A red minibus?' Kissie said. 'What happened to our rusty white one?'

'Get there as quickly as possible,' Angela said, ignoring her question. The rusty minibus had been a standing joke among the team since they arrived.

'You want me to go now?' Kissie asked, frowning. A sense of vulnerability came over her. The hairs on the back of her neck bristled, causing her to shiver. It was roughly two kilometres back to the road. It was uphill and there were no paths. She had two heavy bags and a tripod to carry, and it had taken two of them to carry it all and set it up. 'Obviously, I'm on my own. It will take me a while to pack up my gear.'

'Leave the equipment,' Angela said. The menacing silence following the order made Kissie shiver.

'You want me to leave all this equipment here in the woods?' Kissie asked, shaking her head. 'It's thousands of pounds' worth.'

'I know how much it costs, Kissie,' Angela said. 'But I need you to leave it and get to the road now.'

'You're frightening me. What has happened?'

'There's been an incident and we need to regroup immediately back at the hotel,' Angela said. 'The equipment will be safe. Those woods are contaminated. No one will touch it.'

'I'm aware they're contaminated.' Kissie chuckled, but it was a nervous laugh. 'Everything here is contaminated. That's why we're here.'

'Leave it and get to the road,' Angela repeated. She didn't share the mirth.

'Okay. I'll set off now. It'll take me fifteen minutes.'

'Make it ten, Kissie,' Angela said. 'You need to run.'

CHAPTER 2

Beb: The Sahara: Fifteen Years Ago

Beb didn't know how long he'd taken to recover enough to compose himself and think straight. It had taken a long time to consider standing and walking, but this was desert time, which is different to time generally. Everything is more urgent in the desert.

In a moderate climate, a human can last three to four days without water, but in the desert, half that. Most people would last no more than a day in the desert sun without sustenance and shelter. Beb was hardened to its extremities, but even so, the clock was ticking, and his strength was sapped by the injury to his neck. His nerves were pinched by the swelling, and it was affecting his left leg. His hip was numb, and the limb wasn't functioning as it should. He was walking as if one leg was longer than the other.

As the sunrise appeared in the east, he spotted the silhouette of a huge dune. It looked to be about a mile away. A mile before sunrise was doable if he left now. If he didn't reach it or it was further away than it looked, he would be in trouble.

His options were limited. The Tuareg had gone over the border for supplies, and they would have returned from Morocco by now, and if he climbed the dune, he may be able to see their fires. He needed to reach them and warn them that he and Damilola had been attacked and the goats were gone. Their attackers would know they were attached to a larger tribe somewhere and they could be fixing to attack the main caravan.

Beb set his sights on the dune and walked in an ungainly manner as quickly as he could.

The sun was hovering on the horizon as dawn broke and the temperature began to rise. Beb was struggling. The dune didn't appear to be any closer, but he knew that was a trick of the light in the desert. Things in the distance shifted and danced and sometimes vanished.

His throat was painfully dry, and he knew he was running on empty. He was in the death zone. His mind drifted back to a time when all he worried about was his homework. A time before he was torn from his mother and father and his sisters. Their faces floated by in his mind, each one smiling, happy, and healthy. He wished he knew where they were now, and he wished he was with them. Sometimes, he heard his mother's voice. Sometimes he could smell her. He wished he could hear her voice again. They were going to London, where the streets were paved with gold. He read that in a book when he was small. His father read it with him. He would find them one day.

An hour later, he was at the base of the dune, and he rested for a few minutes before he set off up the ridge towards the top. His feet were sinking into the soft sand, making it hard going, and his breathing was quick and shallow. Every breath burnt the delicate tissues in his lungs. The progress was slow, but eventually, he reached the top. He turned three-hundred and sixty degrees, looking for plumes of smoke, but there were none. He sat heavily in the sand and stared at the never-ending dunes which stretched to the horizon in every direction and his tears left tracks across his cheeks; they dripped from his chin into the sand and vanished instantly.

CHAPTER 3

Damilola: London

Damilola took the Tube to St John's Wood. He took the park exit from the station and walked past Lord's Cricket Ground and entered Regent's Park through the west entrance. It was cold and overcast and the traffic was light. In the park, there were several gatherings taking place, a group of mothers with pushchairs were laughing at something, a group of joggers were planning their route, some of them jogging on the spot, which amused him, and a group of teenagers were arguing with a dog walker about a burst football. His Staffordshire Bull Terrier had attacked it and he was claiming they shouldn't have kicked the ball towards him. The teenagers were insisting he should have his dog on a lead, and they wanted financial compensation for the ball. The Staffie was snarling like a demon and the teenagers kept their distance.

He spotted two dog walkers to his left and several people reading on benches, but none of them were the people he was looking for. He was nervous and excited and sweat trickled down his back. This could be the opportunity for him to break away from his adopted family. He was a cuckoo, after all, and it was time to fly the nest. They had served their purpose and transported him from his servile life in the desert, wandering eternally with only the goats as friends, to this cosmopolitan metropolis, where opportunity abounded if you had money. He didn't have money, but Kalu did, and he had stolen two of his credit cards and acquired three of his own online, bringing his stake to twenty-two thousand pounds. Kalu would soon notice his cards were gone, as he wasn't a stupid man by any stretch of the imagination but by that time, Damilola planned to be on the way to having a place of his own, with a pocket full of cash, a BMW, and all the designer clobber he wanted. This was his shot at the life he'd desired for as long as he could remember. A life of riches and luxuries, earned easily by buying and selling class-As. It involved no studying, no revision, and no hard work.

Damilola had arranged the meeting through an Algerian woman he'd known for a few months. They called her Jet, and she knew everyone worth knowing in the local underworld. She was at the top of her tree. He'd been buying sniff from one of her minions for over twelve months before he was trusted enough to be introduced to her. After a few months of chatting, he'd been badgering her to be part of her network, but she was reluctant and distrusting of anyone she didn't know well. He explained how he'd spent years enslaved by nomads in the Sahara and how he came to be in London. She didn't believe him at first, but when he told her how his mother and sisters had drowned attempting the crossing, she looked at him with different eyes. It softened her attitude towards him.

When she told him she would consider it if he could produce a twenty-grand investment to get him started, he jumped at the opportunity. Of course, he didn't have twenty-grand, and he had no means of borrowing such an amount, so he used his initiative and acquired ten-grand of credit across several cards in his name and stole the rest from Kalu.

He took the path to the right and kept walking, his hands shoved deep into his pockets, his collar up to keep the cold from his skin. This climate was shit. He could never get warm. His years of walking barefoot and topless in the sand had made him sensitive to the cold and dampness of London. He hated the place. Most of it was a shithole, and he had plans to move to California or Florida, where the sun was always shining, and all the women were beautiful. That was the plan. It would take a few years of working for Jet, but he would do some wheeling and dealing himself on the side and build up his pot. She would never know the difference.

He'd already made a few enquiries about shifting crack cocaine in kilo bundles to a crew of Albanians who worked over at Finsbury Park. They said they would take whatever he could get at the right price. They seemed like nice guys. Everyone told him to avoid them as they were dangerous and absolutely ruthless when it came to business, but he had made a connection. He thought they liked him because he was an immigrant like them, trying to make his way in a foreign land with no education and no assets. Maybe they respected that. Whatever the reason, they were keen for him to bring them some drugs. One step at a time, he would get to where he wanted to be.

'Hey,' a voice called from his left. He turned to see a pretty black woman, about nineteen to twenty-ish. Her hair was dreaded but short. 'Are you Beb?'

'Nice bangs,' Damilola said, commenting on her hair. He was instantly drawn to her. 'I love your hair.'

'What are you, an image consultant?'

'No. I'm just saying,' Damilola said, smiling. The woman didn't smile back. 'Come on. It's nice to be nice.'

'Are you Beb?'

'Who's asking?'

'Don't play games. Jet sent me,' the girl said, walking away. 'Follow me.'

'What's your name?' Damilola asked. He jogged to catch-up with her. She strode on without answering. He clocked how good her ass looked in her jeans and decided she was a ten out of ten. 'Where are we going?'

The woman took a narrow path which ran downhill towards a subway beneath the main road. A troop of skateboarders were tick-tacking near the entrance, using the slope to gain speed. Damilola felt uneasy about entering the subway. It was a concrete tube with no way out if there was trouble. Once he was in, he'd be a sitting duck with no escape. His money was in his coat, and he wasn't carrying a weapon. He sensed danger.

'Listen to me, whatever your name is.' he said, stopping. 'I'm not going on a magical mystery tour with you or anyone else, so either tell me where we're going, or this doesn't happen.'

'Fuck you, goat boy,' the woman said without turning around. 'Jet has her routines in place for your safety and ours.'

'And I have mine too,' Damilola argued. 'I'm not going through a subway with someone I've never met.'

'We have protocol. The Dibble are forever sending UCs our way. You could be police.'

'I'm not police.' He laughed. 'Do I sound like police?'

'Do it our way or no way, goat boy.'

'Goat boy?' he muttered. 'The best-looking woman I've seen in ages has just called me goat boy.' Damilola shook his head, disappointed his demand hadn't had any impact. The woman clearly didn't give a fuck if he followed her or not. He reassessed his position in a microsecond. This was a gamble with high stakes, and he had to make a decision instantly. The woman was approaching the subway entrance. 'Wait a minute,' he said. He jogged to within five yards of her. She turned to look at him. 'This goes under the road. I'll meet you on the other side,' he said, climbing the bank. The woman walked past the skateboarders and into the concrete tunnel.

Damilola climbed up to the road and waited for a gap in the traffic. He ran across the road, narrowly avoiding a black cab and a double-decker bus. He reached the *up* ramp from the subway as the woman was exiting. She climbed the steps and turned right towards the Tube station, and he followed her, jogging to catch-up. Her perfume reached him. Chanel. He came level and touched her arm. She shrugged him off and glared at him.

'Don't touch what you can't afford, goat boy,' she snapped, pulling a switchblade. It clicked open, and she kept it down by her side where passers-by couldn't see it.

'Sorry. Can we start this again?' he asked. 'I think we got off on the wrong foot.'

'Don't ever touch me again, goat boy,' she said, without any expression on her face. 'Do you understand me?'

'Please don't call me that,' he said. *She's ice-cold and highly strung*, he thought. Not girlfriend material, no matter how gorgeous she was. 'It's so disrespectful.'

'You have to earn respect, goat boy.'

'For fuck's sake,' he whispered to himself.

They were level with a bus stop and a single-decker pulled up. She pushed to the front of the queue and climbed on board, showing a bus pass.

'Where are we going?' Damilola shouted. She ignored him and sat near the rear of the bus. He waited his turn and bought a ticket to the end of the line, which was Gatwick Airport. He walked along the bus and sat next to the woman. She looked out of the window, oblivious. 'I bought a ticket to the end of the line because I haven't got a fucking clue where I'm going.'

'That's the general idea,' the woman said.

'It's all a bit unnecessary, isn't it?'

'Nope.' She turned towards him. 'I don't know where we're going yet, so you've got no chance of knowing. Sit still and don't move a muscle.' She put her hand between his legs and squeezed, then moved down each thigh in turn. Her other hand went beneath his jacket and felt up his back. 'You're not wearing a wire, are you?'

'No,' Damilola said, frowning. 'Of course, I'm not wearing a wire!'

'People do,' she said, finishing her search. She stood up and pressed the stop button. The bus came to an abrupt halt at the next stop. She opened the door and jumped off. Damilola nearly tripped over the step trying to keep up. She waited next to the kerb as the bus pulled away.

'Cross here,' she said, pointing to a zebra crossing. They crossed the road as a double-decker approached the closest bus stop. She flashed her pass and climbed on. Damilola paid for five stops and followed her to a seat near the rear.

'Is this really necessary?' Damilola protested. She didn't answer as the bus pulled away in the direction they'd come from. Three stops on, she pressed the *stop* button and jumped off. Damilola followed her as she headed for a large McDonald's. She entered through the side door, crossed the dining area, and exited on the opposite side of the building. One more bus ride for six stops and they were on a busy section of Oxford Road.

'I could murder a cheeseburger and a Coke,' he said, pointing back at the restaurant. 'Fucking about on buses makes me hungry.'

A Mercedes jeep pulled up next to them. The back door opened and a black man the size of a bear climbed out. He was wearing shades and a parka.

'Get in,' he growled. The woman opened the front door and climbed into the passenger seat. 'Now, goat boy,' the man grunted.

'There's no need for this goat boy shit,' he mumbled.

Damilola reluctantly climbed in, sitting next to another man who could have been the twin of the first. Both men had bangs similar to the woman. The driver sported the same hairstyle.

'Cool bangs,' Damilola said, looking around at the men. 'I get it. The bangs are like a gang thing, innit?' he asked, smiling nervously. He made a gun with his fingers as a joke, but no one smiled. 'This is all very serious,' he added, shaking his head.

'Do you have the money?' the woman asked, without turning around.

'Yes. Of course,' Damilola said, nodding. He felt dwarfed by the meatheads on either side of him.

'Check it,' she said, turning around.

The men grabbed his arms and patted him down. 'Wait a minute,' Damilola said, trying to break free. His arms were pinned to his sides, and he couldn't move. The man to his left found his money in his inside pocket. The bundle of twenties was wrapped in cellophane. 'Get your fucking hands off my money.'

A hard punch to the side of his head stopped him struggling. His ear went numb but felt like it was burning. The man let go of his arm and ripped open the package.

'There's a thousand twenties in that bundle,' Damilola said, rubbing his ear. 'Is this bruiser going to check every one of them?'

'Yes,' the woman said. The vehicle stopped down a side street and the man to his right opened the door and climbed out. 'Get out,' she said.

'What?' Damilola said, shaking his head. 'What about my money?'

'We'll be in touch once we know it's legit,' she said. 'Get out.'

'This isn't what I agreed with Jet...'

The big man reached in and grabbed his arm. He was pulled like a rag doll and tossed onto the pavement, falling heavily to his knees. The man climbed back in and slammed the door closed as the Mercedes roared away. Damilola watched it slow down and slip into the traffic before it disappeared around a corner. He rubbed his ear and picked himself up. 'We'll be in touch,' he muttered to himself. 'You better be in touch, lady, or this goat boy is going to bite you on the arse.'

CHAPTER 4

Kissie: Ukraine

Kissie put the dosimeter back in its case, hung her camera around her neck, and set off towards the road. She kept looking back at the equipment, feeling guilty about leaving it there, but Angela had sounded so concerned, she did as she asked. Her heart was beating quickly, and she was trying not to panic, but the traumatic experiences of her childhood were bubbling to the surface. The journey from Monguno to Tripoli had been fraught with danger, anxiety, fear, and devastating loss. The doctors said she had PTSD and she must avoid stressful situations and so far, she had done.

She jogged up the hill, trying to avoid fallen branches and brambles beneath the undergrowth. It was painfully slow going and her brain was telling her to sprint as fast as she could, but it was too far to travel at full speed. She was young and fit, but not fit enough to sprint two miles. She would be out of breath in a few minutes and there were so many trip hazards. She would fall and bash her head on a tree or something. Surely things couldn't be so bad she needed to run all the way. Angela said run, and she was an experienced woman who had worked on projects in unstable countries all over the world. She didn't spook easily, but she'd sounded different. Concerned. Frightened even.

Kissie persevered and trudged through the undergrowth as quickly as she could safely. She reached the crest of a small hill and looked down at a deep hallow. At least the rest of the distance was downhill. The trees were thinning out and she could travel faster, but she still had over a mile to cover before she would see the road. Movement to her left caught her eye, and she had to focus to distinguish human forms. They were wearing camouflage. Soldiers. A unit of four or five were spread out, weapons at the ready, making slow progress through the trees from her left. The more she looked, the more soldiers she could see. Ten, twelve, twenty maybe. More to her right. They were between her and where she needed to be. She stopped and hid behind a tree; the urge to pee came over her, it was swift and powerful. Her heart was in her mouth and her breath was stuck in her chest. She closed her eyes and tried to blend into the tree. There was no way she could carry on without being seen. She stepped out of the foliage with her hands splayed to her sides, so they could see she was unarmed.

'What are you doing here?' a female voice asked in Ukrainian.

'I speak English. I'm a scientist,' Kissie answered, showing her ID on a lanyard. The woman was dressed in full combat gear. Her face smeared with camo-paint. She carried an automatic rifle. Kissie had no idea how she'd got so close without her seeing her; they were clearly well trained. Two more soldiers approached from her left. Three more from her right. They came out of the trees and bushes as if by magic. 'What is going on?' Kissie asked.

'Russian paratroopers have landed. They're everywhere,' the woman said in decent English. 'They're trying to take the power station. Where are you going?'

'West to the Pripyat Road,' Kissie said. 'There's a minibus coming for me.' The soldiers exchanged glances and spoke in Ukrainian. One of the men barked orders, and the soldiers moved on to the east, towards the river.

'Go quickly,' the female said, pointing. 'If your bus isn't there, make your own way to wherever you're going. Don't wait here, understand?'

'Yes,' Kissie said, nodding. She felt like she was going to wet herself.

'Go,' the soldier said. 'Go now!'

CHAPTER 5

Monguno, Nigeria: Present Day

She stared at the ceiling while he grunted in her ear, thrusting inside her. He wouldn't be long. He never was, which was the only positive she could take from his lovemaking. It was quick and not very often. When the urge took him, he would grab her by the back of her neck and lead her to their mattress in their two-bedroom shack. He would herd the children out of the room and close the door. There was no foreplay or emotion involved. He could be sticking his thing into a hole in the mattress. A little piece of her died every time he forced himself inside her and she would lie there and wish she hadn't been pulled from the sea and saved from drowning. Her life had been so happy when she was young. Before the Boko had invaded her town and driven them out of their homes.

Her father had anticipated they would come one day, and he had a vehicle stocked and prepared on the other side of the jungle. He'd kept it in a lock-up, so no one knew it was there. He was a clever man and his preparations had saved her family from certain death. They had headed north towards the desert, where her younger brother, Beb was taken by thieves and presumed dead; then they bought passage on a boat from Tripoli sailing towards Malta and Italy. It didn't matter where they landed as long as it wasn't Africa. Europe was their goal, but the traffickers were pirates, and the boat was dangerously overcrowded. Her father would never have allowed them to board that deathtrap, but they were forced onto it at machinegun point. The boat sank and her parents, Kalu and Esse, and younger sister, Kissie, drowned.

She was dragged from the sea by a Libyan fishing boat, which had come to help. Help. That was a joke. They had rescued Oke and Isime and a few others from the foaming water and said no one else survived. Surviving should have been a blessing, but it was a curse. They'd been taken back to Libya, where they were raped and claimed as property and driven south towards the desert and the borders of Chad. They were sold to slavers and assaulted again before being trafficked back through Niger. On the border of Nigeria, the slavers were attacked and killed by a platoon of Boko Haram and the sisters were given to two of the soldiers as wives and, ironically, they were taken to Monguno to live. They were forced into marriage to men twice their age and used as breeding stock. As the wives of extremists, their existence had been a living nightmare since. Isime was traumatised by the experience and, despite dealing with her own demons, Oke mothered her as much as she could.

Living in Monguno should have brought comfort, but it brought none. All the women in the community had suffered the same experiences. The rape of women was as much a part of daily life as eating and sleeping. She learnt to switch off and go to another place while he relieved himself.

Oke felt him climax and waited for him to climb off her without a word. He left the room, and she went to the tiny bathroom and cleaned herself, but his stink was still on her. His stink was everywhere. It made her gag. Washing wasn't a priority for him. Oke went into the other room, where her three children were playing. The youngest ran to her, clinging to her leg. A knock on the door made her jump.

'Come in,' Oke called.

Isime opened the door, her eyes wide and frightened.

'Oke, help me. Come quickly,' she said, in a panic.

'What's the matter?' Oke asked, walking towards her. They kissed, and she held her sister. Her body was shaking. 'You're shaking like a leaf. What is it?'

'Droon has a terrible cough, fever, and diarrhoea. It's the worst I've ever seen,' Isime said. 'He's so weak, he can't move. Now Mahid has started to cough. I don't know what to do.'

'How long has Droon been sick?' Oke asked.

'Since yesterday morning. He came back from a patrol the night before and fell sick a few hours later. His cough is so bad, it sounds like he has water in his lungs. He can hardly breathe. Some of the others who were on the patrol with him are ill too. They all have a cough and a fever. He can't even take water and keep it down, but the sickness won't stop,' Isime said, shaking her head. 'He won't give me money for medicine.'

'I have some hidden,' Oke said. 'Don't panic. Tell me his symptoms.'

'A barking cough, fever, sore throat, and thirsty all the time, but he can't keep anything down,' Isime said. She lowered her voice. 'He's passing fluid like coconut water.' She glanced at the children, trying not to be heard. 'It has blood in it, too.'

'That doesn't sound good,' Oke said. 'He needs medicine.'

'But he won't take it. You know what he's like,' Isime said.

'Droon is a man. He can make up his own mind, but Mahid is a child,' Oke said. 'If Droon doesn't want to get better, that's up to him, but we need to treat Mahid.'

'What about the others who are sick?'

'How many are there?'

'There was thirty of them on patrol,' Isime said, shrugging. 'I don't know. I heard some of them are sick, but not how many.'

'I don't have enough to treat them all, and if I say I have medicine, they will confiscate it and punish us,' Oke said. 'I'm not letting them beat me for trying to help my nephew.'

'But if it's contagious, it might spread through the town,' Isime said.

'If it is, we can't stop it,' Oke said. 'Do you want to try to save your boy?'

'Yes. Of course.'

'We say nothing and treat Mahid.'

CHAPTER 6

Beb – Sahara

The sun was climbing from the east when Beb began walking west. To the north was nothing but sand for a thousand miles; south was five-hundred miles through bandit country before he would stumble across settlements if he was lucky. West was his only option. If his bearings were correct, the Moroccan border was west, and it was frequented by nomads buying supplies before they set off into the wilderness of the desert again. Without water, he had no other option but to try find other humans and pray they were the type who would help. There were pirates in the west, but it didn't matter. He had nothing of value but his life.

Beb put the blanket over his head, turned his back to the sun, and walked in the opposite direction. He kept his eyes from the horizon and focused on the ground in front of him. It was the only way to keep going and stay reasonably sane. Looking at the never-ending sea of sand dunes was enough to drive the strongest people crazy. The urge to lie down and sleep was overwhelming. It would be simpler to give up and die than to struggle on through the burning thirst, exhaustion, and hunger. The heat was increasing and sweat oozed from every pore, dilapidating his fluid reserves further still. It was an unsustainable situation, yet he plodded on, one foot in front of the other. The pain from his neck was sapping what little strength he had left.

A familiar grunting noise drifted to him on the breeze. He listened carefully, trying to pinpoint which direction it had come from. Again, the grunt came to him. A camel. Beb scanned the horizon and saw a line of people in the far distance, dots against the sand at first. He kept walking in their direction and soon, he could make out three camels with riders, but no goats or children walking with them. They were not part of a tribe, which meant they were pirates or a scouting party, possibly men, who drifted across the desert looking for migrants to rob. Beb felt his stomach churn; butterflies turned to elephants in his guts as anxiety spread through his veins. He had no choice but to ask them for help. If he didn't, he was dead anyway.

CHAPTER 7

Damilola checked his phone for the millionth time in four hours. The screen was blank. The number he'd been using to communicate with Jet was disconnected. Not engaged, not switched off, disconnected. He felt sick to the core. If Jet had decided to take his money and renege on the deal, there wasn't a lot he could do about it apart from finding her and asking her to return it or fulfil the order. She had security upon security upon security, more muscle than any normal person required. He couldn't mess with them. If he decided to hurt her, he knew where she drank, he knew where she did business, he knew where she frequented when she was looking for pussy to take home to her bed. Finding her wouldn't be an issue but leaving in one piece would be. Violence wasn't the answer here. Convincing her not to rob him was the only solution. He was an insect walking through a land of giants where he could be swatted at any moment, and he knew it.

Stepping into the big league was fraught with danger, but he was confident he could handle it until he was thrown onto his arse from the back of a cab. This wasn't the first time he'd felt helpless. Being driven from his home by Boko and watching his family being executed when he couldn't lift a finger to stop it was a devastating experience. When everything you've known and loved is swept away in minutes, it makes you realise in no uncertain terms what being helpless is. He was helpless then, and he was helpless now.

His phone beeped, and he looked at it. It was a call from Kalu. He pressed the *reject* button and sent him to voicemail. The knot in his stomach tightened. Things were going from bad to worse. Had he noticed his cards were missing? Surely not yet. He had taken them from his second wallet. The one he used as a parachute in case he ever lost his primary and had to cancel all his cards. Kalu was always prepared for a disaster to happen. It was the way his mind worked. Just in case. Everything was just in case. Kissie had talked many times about their escape from Monguno and of course, he had pretended to remember everything when he remembered nothing because he wasn't there. Kalu was a kind but cautious man. He had the foresight to give his children a gold coin to keep in case of emergencies and if they became separated. Beb had told him about his coin and ultimately, that sealed his fate. Damilola felt no guilt or regret for taking it and taking his life and taking his place in the world. It was survival of the fittest. Dog eat dog. Kalu knew this and tried his best to protect his children. It was his mindset which had allowed them to escape Monguno when so many were slaughtered.

His phone vibrated again, and he looked at the screen. A text message appeared.

Euston Station. The Cornish Pasty Shop.

Damilola clenched his fists. 'Yes!' he shouted. He hailed a black cab and headed across the city to Euston. The relief flowed through him, and he felt excited again.

CHAPTER 8

Kissie made her way through the woods as quickly as she could. She encountered two more units of soldiers before she reached the road. They were edgy and focused on finding the enemy paratroopers. They asked her the same questions, and she gave the same answers. She was told to get away from the area quickly on each occasion. Her heart felt like it was going to punch through her chest. Fear and anxiety bubbled beneath the surface, threatening to take control. She was relieved when she heard engines and saw traffic through the trees, but her relief didn't last long. The traffic was a convoy of military trucks heading north towards the Belarus border. Ukrainian defenders were on the move, just like the troops in the woods. It was obvious that the military had been mobilised. It saddened her deeply to think of this peaceful nation being invaded on the whim of a megalomaniac. Kissie had witnessed the horror of war firsthand and she didn't wish to see it again. She increased her pace and stumbled out of the bushes near a bend in the road. The army trucks were in the near distance, the engine noise fading, and the road was quiet. Too quiet. Her breathing was controlled, but she was far from calm. She wiped sweat from her brow and checked her mobile. There was no signal. She needed to talk to Kalu. He would be watching the news, monitoring the deteriorating situation, and if he saw that Russian paratroopers had landed at Pripyat, he would be beside himself for her safety. She glanced at the convoy as it reached the crest of the hill.

From the north, she heard a whooshing sound. She looked up but couldn't see anything, and then the truck at the rear of the convoy exploded. It left the asphalt for several seconds, a huge candle-shaped flame sprang skywards, the deep orange colour of the evening sun. Smoke billowed, the tendrils twisting and folding into themselves as they climbed from the wreckage. She covered her mouth with her hands as if breathing would attract attention.

'Oh, fucking hell!' she said, fixated by the carnage. 'No. no, no.'

From the smoke, a red minibus appeared, travelling at speed towards her. Kissie looked skyward and closed her eyes in a silent prayer. She had seen death and destruction while trying to leave Africa. She didn't expect to see again. Not in Europe. The unthinkable had happened. Kissie took a deep breath and tried to settle her nerves. In a few minutes, she would be on the bus, heading for the safety of their hotel. From there, they would have to make their way out of northern Ukraine; Angela would have a plan. She always had a plan.

The minibus approached and she could see the front seats were occupied. She didn't recognise the passengers. The rear seats looked empty. She waved at the driver, Omar. He flashed the headlights a hundred yards away. There was another whooshing sound, louder this time, and the red minibus disintegrated in a white flash. The heat burnt her eyebrows and singed her skin and the blast hit her like an express train throwing her backwards into the bushes. Kissie landed heavily on her back, winded and stunned. She saw a drone and white clouds scurrying across the sky, tinged with grey and red. Red filled her vision, and she knew it wasn't clouds. It was her blood. Then darkness engulfed her as she lost consciousness.

CHAPTER 9

Oke: Monguno

Oke took her children to a neighbour's and asked her to look after them for a while. She explained there was sickness in her sister's house and the neighbour said she'd heard that the men who went on the patrol the night before were ill. Oke asked how many and she said more than twenty had taken ill. Oke and Isime thanked her and walked through the town quickly. There was a lot of activity. Technical trucks, which were pickups with heavy calibre machineguns mounted on the flatbeds were speeding around, loaded with men. The Boko men were always aggressive, sporting shades and berets, snarling at anything that moved, but they appeared to be increasingly on edge. The sisters walked arm in arm, heads down to avoid eye contact. They were both wearing black burkas with veils, as did all the females in the Boko community. They didn't stop to talk to anyone along the way, moving with purpose. Conversation between females in the street was frowned upon. Oke had a million questions to ask Isime and more came to her every passing minute but she kept them to herself until the road was empty of traffic.

'What have you been giving them?' Oke whispered.

'I have some wormwood tonic, which I made yesterday,' Isime said quietly. She showed Oke a reused Coke bottle, which was hidden in her clothing. 'It's good for the chest, but it's not touching their coughs.'

'Good. It's better than nothing, and you can use it to keep Droon from watching me. When we get there, you can try to give some to Droon. I'll give Mahid the medicine while you distract him,' Oke said. 'Are they in the same room?'

'Yes. Droon insisted I move him when Mahid showed symptoms. As soon as he coughed, he knew he was infected.'

'That's odd,' Oke whispered.

'Not really. His mother is getting frail, and he said he didn't want her getting sick,' Isime said. 'Of course, she's been telling me everything I'm doing is wrong. The woman doesn't stop complaining, but she does nothing to help me.'

'You're missing my point.'

'What's your point?'

'That means he thinks he's got something contagious,' Oke said, shaking her head. 'How does he know it's contagious?'

'I don't know, but now you mention it, he did act as if it was automatically contagious.'

'Why would he think that unless he knows something?'

'I don't understand,' Isime said.

'Droon was protecting his mother at the expense of his son because Mahid was already coughing, yes?'

'Yes. I suppose so,' Isime agreed.

'That's because he knows he has something contagious,' Oke said. 'What can make all those men so sick at the same time?'

'What are you thinking?'

'It has something to do with where they went to.'

'Like what?'

'I don't know. Where did that patrol go to?' Oke asked. 'Did Droon mention it?'

'No. He never says where they go.'

'Wherever it was, they brought this back with them, and they know what it is, and they're scared of it spreading.'

'But I've been nursing them all night,' Isime said. Oke nodded silently. 'I'll be infected. You must stay away from me.'

'It's too late.'

'What is it?' Isime asked.

'I had sex with Rashid this morning,' Oke said. 'If he has this, so do I.'

'We're going to get sick, aren't we?' Isime said.

'Maybe not,' Oke said. 'Father made sure we had every inoculation available when we were children. Let's hope one of them gives us some immunity to whatever it is.' Oke nodded. 'We didn't get the flu ever, nor covid.'

'That's true. I hope you're right,' Isime said.

'Oh no,' Oke said as they turned the corner onto the street where Isime lived. The houses had three bedrooms and en suite bathrooms because her husband was further up the ranks than Oke's. Their childhood home wasn't far away because Kalu had been a GP. The area was the most affluent part of the town back then. The local bank manager had lived in Isime's house when they were children; it had been a nice area for professional people. Oke wasn't in the slightest bit jealous of her sister for having a bigger house. Her husband, Droon, was a pig. He regularly beat Isime and their child, often for nothing more than sport or because he was having a bad day. He said discipline was good for them.

'What is it?' Isime asked, staring at a group of men and army trucks.

'The Mullah and his men are outside your house.'

'No!' Isime said. 'Surely, they're next door.'

'They are, but they are at yours too. I don't think they're in just one house,' Oke said. They approached a small gathering of neighbours. They looked at Isime with suspicion in their eyes. 'What is going on?' Oke asked.

'There is sickness in the town. It has killed two of the men who went on patrol the night before last,' one of the women said.

'Where did the patrol go to?' Oke asked.

'How would I know?' the woman said, shushing Oke. 'You will be in all kinds of trouble asking questions like that.'

'They are quarantining the houses of everyone who went on patrol and everyone who has been in contact with them.' Another woman interrupted. She pointed at Isime. 'What are you doing out of your house?' she said to Isime.

'She hasn't been in there while they've been sick,' Oke said. 'She has been with me. Droon insisted on her leaving and leaving his mother to tend to them.'

'Rubbish,' the woman said. 'You're protecting her.'

'No one is protecting me. I am going into my home. I need to see to my son,' Isime said. She looked at Oke and shook her head. 'I can't leave him in there without me.'

Boko soldiers spotted them talking. One of them looked angry and marched over. 'What are you doing here, women?'

'Gossiping,' another barked.

'I was gathering leaves to make a tonic,' Isime said. She showed him the bottle. He nodded and pointed to the house.

'Go and take care of your family.'

'Wait,' Oke said. She hugged her sister and slipped the tablets into her hand. 'Take some yourself and give the rest to Mahid. I'll see you when this passes,' she said. Isime nodded and turned away, wiping a tear from her eye. Oke felt a shiver run down her spine as she walked up her path and into her house. Their eyes locked for a few seconds. She caught the look in her eyes as she closed the front door. Isime was terrified.

CHAPTER 10

Beb twirled the blanket above his head in a circle. The small caravan would see a lone figure on foot coming from the east, where there was nothing but sand, trying to attract attention. There were two scenarios: he was in dire trouble, or it was part of an elaborate trap. Not much elaboration went on in the desert, so anything was worth a try. Beb continued to wave the blanket until his shoulder muscles were burning, but the camels didn't change direction. He was exhausted and ready to give up. Just when he thought it was too late, the caravan changed tack, and the camels were trotting now, heading towards him. The relief was immense, despite the danger. If they killed him, there was nothing to gain but his corpse and even the pirates were beyond cannibalism. He staggered towards them, and it seemed like an age before they were close enough to see he was an adolescent, undernourished, and close to death. His face was blistered, lips chapped, and his eyes were dull and unfocused.

One of the men climbed down from his camel and opened a goatskin flask. He put the nozzle to Beb's lips and let him drink.

'Sip it,' the man said. He spoke Tamashek, which was the language of the Tuareg and parts of Mali and Algeria. Beb studied the men and realised one of them was a young female. Their blue clothing and discoloured skin told him they were Tuareg, but he didn't know them. They looked concerned at his condition.

'Thank you,' Beb replied in their language.

'You speak Tamashek?' the man asked. He allowed Beb to take more water.

'Yes,' Beb said.

'What are you doing out here alone?' the man asked.

'I was with a caravan belonging to the Othman families.'

'But you're not an Othman.' The man noted Beb's skin. 'You're Nigerian?'

'Yes. I'm from Monguno in Nigeria but we were driven from home by Boko, and we tried to get to Tripoli, but I was kidnapped along the way and sold to Tahenkot Ult Othman.'

'We know of him.' The man frowned at the name. His colleague nodded, and his expression was one of distaste. 'What happened to your family?'

'I have no idea. I have been a slave in the desert since then.' Beb sipped the water. 'I have travelled with his caravan for many years, but my friend and I were attacked while we slept. They buried me for dead and when I came around, they were gone.'

'And your friend?'

'Damilola. He was gone too, and the goats.'

'When was this?'

'The day before yesterday,' Beb said. 'They left me with nothing.'

'You don't need anything in the grave,' the man said, grinning. 'If they thought you were dead, why would they leave you with anything?' He took some dried meat from his bag and handed it to Beb. He ripped at it with his teeth and chewed hungrily. 'Take it easy,' the man said, 'or you'll be sick.'

'I'm very grateful,' Beb said, sipping the water and chewing. 'I wouldn't have made it through the rest of the day.'

'You're a strong man to make it this far.'

'I was ready to give up. I can't thank you enough.'

'You can travel with us for a while. Maybe we'll come across your owner,' he added, frowning. 'Although, maybe it's better to travel as a free man and make your own choices?'

'Is that what you are?' Beb asked, slurping water to wash the meat down.

'Yes,' the man said. 'We're free men and this is my daughter, Amira. Our chief demanded her as his wife, so we left the family.'

'Isn't that normal for the chief to pick his wives?' Beb asked, eying Amira.

'Yes, but our chief was also my father. And now we have no chief. We take no slaves, male or female.'

'I'm Beb and I give you my thanks again.'

'I'm Mohammed Ag Salla and this is my brother Katouh, and you're welcome, Beb.'

'I'll travel with you a while if I may,' Beb said, glancing at Amira again. Her eyes were the most beautiful he'd ever seen.

'We would be honoured.'

'Thank you.'

CHAPTER 11

Damilola: London

Damilola walked between the gatehouses at the front of Euston Station. The buildings had been converted to a wine bar and a trendy real-ale pub. The tables outside were busy with commuters passing an hour before boarding their trains and local employees taking a break from their desks. Empties littered the shelves and tall tables and a barman wearing an apron was hurriedly collecting as many as he could. Damilola pitied him for working so hard serving others and tidying up after them for a pittance. He wasn't going to be enslaved ever again.

The smell of ale and cigarette smoke drifted to him; both teased him to enjoy them himself for a while. He could murder a pint and a cigarette or two. Alcohol and tobacco were two of his favourite discoveries after moving to London. Kalu disapproved and Kissie nagged him about his drinking, but they didn't stop him from doing what he enjoyed. He read the chalkboards advertising today's offers, which were the same as yesterday and the day before. Sampling their wares was tempting, but there would be plenty of time later on. His mouth was dry, and his nerves were tingling as he walked up the ramp to the food court. It was as busy as he had ever seen it. Litter spilled from the bins and discarded cups and plates were dotted across the paving stones. It was a shit-hole. He hated this city.

The smell of pizza, burgers, fish and chips, Indian spices, Chinese, and pastry mingled into a mouth-watering odour, spoilt only by the whiff of diesel engine fumes. One of his friends said London smelt of kebabs and diesel and he wasn't far off the mark. He spotted the pasty outlet and headed for it. All the tables were full and there was no one obvious to focus on. He skirted the tables and went to the counter, where he waited five minutes in line and ordered a coffee. The server was a black male with bangs and Damilola stared at him expectantly, waiting for him to acknowledge him; he took his payment on a card and handed him his latte, a stirrer, a napkin, and a paper flyer. Damilola was disappointed and walked towards the bin to dump the flyer.

'You don't want to throw that away, goat boy,' a familiar voice said. He turned to see the pretty face of the woman he'd encountered earlier. She winked at him, but there was no amusement in her eyes. 'Read the offers. They're worth trying.' She pointed to the flyer. Damilola looked at the printed side and then turned it over.

Left luggage locker. The key is in your coffee.

Damilola shook his cup and felt something which didn't belong in there. He looked up to speak to the woman, but she was gone. He caught sight of her bangs as she entered the station. There was no point in following her. If she had anything to say to him, she would have done so. Her purpose was to make sure he got the key to a locker. Removing the lid from his coffee, he tipped the contents into the bin and removed the key. He made his way to the entrance hall and checked the station layout. The left luggage lockers were at the top of the ramps near platforms 16-18. His palms were sweating as he entered, and the echoing noise of the station engulfed him. The platform announcements followed, one after the other, blending into one long blurb of information. A woman dragging a suitcase cut across him, the wheels running over his foot painfully. She carried on regardless of the collision. He swore beneath his breath and weaved his way across the cavernous ticket hall. The kiosk was signed as the concierge. He was confused. There didn't appear to be any lockers.

'Can I help you?' the assistant asked. She was a tiny female of Chinese origin.

'I have left my bag in this locker,' Damilola said, showing her the key. The assistant frowned.

'Is that a key?'

'Yes, of course.'

'I'm sorry,' the assistant said, shaking her head. 'We use a ticket system here. There are no storage facilities using keys here.'

'What about somewhere else in the station?' Damilola asked, blushing. The elephants were back in his guts, stomping around. He felt sick. She shook her head.

'Only ticket systems nowadays,' she said, grinning. 'How long ago did you leave your luggage?' Damilola was stunned into silence. Anger boiled inside. 'Was it in the nineties?' She giggled.

'Fuck you,' Damilola snapped. 'It's not funny, fucking idiot,' he added as he turned and walked away. He headed across the hall and exited next to the pasty outlet. The queue was ten deep. There were two females serving and no sign of the male who had given him the loaded cup. He checked his phone. Nothing. His heart sank as he realised he had been tricked again.

Chapter 12

Kissie woke up choking. Blood was running from her nose and congealing at the back of her throat. She turned onto her side and vomited, tasting copper and bile. It burnt her tonsils and made her vomit again. She blinked her eyes, trying to work out why she couldn't see. Was she blind? She rubbed at them with the back of her hands and realised it was blood pooling. With her right hand, she reached for her water bottle and twisted the cap. She sipped from it and rinsed her mouth and then poured some into each eye in turn, wiping them with the lining of her jacket. She felt blood trickle from her forehead, and she felt for the source with her fingers. There was a two-inch gash just below her hairline. She knew her nose was broken but couldn't feel any critical injuries to worry about. Kissie had dated a fireman, and he had told her about people losing limbs and not realising. She had all four of hers. She remembered a blur before the impact. Something globe-shaped had hit her square in the face and knocked her unconscious for a few minutes. She looked around and focused on the severed head of a middle-aged man. His beard was smouldering, and she could smell burning hair. The eyes had rolled back, giving him a sightless stare. She wondered if that was what hit her in the face and realised it was such a bizarre thought. Was she head-butted by a severed head? It was a dreadful theory, and she vomited again and tried not to look at it, but her eyes were drawn to it. The memory of watching the minibus explode into a fireball returned, and she stood up and looked around. She was surrounded by foliage and smoking metal. There was no sign of life.

'Oh, no, no, please no,' she whispered as she tried to walk. 'Don't do this to me again.' She prayed to a god she didn't believe in. 'Not again. Give me a break.' She checked her pocket for her mobile, but it wasn't there. She patted her jacket and jeans multiple times, but every time she searched, they were still empty. 'Fuck, fuck, fuck!' she muttered. 'Think, Kissie.' She tried to settle her breathing. Her comms unit was clipped to her belt. She reached for it.

'Angela. This is Kissie,' she said. The unit clicked.

'Kissie?' Angela's voice answered. 'Are you on the minibus?'

'No.'

'Why not?' Angela asked. 'Omar said he could see you by the side of the road.'

'The bus was hit by a missile,' Kissie said, whispering. She was frightened of being heard.

'What?'

'The minibus was hit by a missile. I saw a drone. It's blown to bits,' Kissie said. 'Omar is dead.' There was silence as she looked at the smoking debris. 'And the others, whoever they were, are dead too. There are troops everywhere. A truck was hit too. It was full of soldiers, and they were blown to bits…' She rambled.

'Okay, keep calm, Kissie.'

'I don't feel calm, Angela,' Kissie said. 'I was hit in the face by a severed head,' she hissed. 'I am definitely not fucking calm!'

'That is terrible, Kissie,' Angela said. She could hear the fear in her voice. 'You have to think clearly. Tell me if you're injured.'

'What?'

'Listen to me, Kissie,' Angela said calmly. 'Are you okay?'

'Something hit me in the face,' Kissie said. 'I think it was a head, so no, I'm far from okay. A fucking head!'

'You're not making sense, Kissie,' Angela said, trying to understand what Kissie had seen. 'I know you're shocked, but are you okay?'

'I've broken my nose, I think, and I have a gash on my forehead, but I'll be okay.'

'Are you sure Omar is dead?' Angela asked. Kissie spotted a red training shoe on the side of the road. It was a Nike with a foot inside it. The leg had been severed above the ankle. He always wore those trainers. She knew it belonged to Omar.

'Positive,' Kissie said. 'There are Ukrainian soldiers in the woods, lots of them. They told me to get away from here as fast as I can,' she sniffled. 'I'm scared, Angela.'

'It's only natural to be scared. You must focus and get away from there. Take a deep breath. Don't think about being scared,' Angela said. 'Can you walk?'

'Yes. My legs are fine,' she said, instinctively touching her thighs. Kissie looked up the road to where the convoy had been bombed. Plumes of black smoke dominated the horizon. 'Don't leave me here on my own.'

'I'm not going to leave you there,' Angela said. There was an explosion in the background and Kissie could hear people screaming. 'Oh, my God!' Angela shouted.

'What happened?' Angela didn't reply. 'What was that?' Kissie asked, frightened. 'Angela! Are they there?'

'No one is here, Kissie,' Angela said. 'A bomb landed across the square. The town hall has been hit.'

'I'm not going to get out of here, am I?' Kissie cried. 'Please don't leave me here,' Kissie said, shaking. 'Please come and get me.'

'I need you to get away from there, Kissie,' Angela said. 'Start walking towards town and I'll send someone to meet you.'

'Okay. Okay. Okay,' Kissie said, trying to pull herself together. 'I'm going to walk towards the station.'

'Okay, Kissie. That's good. Stay near cover,' Angela said. 'I'll send someone to pick you up as soon as I can.'

'Can't you send someone now?'

'Yes. I will send someone now. Just keep walking.'

'Okay,' Kissie said, trying to keep it together.

'I'll make some calls and get back to you as soon as I have arranged transport for you, okay?'

'Yes.' Kissie sniffled again. 'Don't leave me out here,' she whispered. 'Please don't leave me out here.''

'No one is going to leave you there,' Angela said convincingly. 'Do you hear me?'

'Yes.'

'Keep walking. I'll call you back,' Angela said.

'Okay.' Kissie put the comms back on her hip.

Kissie was in shock and frightened and she wanted to speak to her father. She needed her phone, but it wasn't where it should be. The phone was in her hand when the minibus exploded. She'd seen a drone against the blue sky when she was knocked over and she had the phone then. She went back into the bushes and scoured the woodland floor, kicking at the twigs and dead leaves. It must have fallen from her hand when she was knocked out. She could see where the leaves were disturbed when she fell. The severed head stared at her, mouth open and beard still smouldering. She felt queasy again and was about to give up when a glint caught her eye. There it was. Kissie picked up the Samsung and looked at the screen. It was intact, but there was no signal. She put it into her pocket and stumbled out of the bushes onto the road. The chassis and wheels of the minibus were fifty yards away, smouldering. The front grill was intact up to the bottom of the windscreen, and the sides of the bus were splayed out, almost flat to the road. The tyres were nothing but melted rubber on the asphalt. The interior – dashboard, steering wheel, seats – were gone, as were Omar and his passengers. She could smell fuel, burning rubber, and roasted pork. The latter she recognised as human flesh from her experiences in Africa. It made her stomach twist, and she recoiled from the carnage, staggering away in the direction of the centre of Pripyat. She was half running, but her coordination was gone, and she weaved as if drunk. It was five miles to the abandoned railway station, which had become a tourist attraction for ghouls and scientists like her. Their hotel was another four miles beyond that. It was the best part of ten miles, which wasn't impossible, but at that very moment, it might as well be on another planet. The familiar touch of fear gripped her as she set off towards Pripyat.

CHAPTER 13

Oke, Monguno

Oke walked quickly to her home and picked up her children from her neighbour, making sure she didn't touch their skin, which was difficult with the youngest, Kareem, who clung to her leg all day long. Jeeps and technicals roared by in convoys, crammed with heavily armed Boko fighters, sunglasses glinting, black skin wet with perspiration, expressions of anger and aggression painted on each face. They were ready to fight, but what were they fighting against? A sickness which was spreading through their ranks or was there something beyond the dusty streets of Monguno which needed confronting? Their behaviour was erratic and made no sense. They were driving in circles around town with no purpose that Oke could see. Whatever the patrol encountered, they brought back a sickness inside them, and men were dying.

Rashid hadn't shown any sign of sickness earlier, so maybe he wasn't infected with whatever it was. The spread and severity of this illness were unusual. To floor a healthy adult male so quickly was a sign of how powerful it was. She had seen nearly everything Africa had to throw at the human race, Ebola, cholera, malaria, and more, but she didn't recognise this, and the symptoms appeared quickly and with severity. Covid had spread through the town like wildfire and killed dozens, but it was a slow burn, symptoms not appearing for days but this was quick and deadly. She had a bad feeling about its source and how it infected those men who had already died. Curiosity burnt inside her. It was in her nature and Boko had tried to beat it out of her over the years. She had worked in the hospital and become a nurse without qualifications. Boko didn't believe in women becoming qualified and textbooks were burnt along with every other type of books. Asking questions had cost her a flaying with a riding whip and her rear end was so injured, she couldn't sit for a week. Rashid had given her black eyes, split lips, and several broken bones for challenging him and asking questions, but she couldn't help herself. It was just her nature. Curiosity killed the cat, they say; it may still kill her, she often thought.

Rashid barked at her day and night as if she was a naughty puppy that needed schooling. She ignored him most of the time and kept her head down. Making eye contact during a lecture resulted in physical reinforcement of his message. They wanted their women uneducated, unresponsive, and obedient. She was none of those things, so beating it out of her was his mission. She would have to tread carefully but to help her sister, she needed to know where the Boko fighters went on that patrol. She was convinced that wherever they went to, was the reason for this outbreak. It was too much of a coincidence to be anything else. They went somewhere and came into contact with an invisible evil.

When she got the children inside, she made some broth from vegetables, spices, and herbs. The eldest daughter, Najma, always helped her to cook and look after her siblings. She spoke to them like they were her children, with her hands on her hips, which made Oke laugh. There was dough proving in a basket, ready to be baked into flatbreads. The oven was old and inefficient, so she kept it on low and turned it up to full heat when she cooked. Electricity bills didn't exist in Monguno anymore as all the metres and substations were hot-wired and the electric company didn't send engineers into Boko territory. It would be a suicide mission. They spent the afternoon cooking and talking, and four hours went by when a loud knock on the door interrupted their chatter. Oke opened it, her three curious children behind her like shadows. Her middle child, Rida, held her hand for reassurance. She was scared of men, including her father.

Two Boko men stood, holding Rashid between them. He was hanging, slack-jawed, his legs buckled. Saliva dripped from his chin and his nose was running green from both nostrils. His eyes couldn't focus on her, rolling in his head.

'Look at the state of him. When did this happen?' Oke asked, opening the door wide. 'Bring him in and put him in the bedroom. Stand back, children,' she ordered. The kids stepped away, Kareem sucking his thumb. Najma shooed the others out of the way. Oke led the way and stripped the bedding, leaving one pillow. 'Put him on there. Tell me what happened.'

'He collapsed on the way to a meeting,' one of the men said. She knew him as Ishmael. He looked drained and disorientated. His eyes were bloodshot.

'When was this?'

'About an hour ago. We gave him water and some soup to give him strength, but he became worse.'

'Some of the other men are sick too?' Oke asked. No one answered. 'I heard some have died.' No reply. 'You look sick too, Ishmael,' she added.

'I don't feel too good,' he said, nodding. He coughed, and Oke instinctively stepped back. 'Can I have some water, please?'

'Najma, bring me a glass of water,' Oke shouted. Najma appeared in the doorway with the water. 'Not my best glass,' Oke said. Najma looked confused.

'But you told me always to give a guest the best glass,' Najma said, frowning.

'I did, but this guest has something contagious,' Oke said, shaking her head. 'Go and bring me water in one of the paper cups from the cupboard.' Najma did as she was asked. 'That girl is so clever. She forgets nothing,' Oke said, eyeing the Boko men. 'Were you on the same patrol as him?'

'Mind your business, woman,' the other man said. She knew he was Muktar, and his mother was not much older than she was. She'd been married off at nine and was pregnant at twelve. He glared at her, his eyes bright and piercing. There was nothing wrong with him, yet. 'Don't ask questions about things which don't concern you, woman.'

'My husband is sick in his bed,' Oke said, pointing at him. 'He was in good health before that patrol, and now he looks like he's dying. Other men are already dead, so I think it concerns me. Now, leave my house,' Oke said, pointing to the door. 'I won't be told what to do in my own home by a boy,' she snapped and pointed to the door again. 'I will speak to your mother about your manners,' she added. The man looked gobsmacked. 'Get out unless you want this sickness.' The men looked worried. 'I lay with Rashid this morning. Whatever he has, I have. Now get out!'

They turned and walked out at speed. Najma handed Ishmael a cup of water and he took it without stopping to say anything else. Oke walked to the living room door. The children were standing against the wall like naughty children waiting for the headmaster.

'Your father is sick, and the sickness is catching,' she said. Kareem looked up at his elder sisters. Rida put her arm around him and kissed his head. 'You do not come into this room under any circumstances, understood?'

The children nodded, wide-eyed and frightened. Rashid coughed and Oke went to him with water. She wiped his mouth and there were flecks of blood in his spittle.

'Open your mouth,' she said. He did as she asked. 'Your mouth is blistered. Did you drink from a stream?'

'No,' he muttered.

His eyes were yellow and bloodshot. She felt his temperature. He was burning up. Oke fetched a clean cloth and soaked it in cold water from the tap. She wiped his brow, and a clump of hair came away from above his forehead. Oke shook her head and grimaced.

'Your hair is falling out,' she said, showing him the clump. 'This is not natural. This is not like any sickness I have seen before, Rashid,' she said into his ear. 'You were well this morning, well enough to lie on me. I can't help you unless you tell me what it is you did on that patrol.' Rashid blinked and looked into her eyes. They were bleary and unfocused, but he understood what she had said. She knew that. 'You and a lot of other men are sick and dying. Where did you go on that patrol?'

'You will get us all killed, woman,' Rashid said, shaking his head. 'Shut your mouth and tend to the children.'

'Have it your way,' Oke said. She stood up and left the bedroom, closing the door behind her.

CHAPTER 14

Beb, Sahara. Present Day

Beb and Amira lay together as the sunrise crept up in the east. He ran his fingers over her breast and down her side to her stomach where he traced circles on her dark skin. She smiled at him, her green eyes sparkling and full of life. She was the most beautiful thing he had ever seen. His heart did a somersault every time he looked at her and nothing could have prepared him for how much he loved this woman. He loved her so much it hurt. Whatever God had done to him and taken from him was worth every moment of pain he'd suffered because it all led to Amira. She was his sun, his moon, and his stars all in one beautiful body. Her smile beguiled him, her laughter transfixed him, and nothing in God's universe was comparable to making love to her. There was nowhere else he could ever be but by her side.

Their daughter slept peacefully on her cot at the foot of their mattress. They held each other long after the heat of passion had begun to fade to the glow that followed. Their love had been instant and earth shattering and the way he felt about Amira was only matched by his love for their daughter, Heba, which translates to *gift of God*. Amira and Heba were gifts from God indeed. A God who had taken everything from him and abandoned him to slavery in the wilderness. He had a plan for Beb, and he had rewarded him with the love of the most beautiful woman on the planet and blessed them with their daughter. There was nothing more he could ask for.

Their instant attraction had been tempered by their domestic situation. Her father had been kind to him, saved his life, and allowed him into the fold. He was an honourable man, and Beb respected him deeply. He couldn't tell him how he felt about Amira at that time, no matter how strongly he felt about her. Amira felt the same way but honoured her father and couldn't disrespect him in any way. Their love didn't go unnoticed by her father and uncle, and they all pretended it didn't exist for eighteen months. It was more than an elephant in the room, more like a brontosaurus in the camp.

One day, their supplies needed to be replenished, and they travelled south to the town of Tawendert on the border of Mali. Mohammed and Amira stayed in the desert while Katouh took Beb to the town, where they bought supplies. When they'd made their purchases, they took some sweet tea at a café and Katouh spoke to Beb man to man. He offered Beb money to travel to the nearest city in Mali, to see if he could trace his family and see if they had survived. He told him to take the opportunity to search for them and possibly be reunited with them, as they wouldn't be close to the border again for a year or more. Beb didn't hesitate to thank him for his offer but declined it. He explained his love for Amira and his intention to marry her and he explained that Europe, London, or anywhere else had no attraction to him. His family had left him years ago and the chances of them being alive were slim. Wherever Amira was, was his home.

Mohammed had been so pleased to see him return, he wept. Amira was so relieved she was almost hysterical. It was an emotional reunion, and it cemented Beb's transition into the family. They were married shortly afterwards and Heba came along two years later. Since then, Amira and Heba had become his world and with Mohammed and Katouh they had bought more camels and some goats to breed and travelled as a family in peace with the world around them. His life was as perfect as it could be.

CHAPTER 15

Damilola, London

Damilola sipped from a bottle of Stella and inhaled a Marlboro. He felt angry and deflated. Jet and her crew had given him the runaround, taken his money, and given him nothing in return. They had robbed him, simple as that. There was nothing else to call it. He was at a loss as to what to do about it. Kalu would find out his spare wallet and credit cards were missing and when he did, he would check the balances on them and realise they'd been maxed out. It wouldn't take long for him to point the finger at him and then the shit would hit the fan. He could hear Kissie's voice in his head. She didn't trust him. He could feel it. She tried, but she didn't. Sometimes, it was as if she knew that he wasn't Beb. She couldn't truly know, but she sensed something wasn't right. Stealing from her beloved father would be the icing on the shit cake he would have to eat. How could he explain what he'd done with the money?

'I invested it in class-As but got ripped off by the supplier.'

His phone beeped, and he nearly dropped his beer looking at the screen.

Take the key to Great Portland Street. The lockers are at the back of the ticket hall.

Damilola punched the air and swore beneath his breath. He used Google Maps to find it on his phone. It was a twenty-minute walk away or five minutes in a cab. He decided to take a cab. His nerves were jangling as he stood by the road, hailing a taxi. Ten minutes later, he was jogging down the stairs, taking them two at a time. The ticket hall was busy, noisy, and smelt of urine. He scanned it, looking for the lockers, and saw a faded sign saying *Left Luggage*. His pulse was racing as he made his way towards it. He skirted the area first, making sure they weren't there watching him make a fool of himself again. There was no sign of anyone with bangs. He caught a glimpse of a uniform, but he was going up the steps to the street above. A man wearing a long raincoat and trilby hat opened a locker and took out a briefcase. He could have been in *Bridge of Spies* or *Tinker, Tailor, Soldier, Spy*. Damilola loved spy films. Especially war-based movies. He walked across the hall and found the locker that matched his key. His heart was beating as he inserted it and opened the lock. He opened the door and smiled. There was an Adidas holdall inside. He undid the zip and looked inside. White powder. Lots of it.

CHAPTER 16

Kissie kept close to the tree line and tried to maintain a fast walking pace. She kept one eye on the sky, searching for another drone. The sound of voices in the woods drifted to her, frightening her. She listened intently to distinguish which language they were speaking. The urge to run was overwhelming, but she controlled it and kept a steady pace. Yaniv Station was on this road and when she reached it, she would have to turn west towards the Hotel Pripyat. She was praying someone would pick her up before that. Her feet were hurting, and her head was aching. The bleeding from her head had stopped now, but she still felt faint. She wanted to lie down, curl up, and go to sleep, but if she did, she might not wake up. Concussion was silent but deadly and she'd been knocked unconscious, for how long, she didn't know, but she had to keep upright and moving forward. She needed Angela to send transport to rescue her. A rescue is what it was. She couldn't thumb a lift, as there was no traffic at all going in the direction of Yaniv. A column of military vehicles passed her on the opposite side of the road, heading in the other direction. No one gave her a second glance. She was a young black woman, and Russian collaborators would be indigenous Ukrainians. The soldiers looked grim, frightened even. None of them were smiling, but why would they be when they were about to engage in a war with a nuclear powerhouse which had enough warheads to wipe out NATO ten times over? It was David versus Goliath in military terms and most of the world would hope the outcome was the same. They had been training for a Russian invasion for years, but that didn't make it any easier to deal with. She could see the anxiety etched into their faces. Kissie had heard the locals talking about it. She had heard the Ukrainian soldiers stationed in Pripyat chatting to other scientists and everyone was of the same opinion. Putin was sabre rattling, but his ego was so great, it made him unpredictable. No one knew what he would do until now.

Kissie saw plumes of smoke on the horizon around the area of the Hotel Polissya, which had been abandoned when the reactor caught fire. It was the tallest building in Lenin Square at the centre of the abandoned town. Several fires were burning and two of them were roughly where she was heading around Kirova Street. Angela had said the museum – which everyone called the town hall – had been hit a block away from the hotel. She was torn between heading for somewhere where there was no smoke or the place where her friends and colleagues would be. Like her, several of them were out testing around Chernobyl. No doubt they would all be trying to make their way back to the relative safety of the hotel, but the truth was, nowhere was safe. That was certain. The drone had hit a military convoy but also taken out a civilian vehicle, too. They were targeting indiscriminately, and they wouldn't be safe until they left the area. Her comms unit clicked.

'Kissie,' Angela said. 'Where are you?'

'I'm about two miles closer to the station from where I started,' Kissie said, frustrated. 'I haven't stopped for a coffee while I wait,' she added, growing angry.

'I know this is scary for you,' Angela said. 'The traffic is backing up. What's happening where you are?'

'There are vehicles on the road, but they're all army trucks and all going in the other direction.'

'So, you're about three miles east of Yaniv Station?' Angela asked.

'Yes,' Kissie replied. 'Is anyone coming for me?'

'Yes, me. I'm on the way,' Angela said. 'The police are trying to stop everyone from driving. There will be a curfew imposed shortly, but I'm about two miles west of the station. I'll be ten minutes if this traffic moves,' she added.

'Why will there be a curfew?'

'There are Russian sympathisers in the area,' Angela said. 'It was them that blew up the museum, not a missile. I heard one of the soldiers saying they're also laser targeting the drones from the ground. They pinpoint a target with a laser, and the drone fires a missile at it. No one is asking for permission to bomb targets, which means no one gives a shit what they hit.'

'That's awful,' Kissie said. 'The minibus was clearly not a military vehicle.'

'They're firing indiscriminately,' Angela said. 'Residential areas have been hit.'

'Where?' Kissie asked. 'All over Ukraine?'

'Yes. They're attacking from the north and the east, all along the border.'

'Wow, this is scary. He's lost the plot,' Kissie said.

'He lost it a long time ago. Listen, the locals are twitchy about the collaborators being in the area. Of course, they're not wearing Russian uniforms, so they're stopping everyone from moving. That way, they'll know who the sympathisers are.'

'Really?' Kissie said, confused. 'What if they stop you?'

'I'm an American,' Angela said. 'Hopefully, they'll know I'm on their side and I'm on a mission of mercy picking up a very frightened scientist from the Red Woods.'

'That's me,' Kissie said, nodding.

'I know. Hang in there, keep walking and I'll be with you shortly.'

'Okay,' Kissie said. 'Thank you.'

CHAPTER 17

Oke, Monguno

Oke sat on the edge of Kareem's bed and touched his leg through the sheet. A ceiling fan rattled gently, creating a breeze which made the heat bearable. He was struggling to keep his eyes open, despite this being his favourite story. She told the childrean a story every night, usually regurgitated from the memory of her childhood when Kalu and Esse would read books to them. Stories fascinated her and gave her so much joy as a child, yet Boko forbade books, especially for girls. Education and developing an imagination could lead to females having an opinion, and that was outlawed. To take such joy from children was wicked, and nothing could justify it. They couldn't stop her from telling them stories from her own imagination as long as they didn't know. Nothing could justify not sharing those moments of make believe between parent and child. It was an evil thing to deny feeding their young minds and letting their imaginations run wild with stories of dragons, princesses, wizards, and werewolves. It deprived the children of so much joy.

Oke despised them and their interpretation of their religion and she longed to return to the Monguno of her youth before Boko drove them from their home and forced them to flee to another continent where the sea claimed her family and dropped her in this living hell. She looked at her children dozing, their innocence shining like an aura around them, and her heart broke for the millionth time. She felt the sting of hot tears as they fell from her eyes and trickled down her cheeks. Her daughters would be taken from her and forced to marry a man much older than them, forced to have sex before they were ready and impregnated while they were still children themselves, and there was nothing she could do to ease their plight. In most civilised cultures, the Boko would be thrown in jail and locked up for a long time, but here it was the norm. Their future was mapped out for them before they were born, and it was not bright. It was dark and filled with hardship and heartbreak, pain and suffering. How could a mother look at her children and not wish for something else for them? Anything else but this misery.

Kareem was a gentle boy with an inquisitive nature. He would be taught to use a machinegun as soon as he was strong enough to carry one and he would be indoctrinated and brainwashed to become a misogynistic pig like the rest of them, strutting around with sunglasses on like rap stars when they were nothing but uneducated thugs.

There were days when she thought about smothering her darling children rather than allowing them to be sucked up into the extremist maelstrom of hatred for anything that wasn't them. Killing them would be kinder. She would take her own life if she could, but she couldn't leave them and she couldn't kill them either. She could only hope for something to change. She only carried on living because of her children, yet she was nurturing them for a life of slavery, especially the girls. There were no locks and no keys, no shackles and no bars on the windows, but they were slaves, nonetheless. It was heartbreaking, and she cried herself to sleep at night thinking of ways to escape with her children.

Escape to where? Her entire family, bar Isime, had died trying to escape to a place where no one wanted them. She had no money, couldn't drive, and there was nowhere to go. If she was caught running, she would have a tyre put over her head, doused in petrol and burnt in the street. The odds were stacked against her succeeding at a million to one. Her life was a disaster, but she wanted so much more for her children. Kareem was the kindest soul, such a beautiful, caring boy, yet she knew he would become an animal, programmed to kill and maim other Africans who didn't subscribe to the Boko way of thinking. That was her legacy, and she couldn't accept it.

Rashid called out for her. His voice sounded thick and guttural. Oke went into the bedroom and turned on the light. She stopped in her tracks. Rashid was bleeding from the nose and blisters had appeared on his cheeks. Tendrils of skin hung from the back of his hand and fingers. It was an image from a horror film right there on her bed. The deterioration was startling.

'You need to fetch the doctor,' he croaked. 'I feel like I'm dying.'

Oke took him some water in a paper cup and handed it to him. He could barely lift his head to sip it. 'You look like you're dying, Rashid,' Oke agreed with him. She put her hands on her hips. 'What did you fools do?'

'Don't call me a fool, woman,' he croaked.

'Or what?' She chuckled, sourly, shaking her head. 'Are you going to chase me and beat me?'

'Do you ever shut up, woman?'

'No. I don't and now you have to listen to me. You are the father of my children and most of the time I could quite easily stab you, but I couldn't wish this on you or anybody else,' she said. Rashid cried. He closed his eyes and sobbed. 'Whatever you did on that patrol, you brought this back with you. I have never seen a man waste away so quickly. This is like poison or something. Tell me where you went to.'

'Shut up and fetch the doctor,' he hissed.

'I don't think even the doctor can help you,' Oke said. 'He's useless at the best of times, but this is beyond him.' Oke put her veil on. 'I'll see if I can get him here. Do you want more water?' she asked. He nodded, and she brought him another cup. His eyes were sunken and glazed. 'What did you do, Rashid?'

'Go, Oke,' Rashid said, closing his eyes. 'Before it's too late.'

CHAPTER 18

Beb, Sahara

Beb heard the goats bleating excitedly. It was the middle of the night, and they should be sleeping. One of the camels bayed, followed by the others. Something had spooked the animals. He scrambled out of bed and Amira woke up.

'What is it?' she asked, reaching for Heba. The sleeping toddler moaned and rubbed her eyes.

'Something is frightening the animals,' Beb said. He grabbed his rifle and went outside. It was an old Enfield 303 from the Second World War. The fog of sleep cleared quickly, and he sensed Mohammed and Katouh before he saw them. They were scanning the dark horizon through binoculars. 'What is going on?' he whispered.

'Someone is circling the camp,' Katouh replied. 'I've counted eight men on camels and three on foot.'

'Eleven men. Are they pirates?' Beb asked, raising the rifle.

'No. I don't think so,' Mohammed said, shaking his head. 'Whoever it is, isn't trying to sneak up on us. They want us to know they're circling us, and they want us to know they outnumber us.'

'Who would do that?' Beb asked.

'I'm not sure,' Mohammed said, looking away. Beb spotted the lie immediately. He couldn't fathom why he would lie.

'What do we do?' Beb asked.

'We wait,' Mohammed said.

'If we start shooting, we'll waste ammunition and hit nothing but sand. They're too far away for us to see them clearly and we don't know who we're shooting at.'

'How much ammunition do we have?' Beb asked. He checked his rifle. 'I have a full clip and two more in the tent.'

'Maybe a hundred rounds between us,' Mohammed said, shaking his head. 'We can't win a battle here,' he added. 'There are too many of them.'

'What is going on?' Amira appeared from the tent, Heba in her arms.

'Get inside and stay out of sight,' Mohammed ordered, concern in his voice. 'Do not come outside until we say it's safe.'

'Beb?' she whispered. 'I'm frightened and so is Heba.'

'Do as your father told you to,' Beb said calmly. 'Someone is circling the camp. I don't know why, but you need to stay inside for now. I'll come for you when we know what's happening.'

'One someone or more than one?' Amira asked suspiciously.

'We're not sure.'

'You're lying to me,' Amira said.

'Okay. More than one.'

'Don't keep me in the dark, Beb.'

'Go inside, please,' Beb pleaded.

'I want a gun,' Amira said. 'I can shoot as well as any of you.'

'We only have three.'

'Right,' Amira said, disappointed. 'If one of you gets shot, I want a gun.'

'You need to make sure Heba is okay,' Beb said, shaking his head. 'I'll do the shooting if any needs to be done.' Amira locked eyes with him. He knew that look. She would leave it for now, but the discussion wasn't finished. She would have her say later when they were alone. 'It's probably nothing. Just go inside, please.'

'Mohammed Ag Salla!' a voice called. 'You have something which belongs to me,' the voice drifted on the night air. 'Is that you?'

No one replied. 'You have stolen from me. I have come to take what is mine.'

'Who is that?' Beb asked. Katouh and Mohammed exchanged glances. 'They know your name. Who is that?' Beb repeated.

'Our father,' Mohammed said.

'Your father, the chief?'

'Yes.'

'Give me what is rightfully mine, Mohammed Ag Salla,' the voice shouted. 'You can't run anymore. Your time is up. You're a spineless thief and your brother is a waste of space, too.' Mohammed looked angry but didn't reply. 'Give me what is rightfully mine, or you will all perish here tonight.'

'What did you steal?' Beb asked.

'We didn't steal anything.'

'Then what is he talking about?' Beb asked, confused. 'What does he want?'

'He wants Amira,' Katouh said.

CHAPTER 19

Damilola

Kalu was working his rounds at Great Ormond Street Hospital. He had chosen to specialise in paediatrics in an attempt to atone for losing his wife and children. His guilt was debilitating at times, and he spent many sleepless nights rerunning the scenarios of their flight from Monguno. With hindsight, he should never have left the truck with Beb asleep inside, not even for a minute. That was the point when things began to unravel. He dropped his guard for a few minutes and paid dearly for his mistake. His kidnap and disappearance killed his wife, Esse, long before she drowned. Leaving that town without their son was the hardest thing he'd ever done, and it haunted him. He could still see Beb's face in the rear window of the truck as the thieves drove it away. It felt like someone was ripping his heart out and he would wake up in a cold sweat. Knowing he was sleeping in the next room helped to soothe his shattered nerves. They had Beb back like the prodigal son returning to the fold, yet Kalu dwelled on his kidnap and it burnt a hole in his soul. The Beb that returned wasn't the same kind-hearted boy who was dragged into the desert and kept captive for years. That was the beginning of the end for Esse, Oke, and Isime. Their lives lost in the foaming sea and Kalu hadn't saved them. He couldn't have saved them, yet he blamed himself for their deaths. Every day was a battle against the pain and guilt he carried with him. The memories of being herded like cattle onto that rickety old wreck of a boat were painful. No husband and father would put their family into a deathtrap like that boat, but they were at gunpoint and the traffickers were killing people on the spot. They watched people who protested being gunned down on the jetty without so much as a word of warning. Sail or die, it was that simple.

Some nights he awoke in a pool of sweat, feeling like he was suffocating on diesel fumes. The screams of the drowning people deafened him and the loudest screams of all were his own as he called for his wife and children. Those voices haunted him, and he felt they always would. The guilt and sense of loss he suffered were his penance for the bad choices he made on that perilous journey. Kissie was the only reason he had survived this far. She was bright and funny and so intelligent. It frightened him, yet that strong, intelligent woman needed her father. He saw it in her eyes every day. They were both traumatised by their experiences, and they carried each other through each day. Helping other children seemed like the natural thing to do.

He worked on the private wards and the NHS wings too, and he did a weekend shift at the A&E at the Royal London Hospital once a month just to ground himself. The level of violence experienced by staff and patients alike reassured him that all people were capable of violence no matter what part of the world they came from. Africa was a continent plagued with violence but being African didn't mean he had a violence gene; but it did mean he had more chance of encountering it when he was there. The white Europeans who swamped the casualty departments of the nation at the weekends were mostly under the influence of drugs and alcohol and were as capable of violence towards other humans as any other race, creed, or colour. It was human nature: black, white, pink, zebra striped, or polka dot, made no difference. Humans had a very ugly side to them at times.

Kalu finished his rounds and went into his office. The BBC News was on a loop announcing the Russian invasion of Ukraine. His heart stopped beating for a second and he felt queasy. Kissie. He grabbed his mobile and scrolled to her name. He clicked on it and waited for it to connect. The tone he heard wasn't familiar, but it was clear her phone was not in range of a signal, or she may have turned it off while she was working, or maybe it was broken. Or was it that the communications networks had been attacked? His mind raced through a dozen scenarios, and none of them were good.

Where are you, Kissie? he asked himself.

He turned up the volume on the television and listened in horror as the reporter showed a map of Ukraine. Russian forces had crossed the borders from Belarus in the north and all along the Dombas region to the south-east, but what stood out in his mind was the large, armoured column that was heading for Chernobyl and the town of Pripyat. Kissie was stationed there with her team while they carried out their research into the long-term effects of radiation on the environment. He had begged her not to go there because of the contamination risk. The nucleoids in the air, soil, and water were still off the scale and the closer to the doomed reactor number four they were, the worse it was. Despite the genius engineering of the sarcophagus which covered the nuclear material remaining, seepage hadn't been completely stemmed. As if the risk of radiation poisoning wasn't enough, Putin had been playing war games on the border for months and most of the experts were warning it was a smokescreen for an invasion.

Kalu had asked her to leave and come home when the other scientists left, but she wouldn't hear of it. She wanted to be there, wanted to be a part of the solution and she was uncovering some dramatic findings, which the West was still to learn. She was passionate that the Russians had tried to smother the true scale of the devastating effects the fire had caused, but the Ukrainian government was keen to expose the lies. The truth was frightening and needed to be told and she wanted to make that happen; she had an emotional investment in the research, and she loved her job.

Kalu listened to the news report but couldn't focus properly. He dialled her number again. The line didn't respond at all this time. Nothing more than a deafening silence greeted him. Kalu wasn't sure what to do. His instinct was to go and rescue his little girl from the peril she was in, but that was impossible. He dialled Beb and listened to it ring, but he didn't answer, and it went to voicemail. Beb had been acting stranger than usual lately. He couldn't make eye contact with him when he tried to talk to him. Kalu suspected there was more than a bit of alcohol being consumed when he was out socialising, which wasn't to be surprised at but was worrying, nonetheless. He wanted to have a chat with him about where his life was going, but now wasn't the time. It was never the right time because he was so glad Beb was there, back from the dead.

****

Damilola took his bag from the locker and switched it. Then he had second thoughts and switched it again. He took the bag from the locker and closed the door. He put the key into the bag and his phone beeped. His focus was on getting away from the lockers quickly and blending into the masses on the Tube trains below him. He would take a couple of detours to make sure he wasn't being set up and then head to Kalu's lock-up, where he kept an old VW Beetle, which he intended to restore. He looked at his phone and pressed the *busy* button. It was Kalu again. He didn't want to talk to him yet, not until he had sold all his gear and could pay off the credit cards. It would leave him with double his starting stake and that was a big chunk of cash to restock and do it again. He could double his money each time, maybe twice a month, and then he could hire some extra hands to expand his distribution network and he would be on the way to the big league. There were always people eager to earn cash quickly, especially on the club scene. Dealing class-As was better than aftershave when it came to impressing the women, so there would be no problem recruiting. They would have to be people he trusted, and there weren't many of them around, but he had a few names in mind. His future was in his own hands for a change and the opportunities were exciting. Jet had given him the runaround to make sure he wasn't an undercover officer or a grass. He understood that now, although it had been very frustrating and stressful at the time. If he could move this stock quickly and discreetly, she would be impressed and maybe, after a few months, set him up with a line of credit. If he could get credit, he could buy some crack cocaine in bulk and sell it to the Albanians. That could triple his money in one afternoon. His phone vibrated. It was a text message from Kalu. He would read it when he got on the train.

Damilola bought a ticket to Elephant and Castle and headed down the escalator to the Northern Line. It was reasonably quiet, and he didn't have to wait long for the train. All the time, he was waiting for a hand on his shoulder and the click of handcuffs on his wrists, but nothing happened. His heart rate settled, and he began to relax. He swapped lines and got off at Waterloo. There was no sign of Jet's people. No bangs, no shades, or leather jackets, no men-mountains or pretty women calling him *goat boy*.

He jogged from the station to the lock-up and walked past it, around the block, and back again before opening the door. The lights flickered on, and he stepped inside. He had a metal toolbox, which he used to stash any drugs he bought. He never took anything home. Kalu was way too sharp to get away with that and Kissie was forever picking up his clothes and putting them in the washing. He would get caught out one day, so he used the lock-up. He did what he needed to do, locked up, and headed back to the station. As a final check, he boarded a train south and exited at Kennington. It was a quiet station where he could be certain no one was tailing him. The platform was deserted but for a Muslim woman with a pushchair who was struggling to get off the train. He leant against the wall and took a deep breath before heading for the escalators. The tension in his body dissipated and the urge to take a dump came over him; he looked around for the public toilets. They were at the top of the first escalator, and he could smell them before he saw them. He wrinkled his nose at the eye-watering stink. But nature was calling and there wasn't much choice.

The floor tiles were awash with water when he stepped inside. A single bulb struggled to light the place. There were two cubicles to his right and a urinal on his left. One of the cubicles had an 'out of order' sign on the door. The other was a scene of disgusting depravity. Toilet paper soiled with excrement and a number of stools were floating just below the seat. The bowl flooded and the U-bend blocked. Damilola needed to go, but not that badly. There would be other toilets. He didn't hear the splash of feet approaching in time to turn around. A hard punch to his lower back knocked the wind out of him, followed by two more. He grabbed at his back and felt warm blood soaking his fingers. They weren't punches he'd felt. The stab wounds pumped blood, and it dripped onto the soaking tiles at a frightening rate. A red puddle spread around his feet. He felt his knees buckle, and the holdall was ripped from his failing grasp. His vision blurred, and he caught sight of his attacker as they headed for the exit. A black female with bangs.

'Cheers for the coke, goat boy,' she called as she left. 'I've been wanting to set up on my own for years!' He heard her throaty chuckle as he slipped into unconsciousness.

Chapter 20

Kissie, Pripyat

Kissie was tired, had a headache, and a burning thirst. Her water bottle was empty, most of it used to clear her vision. She wished she'd saved some, but she hadn't expected to be walking so far. The constant trickle of military vehicles heading north had become a solid line of lorries, jeeps, and trucks, interspersed with the odd tank. Ukraine was planning a fightback few might have expected.

Her feet were sore, and she'd slowed her pace to a painful trudge, feeling the blisters with each new step. The sound of an almighty explosion came from the north, followed by two more in quick succession, and a plume of black smoke climbed above the trees. The convoy came to a halt, brakes squealing. She heard radio chatter coming from a vehicle nearby and the tanks broke from the formation and hurtled north on the wrong side of the road.

Anyone coming the other way would be in for a shock, she thought. With the best will in the world, Angela couldn't leapfrog a column of trucks loaded with soldiers and munitions, and it was at a standstill. Kissie couldn't see how she would reach her at all. She focused on the road directly in front of her and put one foot in front of the next.

'Hey. Are you okay, lady?' a voice called from one of the jeeps. He spoke Ukrainian.

'Do you have any water, please?' Kissie asked.

'You speak English?'

'Yes,' Kissie said, nodding.

'You look a little banged up,' the man said. 'What happened?'

'There was a drone strike on a minibus about two miles up the road,' Kissie said. He was wearing a Red Cross armband. The logo was on the passenger door too. 'You're Red Cross,' Kissie said, relieved to speak to another human.

'How did you guess that?' the man joked. Kissie smiled. 'We heard about the drone strikes. It was reported there were civilians onboard?' Kissie nodded, her eyes filling up. 'Did you get caught in the blast?' Kissie nodded again. 'Let me take a look at that head wound,' he said, giving her a bottle of water. She twisted the top off and slurped from it. The man took an alcohol wipe and dabbed at the wound. Kissie winced at the pain. He frowned. 'I'm Oleg, by the way. What's your name?'

'I'm Kissie.'

'Hello, Kissie. You have something stuck in this gash. Let me take a look.' He led her to the jeep and sat her on the running board. He took some tweezers from his kit and swilled alcohol around the wound, clearing the congealed blood. 'I can see it,' he said. He pulled at the embedded object with the tweezers and Kissie winced again as he pulled it free. He inspected it and showed it to Kissie.

'What is that?' she asked, frowning. She knew what it looked like but didn't want to confirm it in her own mind.

'It's an incisor,' he said, frowning. 'And it looks human,' he added matter-of-factly.

Kissie realised she'd had a tooth stuck in her forehead and vomited on his highly polished boots.

CHAPTER 21

Oke & Isime

Isime gave water to her son, Mahid, but he regurgitated it immediately. That was the third time in as many minutes. He was crying constantly, but she couldn't give him any relief from the pain and discomfort. There was nothing more heartbreaking than hearing her child in distress and not being able to help him. His cough was constant, and she could hear the phlegm settling in his lungs. It was becoming worse. She feared it could turn to a severe chest infection if he wasn't given medication of some sort. Her husband, Droon, had been delirious for over two hours now. His eyes were bloodshot, more red than white, his nose was bleeding, and he had blisters in his mouth and on his cheeks. The tonic she gave him had no effect apart from making him violently sick. She touched his head and strands of his hair stuck to her fingers and she stared at them, horrified. Isime was terrified. Nothing she'd heard of did this to a person and she didn't know what to do.

She kissed Mahid on the forehead. The perspiration on his skin had a strange odour. Her boy didn't smell the same. She went into the hallway and closed the door behind her, needing a few minutes away from their suffering and time to think about what to do.

The Boko soldiers were still outside on the street making sure no one left the houses. She wished Oke was there. She always knew what to do but, in her absence, she needed to ask her mother-in-law for advice. It wasn't like her not to be interfering, and Isime wondered where she was. His mother was a horrible woman, but she was old and wise and had seen more than Isime; she may have seen something like this before. She had a lotion or potion for every ailment to the point the Boko men called her a witch but not to her face. No one dared provoke a curse. She was constantly criticising Isime on her domestic skills and how she treated Mahid, so maybe she might know how she could give them some relief from whatever it was. There must be something she could do apart from sitting with them, reassuring them everything would be all right, when it clearly would not be. They were getting worse by the minute. She took a deep breath and went to the living room. It was empty. Isime wondered if the old crone had gone to bed.

She went down the hallway, passing the bathroom as she went. Something caught her eye. Isime retraced a few steps and looked inside. There was blood on the toilet seat, splattering the pan and discolouring the water in the bowl. It was dark red, as if from deep inside the bowels. She looked at the sink and it was splattered with red drops, in a spray pattern, as if someone had sneezed blood onto the porcelain. That wasn't good in any shape or form. Droon and Mahid hadn't moved from the bedroom.

'Magda,' Isime called out to her mother-in-law. There was no answer. She walked down the hallway to her bedroom. The door was open, and the old lady was lying on her back on the bedroom floor. Blood ran from her ears, eyes, nose, and mouth. Her lifeless eyes stared at the ceiling; her mouth twisted in a silent scream.

****

Oke went to the front door and opened it. She saw three Boko men at her gate. A technical mounted with a fifty-calibre machinegun was parked in front of her house. They were smoking cigarettes and chatting when they heard her opening the door.

'Where do you think you're going?' one of them barked.

'Rashid is dying,' she replied. 'He needs the doctor, and he needs him now.'

'There is no doctor. Go back inside.'

'Didn't you hear me?' Oke protested. 'Rashid is dying. He needs the doctor.'

'There is no doctor anymore,' another man added. 'Go back inside and do what you can.'

'What do you mean?'

'The doctor got sick and died, just like the others,' the man said. 'No one has recovered from this sickness, no matter what the doctor did. They are planning to move all the infected to the old school to stop it from spreading further.'

'And who decides who is infected?' Oke asked, shocked.

'Anyone who has come into contact with a sick person will be taken to the school,' he answered. 'You might want to pack some things to take with you. Rashid, you, and your children are all on the list.' He lit another cigarette. 'We'll be moving you before dawn.'

CHAPTER 22

Beb, Amira, & Heba

Beb wasn't sure what to think of the situation, but he was on the verge of panic. He analysed what was going on around him and tried to plan the best way forward. They were being circled by men from a huge tribe whose chief wanted to take his wife for his own. Someone trying to take his family from him wasn't something he'd dwelled on before, but the thought was terrifying. Mohammed had always been honest about the reasons he left his father's caravan, and that reason was that his father was the chief of the tribe and had his pick of the females to be his wives. It was an ancient tradition which cemented families to a caravan. Having a daughter chosen to be the wife of an elder was a great honour, but marriage to the chief was the ultimate honour. Times had changed, but Mohammed's father had not. Picking Amira, who was his granddaughter, went against everything Mohammed believed in. There was no need to take a female so young and so closely related as a wife. He already had fourteen wives and over forty children. Taking Amira away from him and turning her into a breeding machine was the biggest insult Mohammed could think of. His father was doing it because he had an unhealthy taste for young women and to spite Mohammed, who challenged him too often.

Mohammed had told Beb he didn't like his father, and he never got on with him. He never respected his father as a man or as a parent and he despised him as a chief. His father was the personification of everything that was bad about having power over others. He was a bully, he was arrogant, and he was a hypocrite. His interpretation of the Koran was twisted to his own needs and desires wherever possible and anyone who argued with him was either killed or driven from the family into exile.

Katouh was Mohammed's younger brother and as boys they were very close. They both suffered at the hands of their father, often chastised in public, humiliated in front of family and friends at every opportunity, and beaten with horse whips on more occasions than he cared to remember. Mohammed had always dreamt of leaving the family, although he never thought he actually would. Life outside of the desert was strange and alien to him. On the odd occasions that they went into town to resupply and buy water and livestock, he found that life was becoming more Westernised every time and he felt that he didn't belong there.

The desert had become a motorway between central Africa and the Mediterranean Sea, but it was all one-way traffic. Africans trying to leave their homes to escape disease, famine, and war. The constant flow of families carrying all their worldly goods on their persons had been too good an opportunity to miss for the thieves and vagabonds who wandered the planes of the sub-Saharan continent. Thousands of pirates now roamed the dunes looking for the weak and wounded to prey upon, and his father often traded with these evil men. He traded gold and silver, jewellery and ornaments, livestock, and worst of all, human beings, all stolen from desperate refugees. There was no end to his father's ability to not care less about other human beings. He wanted to take Amira as his wife not for any other reason than she was a beautiful young woman, and he was attracted to her. Had it been anyone else's daughter, Mohammed would have been disgusted and saddened by his father's decision to marry her. The fact that it was his daughter who his father planned to turn into a sexual slave was intolerable and Mohammed vowed that this would never happen while he had breath in his body.

For years, they'd roamed as free people, happy with their lot and at peace with the world. They crossed nobody, they stole from nobody, they wronged nobody, and all they asked was that they be left alone to live out their lives as they wished.

Amira was no longer a child. She was a woman with her own mind, her own dreams, her own plans for the future. The arrival of Beb in their lives had been a gift from above, and God granted Amira the love of a good man and the arrival of their daughter, Heba. It had been so long since he'd even thought about his father and the other members of the caravan that he'd almost forgotten they were on the run and always would be. His father was the type of man who was easily offended and found it impossible to forgive and forget. He held grudges and he would seek revenge at every opportunity. Justice was a word he didn't understand. The only justice in the tribe was what he deemed fit to dole out, and it was usually swift and brutal. The threat of meeting him again one day had hung in the back of Mohammed's mind like a dark cloud in the mist of time but now he was here, and he was demanding Amira once again.

'Mohammed. I need your answer,' his father shouted.

'Is that my grandfather?' Amira asked, poking her head out of the tent.

'Stay out of sight,' Mohammed whispered. 'Don't let him hear your voice.'

'What is he doing circling us as if we're strangers?' she asked, whispering. 'And what does he mean by "you stole something from him"?'

The men looked uncomfortable. Beb wanted to speak, but Mohammed held up his hand to stop him. 'Your grandfather is a very bad man,' Mohammed said. 'He is the reason we left the caravan.'

'I know that, but why is he here?' Amira asked. 'What did you steal from him?'

'We didn't steal anything from him,' Katouh said.

'I want what is rightfully mine, Mohammed!' his father bellowed across the sands. 'You can't run anymore. Return what is mine to me and that will be an end to it.'

'What does he want?' Amira asked.

'You, Amira,' Beb said, tiring of the charade. 'Your grandfather wanted to take you as his wife, but your father wouldn't allow that to happen. So, he took you away from the tribe.'

'Is that true?' Amira asked, shocked. Mohammed nodded. 'But he's my grandfather.'

'That's why we left.'

'He's a disgusting pig,' Amira said. 'I would rather die than be married to him. Anyway, I'm already married. He can't change that.'

'He can if your husband is dead,' Mohammed said.

'Well, he isn't dead,' Amira said innocently.

'He could fix that very quickly,' Katouh said.

'You must be joking,' Amira said. 'Are you saying my grandfather would kill my husband and force me to marry him?'

'Exactly that,' Mohammed said.

'Your grandfather doesn't give up when he wants something,' Katouh said. 'That man would do anything to get what he wants. I wouldn't put anything past him.'

'Then shoot him,' Amira said angrily. 'Go and shoot him, Beb.'

'We will if he shows himself, but that's unlikely,' Mohammed said.

'If you give me a gun, I will shoot him myself,' she said.

'I don't think it will be that simple,' Mohammed said.

'What are we going to do?' Beb asked.

'We wait,' Mohammed said.

'Mohammed, my son. Meet me on the sand if you are man enough,' his father shouted. 'Or are you still the quivering coward you always were?'

Mohammed closed his eyes in silent prayer. He stood up.

'Father!' Amira gasped. 'What are you doing?'

'I'm going to speak to him,' Mohammed said. 'I'm going to apologise for our behaviour and give him the opportunity to show us mercy and leave us alone.'

'And what if he doesn't listen?' Beb asked.

'Then I'll kill him.'

CHAPTER 23

Damilola & Kalu

Damilola was found by a Danish tourist who needed to use the toilet. He was lucky, as the Dane was an ambulance worker in Copenhagen. He managed to apply plugs to the knife wounds using pieces of clothing and stem the bleeding while he ran up to the ticket hall to raise the alarm. His speedy actions kept Damilola alive until the paramedics arrived. They put fluids into him, but as fast as they were putting them in, he was losing blood internally. He was taken to King's College Hospital, which was a short drive away with the sirens blaring and the blue lights flashing. The A&E doctors whisked him into theatre, where they worked frantically to stop the bleeding.

Damilola had his wallet and several forms of ID inside, and Kalu had been identified as his father and tracked down within an hour. Kalu had been carrying out a clinic at a private hospital forty minutes away. The traffic was horrendous as he tried to make his way across the river, and a crash on the Vauxhall Bridge slowed traffic to a standstill. Kalu had tried to reach Kissie more times than he could remember, without success, and he was on the edge of insanity when the call came that Beb had been stabbed. He was in a public toilet in a Tube station that he had no cause to be in. Kennington Station had a domed entrance hall, which he had seen before but never had a reason to use the Tube from there. There was no reason for Beb to be in that part of the city. He had a car, which cost Kalu a fortune to run, so why was he in a Tube station south of the river?

Beb had been enslaved as a young boy and held captive by the desert for years until he could escape, to find his mother and older sisters had perished and after all he'd endured, would his life be extinguished by an attack in a public toilet? Kalu wept like a baby as he sat in traffic, praying for the lives of both his children. He wondered what evil he had done in a previous life to be punished so harshly in this one. His phone rang, and he answered the call on hands-free.

'Hello,' Kalu said.

'Is this Dr Sami?'

'Yes. It is,' Kalu said.

'This is Dr Mumford at Kings,' the accent was Irish. 'I've been asked to contact you as a courtesy. It's about your son Beb.'

'How is he?'

'He's not out of the woods yet,' Dr Mumford said. 'We've been trying to find a bleed near the right kidney, and it's been a bugger, but we think we have the little bastard now.' Kalu closed his eyes and took a deep breath. 'We've been pumping bags of A-negative into him like it's going out of fashion, so we have, but it was coming out faster than we could get it in. He's not leaking anymore, but you know the score. There are three deep-penetrating injuries, and we can only hope we've got everything that was nicked. It was a six-inch blade at least,' he explained, talking quickly. 'Are you on your way here?'

'What did you say about A-negative?' Kalu asked, confused.

'I said we've been pumping bags of A-negative into him like it's going out of fashion,' Dr Mumford said with a chuckle. 'Apologies. It's an old saying my mum used to use.'

'My son is O-positive,' Kalu said. 'We all are.'

'With all due respect, Dr Sami, we know how to type a patient,' Dr Mumford said with a snort. 'The patient on that table is A-RhD negative.'

'If he is, then that isn't my son,' Kalu said, slamming his fist on the horn as a cyclist cut him up. 'Fucking idiot!' he shouted out of the window. The cyclist flicked him the finger and carried on. 'I'm not far away, Dr Mumford. Can you tell me how he was identified?'

'He had his wallet in his pocket,' Dr Mumford said. 'I believe his driving licence was in it.'

'He must have stolen my son's wallet,' Kalu said, relieved. 'Beb, his sister, and I are all O-RhD positive.' He sighed with relief. 'I did wonder what he was doing in that part of the city,' Kalu said, shrugging. The anxiety was lifting. 'That cannot be my son.'

'Okay, we'll sort it out when you get here,' Dr Mumford said. 'Your son was lucid for a short time when we were prepping him. He said his name was Beb.'

CHAPTER 24

Kissie, Pripyat

Kissie sat in the back of the Red Cross jeep as it pulled out of the convoy and headed in the opposite direction towards the town. Oleg had decided that in her weakened condition, and with a head injury, she was a priority. The convoy was static and wasn't moving north anymore. They'd heard the sounds of explosions and seen the rising plumes of black smoke and they could only assume the worst, which was there had been a missile attack on vehicles near the front of the column.

Driving Kissie a few miles to safety wasn't going to affect the militarised response. Kissie was all but shattered and she told the Red Cross man that the professor leading the research team was trying to reach her. They'd only gone a few miles when they saw a red Lada approaching on the wrong side of the road and waved them down as they neared. Kissie saw that it was Angela driving. Oleg got out of the Jeep and helped Kissie to get into the passenger seat of the Lada. She mumbled how grateful she was, and the Red Cross man waved and smiled. In different circumstances, they could have become friends, but this was a war zone now and any friendships made were fleeting and fragile.

'I'm sorry it took me so long to get to you, but the road is blocked near the station,' Angela said. 'The police and military have set up roadblocks all around the town, and it's virtually impossible to get anywhere. I had to rant and rave and stamp my feet and I even said the F-word a few times so they would let me through.'

'It's okay, Angela,' Kissie said. 'It's not your fault that wanker Putin has invaded the country. I cannot believe that they're targeting civilian vehicles.'

'Not just civilian vehicles, they're targeting anything and everything they can. We're hearing reports that entire residential tower blocks have been hit with the loss of all the people who lived in them.'

'It's absolutely disgusting. Surely, they can't allow him to do this. Other countries will come to help Ukraine, I'm sure they will. They have to.'

'I wouldn't be too sure about that at the moment,' Angela said. 'NATO will be reluctant to get involved as things will escalate and nobody wants a nuclear war, as there will be no winners. I think Ukraine will have to face this battle alone as far as boots on the ground go. No one else will send their troops or tanks to fight directly against the Russians, as Putin has already threatened an unprecedented response to any interference from the West.'

Angela turned the vehicle around and they headed back towards the abandoned town. As they passed the old railway station, which had been closed since the reactor fire, they saw people standing on the platform with suitcases.

'Why are those people standing on the platform?' Kissie asked.

'Because the people on the radio are advising listeners to get to their nearest railway station even if they've been out of use. I don't understand why they're telling people to do that. It's not as if trains are suddenly just going to appear to evacuate people. This country is huge.' Angela shrugged and reached for her cigarettes. She lit one without asking if Kissie minded her smoking in the car. 'I'm guessing that they're hoping people may use the tracks to walk to the next city or nearest town as long as they're moving away from the Russian attack.'

'I can't believe this is happening. It's one thing telling people to leave their homes and go to the next town or city as long as it's in the opposite direction, but where do these people go?' Kissie opened the window. She reached for Angela's cigarette packet and lit one of the cigarettes. Angela looked at her and smiled.

'I didn't know you smoked,' Angela said.

'I don't, but at this moment in time I'll try anything to calm my nerves,' Kissie said, inhaling. She coughed and spluttered, and they both laughed. 'How on Earth do you smoke these things?' Kissie tossed it out of the window. 'They're disgusting.'

They drove on for a while, both lost in their own thoughts, both looking at the faces of the men and women in the military vehicles on the opposite side of the road. Some of them looked frightened, while others laughed and joked. Many were on their phones, probably checking how their families were and what was going on in different parts of the country. The line started moving again as they approached the abandoned city. They drove through Lenin Square past the Hotel Polissya. They were stopped three times at roadblocks but were waved through very quickly. The sense of relief when they reached their hotel was indescribable. Although they were far from safe, it was safer than where they had been. There were hundreds of Ukrainian defenders between them and the Russian advance, which they both thought would give them a window of time to plan their escape from Pripyat, although the clock was ticking, it gave them a bit of flexibility.

'Is everybody else accounted for?' Kissie asked.

'Yes. You were the last one to be rounded up,' Angela said.

'So, what do we do next?'

'We have a meeting with the security company who looks after all the foreign workers, so we weigh up our options,' Angela said. 'It's three hours or so to Kiev, but we don't know where's safe and we're not likely to know. This is going to be an ongoing situation, changing hour by hour.'

'Will we be able to fly out of the country?' Kissie asked.

'No,' Angela said. 'We've already explored that avenue and we've been told that the Russians are attacking the airports, both military and civilian, and all commercial flights in and out of the country have been stopped.'

'So, we're gonna be limited to road or rail,' Kissie said. 'Trying to escape by road will be a huge mistake because everybody else will be doing the same and the roads in this country are not great at the best of times, but with thousands of people displaced, they will become car parks. I know what it's like to be in a truck with tanks advancing behind you. It's a nightmare and so many things can go wrong and do go wrong, and people panic and when they panic, they're unpredictable. And I know this from experience. I've been here before.'

CHAPTER 25

Oke & Isime, Monguno

Oke dipped a cloth into a pan of cold water and dabbed at Rashid's brow. His skin had become as thin as tissue, and she was scared that it was going to tear. He groaned in agony and his eyes flickered open for a second. There was recognition in them just for a moment, and then the recognition turned to fear. He tried to speak, but his tongue was so swollen and sore that his words were garbled and unintelligible. Oke tried to soothe him, but there wasn't really anything she could do to take away his pain. His body was deteriorating at a frightening rate. She left him, closed the bedroom door behind her, and went to see if the children were okay. The girls were tucked up in their beds and Kareem had climbed in beside Rida and she held him in her arms, his head on her chest as he slept.

'I need you to pack some things, Najma,' Oke said. 'Put all the fresh underwear into that basket and pack some warm things in case it's cold at night.'

'Where are we going?' Rida asked.

'You know your father is very sick and there are other men in the town who are also sick. The town elders are setting up a hospital to take care of them all and we have to go with Father to make sure that he is okay.'

'Will there be doctors there to make him better?'

'Yes, there will be doctors there and nurses and they will have medicine that will help Father to breathe and stop being sick,' Oke lied. 'Your uncle Droon is very sick, too. And your cousin Mahid has a really bad cough and a sore throat, so I think your auntie Isime will be at the hospital too.'

'And where is the hospital?'

'They are setting it up inside the old school on the hill,' Oke said.

'But it stinks in there. One of the farmers kept his goats in there and it smells of wee and poo,' Najma said.

'And how do you know what this building smells like, young lady?'

'I went there with my friends one day when we were exploring and we saw a cat and followed it and it went inside the school through a gap in the door,' Najma explained. 'And then we went to the gap, but the snow was too bad, and the gap was too narrow for us to get in, so we looked through the window. The farmer was sleeping on the floor and the goats were just walking around. I hope they have cleaned it before they take Father there.'

'Why don't they take them to the proper hospital?'

'Because no one knows what is wrong with them or why they are so sick and because it's contagious and other people are catching it,' Oke explained. 'That is why we have to go too, just in case we get sick. So that we will already be in the hospital where they can look after us. Are any of you feeling poorly?' Oke asked. The children all shook their heads, even Kareem, who just copied everything his sister said, anyway. 'Good. You must tell me if you start feeling poorly, if your throat gets sore, or you start to cough even just a bit. And when we go on the journey to the hospital, you must not touch your father. Or anybody else, for that matter. Do you understand me?' The children all nodded again.

'When will we be going to the hospital?' Rida asked. 'Maybe we could help the doctors and nurses to make Father better.'

'It's a very kind thought that you might help other people, but the people who are going to this hospital are so sick that some of them will die. And nobody is quite sure what type of sickness they have, but they do know that it can pass from one human to another, so you will not go near anybody who is sick. Do you understand what I am saying to you?'

Her children nodded that they understood but the expression on their faces told her that they didn't have a clue what was going on or why they had to leave their home.

****

Isime stood over the body of her mother-in-law and tried to make sense of what had killed her, but there was no sense or reason for it. She had bled from her eyes, ears, nose, and from her mouth. That meant that something catastrophic had happened to the cells in her body. It had to be connected to the sickness affecting her husband and her son, otherwise it was too much of a coincidence that she would suddenly develop an illness that would do so much damage in such a short time. She was desperate for answers so that she could help her child. But the armed men outside the house had different ideas. They were trying to contain whatever it was affecting people by leaving them in their homes to suffer and die. She had to speak to someone, but there were no phones and no mobiles in the town unless you were a senior member of the militia. They all had iPhones or Samsungs, and she'd heard that some of them had internet access. It was one rule for them and another rule for everybody else. That is just how it worked.

Being a Boko wife meant that your life had no value. The men didn't value their own lives and were prepared to risk them to fight against the government troops whenever possible. They loved war. They loved to fight anybody who wasn't them. Boko was their everything.

But rules were rules, and she understood she couldn't question them, and she had to follow them to the letter, or her life would be in danger, but the life of her son was more important to her than her own.

She went back to the bedroom where her husband and son were lying. She went to her son first and checked him. He was sweating and burning up with a fever, his eyes were bloodshot, and there were blisters on his lips and around his mouth. His cheeks were pink and wrinkled, as if his skin had been in water for a very long time. It was as if he'd been burnt in a fire or had acid on his skin. She had never seen anything like it, and she felt so helpless she thought her heart would break.

Her son was dying in front of her eyes and there was absolutely nothing she could do about it.

CHAPTER 26

Beb, Mohammed, Amira, & Heba

Beb's hands were shaking as he checked how many bullets he had in the rifle and Amira clung to their daughter as if someone was threatening to drag her away. There was fear in her eyes and Beb could see sweat trickling from her temple down her cheeks. He was trying to remain calm for her benefit and the benefit of their daughter. Although he was cool on the outside, inside was a maelstrom of anxiety, fear, and confusion. Everything had been so perfect for so long and now this man, who he had never met before, was threatening to take everything from him and he was never going to allow that to happen. They would die first.

'I'm coming with you,' Beb said.

'No. You will stay here with my daughter and my granddaughter, and you will protect them with your last breath,' Mohammed said. 'I will face him alone.'

'If you go out there alone, he will kill you and you are our best shot,' Katouh said. 'We won't stand a chance against them without you. I will go and speak to him. He might listen to me.'

'Why would he start to listen to you now?' Mohammed asked, shaking his head. 'He never listened to us before, so what makes you think things have changed?'

'What if I go and speak to him alone?' Beb said. Mohammed shook his head, and Katouh did the same. 'He has history with both of you and he feels as if you have wronged him and if he is as stubborn and malicious as you say, he is unlikely to agree with anything you offer. I may be able to make him see sense.'

'You have no idea who our father is or what he's like,' Mohammed said. 'The man is a megalomaniac with narcissistic tendencies and all the judgement of a psychopathic lunatic. In a different society, he would have been locked up by now.'

'Why don't we all go to speak to him together?' Amira said. 'If he sees me and Heba and I tell him how happy I am, he may relent.'

'You are both badly mistaken. You're not listening to a word I have said to you,' Mohammed said. 'This man will not stop until he has what he came here for, and that is you, my daughter. If we all go together, he will see that you have a child. The child that you have borne to another man. Do you have any idea what that means to a man like him?'

'He will see it as an insult to his authority,' Katouh agreed.

'That may be a good thing,' Amira said. 'If he realises that I am no longer the innocent young girl he once knew and that I have a husband who is a good man and that we have started a family, maybe he'll see sense and decide that I am no longer a suitable wife for him.'

'You were never a suitable wife for him,' Mohammed said. 'You are his granddaughter. The only reason he chose you in the first place was that he was sexually attracted to you.'

'Please don't speak like that, Father.' Amira cringed and shook her head. She couldn't look her father in the eye, and Beb could see how frightened and disturbed she was.

'You must understand that what he wanted to do was not right on any scale. He did not need another wife. He has more children than any man could want or need. This marriage was never for the benefit of the family or the people of the caravan. It was all about the selfish needs of the wicked old man. He is a pervert.'

'Stop saying that,' Amira said. 'You're making me feel sick.'

'I would not let him near you then, and I will not let him near you and your daughter now. There are many good people travelling with my father and many of them were disappointed with his decision to marry his granddaughter. Those people will still be of that opinion and maybe if I talk to him, I can make him aware of just how many people disagreed with him.' Mohammed shrugged and checked his weapon again. 'I am his eldest son and heir. If I cannot make him see sense and he insists on trying to take you away from us, I will have to kill him and put myself at the mercy of the rest of the family for the crime.'

'If we cannot come up with a different solution, which does not involve you meeting him on the sand, then I am going with you whether you like it or not,' Beb said. Mohammed made to protest, but Beb raised his hand and cocked his rifle. 'I will go alone and speak to him myself before I let you leave here on your own. If your father has such venom for you, then he won't see how foolish he is being. Maybe if he hears it from the husband of your daughter and the father of her child, it may resonate a bit clearer.'

'Mohammed, I have given you enough time to make your decision. Meet me on the sand and we can talk like father and son to resolve this issue.' The voice echoed across the dunes. 'My marriage to Amira has been delayed far too long already. You have deprived me of a wife, and you have deprived me of the children we would have had if you hadn't run away like a spoilt child.'

'That's enough.' Beb couldn't listen to his inane ranting any longer and he began walking towards the centre ground between the two groups. Amira tried to call him back, but he carried on walking.

'What are you doing?' Amira shouted.

'I've heard enough,' Beb said. 'If he wants to talk, then I'll talk to him and explain we're married. And if he doesn't like it, I'll end him.'

'If he doesn't listen to you, Beb, shoot him,' Amira said. 'I love you.'

'I love you too and I'll be back shortly,' Beb said. Mohammed caught up with him and the two men exchanged glances but needed no words to communicate what needed to be done. They walked shoulder to shoulder into the night.

CHAPTER 27

Damilola & Kalu

Kalu arrived at the hospital and made his way to the reception to check which ward the man with Beb's driving licence had been moved to. He wasn't anxious anymore; he was furious that this man had Beb's wallet on him. Pickpockets were as rife in the city now as they ever had been. Fagin and the Artful Dodger weren't a patch on the organised gangs who worked the streets nowadays. He intended to clear up the identification and report it to the police. He would be pressing charges, no doubt about it. There would be police officers there, as the man had been stabbed. They would need to speak to the next of kin to gain background on the movements of the victim.

It was curiosity more than anything that made him come to the hospital at all. He'd stopped worrying that it was Beb once he realised the blood type was wrong and it couldn't be his son who'd been stabbed.

When he had first heard the news about the attack, he'd been devastated. The guilt which surrounded Beb being kidnapped was so consuming that he treated his son as if he could do no wrong, as if just being alive was enough. He could not contemplate losing Beb for the second time in one lifetime. That would be too cruel to comprehend and something that no parent should have to endure. When Dr Mumford had said that they were pumping A-negative blood into him,

Kalu realised the injured man couldn't be his son and, however selfish it may appear, he was glad it was somebody else's son and not his.

When Kalu arrived at the ward, he sanitised his hands and went to the nurses' station. The ward sister was at the desk, handing out orders in all directions in her Nigerian accent. She spotted him walking down the ward and stood up to intercept him. It was obvious she was expecting him. There were police officers further down the ward, standing and drinking coffee outside a private room.

'You must be Dr Sami,' she said, smiling. Her smile lit up the ward. 'I have been waiting for you. Dr Mumford said you were on your way and that there is some confusion about the identity of your son?'

'Dr Mumford may be confused, but I am not,' Kalu said. 'The man Dr Mumford operated on was blood type A. Myself and all my family are the same blood type. We are all type O. The injured man cannot be my son. It's a physical impossibility.'

'We both know that it is impossible to get a blood type wrong, especially when the patient needed nearly ten litres of it,' she said. 'There must be an explanation.'

'I think the best thing to do is let me see the patient and confirm he isn't my son, then we can take it from there,' Kalu said. 'I'm in a bit of a rush, so if we can hurry this up, I would be very grateful. Of course, I will have to speak to the police about this man having my son's wallet. He must have stolen it. I just want the wallet back. I don't want to press charges. He's got enough to worry about. Poor bugger.'

'Of course, you will have to speak to them and get the wallet back, Dr Sami,' she said. The ward sister didn't look overly impressed with his prioritising. 'If you follow me this way, I will show you to his room and you will be able to see him from the window. And then we can clear this up once and for all. It won't be the first time we've had people on this ward pretending to be somebody else. I'm sure it's happened to you before now. People will tell you anything if they think it will get them out of trouble and the police might be involved,' she added as they approached.

'I can second that,' one of the officers agreed.

'Last week, we had Brad Pitt, George Clooney, and Winston Churchill all on the same ward. Can you believe that?' She laughed.

'Every day of the week,' the other officer said.

'Let the dog see the rabbit,' she said. They approached the room and looked through the window. 'Here he is, sleeping beauty. He's had enough anaesthetic to knock out a horse for three days, so I wouldn't expect him to be waking up any time soon.'

They looked through the window at the man in the bed. His eyes were closed, and his face was tilted towards them. Kalu felt sickened to the core. There was absolutely no doubt in his mind that the man in the bed was Beb. And yet he knew in his heart of hearts that it was a physical impossibility for that man to be related to him. There was no way that a son or daughter of his and his wife could have that type of blood. He knew the blood type of his children from the time they were born and there were no anomalies whatsoever. It could mean only one thing.

The man in the bed, who had returned from the dead and said he was Beb, was a liar and an impostor and quite probably a murderer.

CHAPTER 28

Kissie

Kissie and the other scientists were gathered in the dining room of the hotel with twelve other international employees from various organisations. There were nearly twenty people in total, including the men who were holding the meeting, who were the security detail for the foreign nationals. One of them was an ex-paratrooper from the UK, another was a Navy seal from the US, two of them were French ex-Foreign Legion, and the others were made up of ex-forces from Poland and Hungary.

Their normal remit was to make sure that none of the foreign nationals were going into the abandoned zones around the sarcophagus, which sealed the doomed reactor number four. Anyone entering that area who stayed for more than a few minutes would be glowing in the dark very quickly.

Their secondary remit was to make sure that if any of the researchers were going into remote areas, they were escorted by at least one armed guard. They were a ragtag bunch and some of them were a bit scary and had a demeanour that made Kissie and some of the other women uncomfortable, making comments in their native tongues and giggling like schoolboys. There wasn't one thing she could put her finger on, but a collection of incidents which gave them the feeling they wouldn't be safe alone with some of the guards. Tom was the ex-paratrooper from the UK, and he was in his 40s with a weathered face and a pugilist's nose. His manner was of a no-nonsense professional, which warned other men not to mess with him. He had hands like shovels, wide shoulders, and was narrow at the hip and when he wasn't working, he was either in the gym or out jogging somewhere. Keeping fit was still a lifestyle for the ex-para, who spoke four different languages. Kissie felt safe around Tom.

Tom had warned her and some of the other scientists not to go anywhere alone with the guards from Hungary or Poland. He said it was nothing to do with them being Hungarian or Polish or pervy; it was that their training and experience was nowhere near as intense as that of a paratrooper or navy seal. He said they were chocolate soldiers, who would melt if the heat was turned up. It had sounded odd when she first heard it, but it did make sense. The scientists used to joke that if they really needed an ex-paratrooper or navy seal to keep them safe, then perhaps they shouldn't go out at all. Of course, the joking stopped when Putin started his war games across the border in Belarus, which was so close to Chernobyl it was merely a leisurely drive away.

The mood in the room today was tense and the security men were all carrying automatic weapons and wearing bulletproof vests. There were no smiles today and no jokes, just the serious business of how to get everybody safely out of Ukraine.

Brad was the ex-navy seal and had been given the authority to take control of the exit strategy by their employer, Whitewater. He was standing at the end of the room next to a whiteboard, which had been borrowed from one of the offices. He'd written bullet points in black marker pen and was ready to start working through them, in order to explain what their options were and why they were the only options available.

'I won't waste anyone's time with introductions. You all know who everybody is, and you also know who is missing,' Brad said. A gloomy silence fell over the room as he began. Of course, everyone knew he was referring to the death of Omar, the minibus driver, and the other civilians who were killed. 'The drone strike which killed Omar is only one of hundreds being reported across the country. The

Russians are targeting indiscriminately both military and civilian vehicles, which is going to make getting out of here harder.'

'We've heard there are local sympathisers using lasers to guide the drone strikes?' Pierre said. He was one of the ex-Foreign Legion men.

'We've heard the same,' Brad said, nodding. 'They're not playing by the rules, which stipulate only military targets can be bombed. Putin is hitting anything. Residential tower blocks have been hit along with schools, hospitals, railway stations, and airports. The Russians have taken out the military airbases, which gives them air superiority and there are no commercial flights in or out of the country for the foreseeable future.'

'Which means what?' Angela asked.

'Which means there will be no flights until the end of the conflict and the withdrawal of all Russian troops and aircraft from the area,' Tom answered. 'We can't trust them not to target passenger planes.'

'It's been left too late, as usual,' a Hungarian guard complained. 'It's a joke and not a funny one.'

'So, there's no business class home?' one of the scientists said. Kissie recognised him as an Israeli called Levi. He was an argumentative man at the best of times. 'Why are there no evacuation flights being arranged?'

'Russian troops have ground-to-air missiles, and they're trigger-happy. They would have no problem bringing down any commercial jet. So flying you out of here is impossible.'

'What about helicopters?' Peter, one of the Polish guards, asked.

'What about them?' Brad asked, trying to be polite.

'Couldn't they get us out of here on a military helicopter before the Russians get here?'

'I'm not sure who you mean when you say "they", Peter?' Brad said, shrugging. 'Do you mean the Ukrainians or the British or the Americans? Because I don't know who *they* are?'

'Whoever the fuck is in charge,' Peter sniped.

'No one is in charge. This is a war zone now, but I will tell you the Germans, French, British, the Americans, and everybody else not directly involved in this conflict won't be sending planes, helicopters, tanks, or any other fucking thing with wings, tracks, or wheels into a war zone when the Russians are the antagonists. Everyone will be shitting themselves about this escalating. Putin has his finger poised over the nuclear button and no one doubts he's crazy enough to use it.'

'We're on our own here,' Tom added. 'There are bigger priorities than moving us to safety. The entire nation is under attack and it's up to us to get you to a safe border crossing.'

'Thanks, Tom.' Brad shrugged and stared at the Pole. 'So, there is no *they* and no one is coming to get us out of Pripyat.'

'As usual,' Peter said. 'No one has our backs. Why would we expect anything else?'

'It's good to hear our security detail is singing from the same hymn sheet,' Levi muttered. 'I'm assuming there is dissension among the ranks?'

'There are different schools of thoughts, but the bottom line is that no one is going to get us out of Ukraine apart from the people in this room.'

'Okay, so what is your plan?' the Pole asked.

'The city of Kiev is a hundred-and-forty kilometres from here, which on a nice sunny day will take us between two to three hours to get to and on a normal day, we'd be able to get a plane or a train from Kiev across the border to Poland or Moldova but all public transport is going to be a no-no for us.'

'Why are you ruling out Romania, Hungary, and Slovakia?' Levi asked, showing off his geography skills.

'Does he like the sound of his own voice?' Angela whispered to Kissie. Kissie nodded and rolled her eyes.

'He's a dick,' Kissie said.

'The security team is not on the same page,' Angela whispered.

'I wish they would shut up and let Brad finish,' Kissie said. 'Peter is doing my head in.'

'We're not ruling anywhere out,' Tom said, supporting Brad. 'Geographically, Poland and Moldova are the closest borders to where we are. Why not listen to what Brad is saying and then we can discuss it?'

'Oh. Sorry,' Peter said, shaking his head. 'You two have put your heads together without consulting the rest of us, but you think we should sit in silence and listen without voicing an opinion?'

'We're paid to protect these people here,' Tom said. 'We're not in the business of consulting with less experienced people.'

Peter thought better about responding. Tom and Brad had been in action many times. None of the others had. 'I've lost count of the number of exit strategies we've put together and we're still here. If we thought you could add anything useful, we would have asked.' Peter flicked the finger and grinned.

'As I was saying,' Brad continued. 'We have to rule out public transport for now.'

'Including trains?' Levi asked. 'Why can't we get on a train?'

'The trains will be full of Ukrainian women and children, as all the men have been ordered to stay behind to fight. We won't be priority for a while. Until they evacuate all the children, at least.'

'This is absolutely crazy,' Kissie said. 'I wouldn't want to be on a train crossing the country while the Russian drones are firing missiles at anything that moves.'

'So, what you're saying is the only way out of this country is by road?' Levi asked.

'Unfortunately, yes, but it's not as simple as it sounds,' Brad said. 'You all know what the roads in this country are like. They were not built for hundreds of people to drive on at the same time. That means that our hundred-and-forty-kilometre drive could take us days rather than hours. We have to assume that everybody close to the border will be heading for the nearest city and obviously Kiev is the nearest to us. We'll be sitting ducks in a traffic jam.'

'What about heading straight for the border?' Levi asked.

'From here to Moldova is four-hundred-and-seventy kilometres and would normally take seven hours by road, Warsaw is eight hundred kilometres from here and would normally take eleven hours, but we have to assume that the roads are going to be gridlocked at points.'

'We would have to go west to Poland and we're too close to the border,' Tom added. 'We need to put some distance between us and the Russian columns, which means heading south first.'

'Sitting in a car for hours on end in gridlock will put immense pressure on us and our supplies. We won't be able to carry enough water and food and sanitation equipment to last for the entire journey. That means we're going to need to set up resupply stops along the way which our military contacts should be able to help with.'

'And how will your contacts know where we'll be and when, if we don't have a clue if we're going to be able to get through?' one of the Hungarians asked.

'The fact of the matter is they won't know, but we can tell them which routes we're planning to take, and they may be able to hide supplies along the route.'

'That way it won't matter when we arrive,' Tom agreed. 'They can bury boxes for us at designated points along the way,' Tom added.

'I can see some of you are looking confused, but this situation does not have a solid set of rules and guidelines we can follow. We don't know where the Russians are today, and we don't know where they're going to be tomorrow. We certainly can't see any further ahead than that. This is all educated guesswork.'

'How fast do you think the advance will be?' Angela asked.

'I'm being told that the Ukrainian army, both the regulars and the conscripts, have been training for this since before the Crimea was annexed eight years ago. Their resistance is going to be organised and determined, and they're being armed with equipment from all over the world. They have anti-tank missiles, and they know how to use them. Without infantry support, the Russians will take heavy casualties and if they make progress, it will be slow,' Brad explained.

'Ukrainian men have to complete national service and serve in the military for at least two years at some point in their lives, which means they're all accustomed to using a weapon. This basically means that every Ukrainian man and some teenagers are now part of the resistance,' Tom explained. 'We're being assured that a Russian advance will be hampered and hindered every inch of the way.'

'Tom is right and if that is the case, then the Russian army will not be taking Kiev in the next two days. I'm certain we can make it there within that time frame. Kiev will act as a shield for the roads and towns to the south and west of the city as the Russians will have to go through the city to access the rest of the country.' Brad pointed to a map. 'If we can get through the city in one piece, we can reassess which border is the most accessible and which is the safest route.'

The room was silent as everybody tried to absorb the shocking facts of the situation they were in. They were effectively trapped in a foreign country and their only way out was to drive or walk.

'We don't have enough vehicles to carry everyone to,' Peter said. 'There isn't enough room to carry us all and enough supplies.'

'We know that,' Brad said, smiling, but there was no mirth in his smile. His eyes bored into the Pole.

'Even if we load them up with enough water and supplies to last us until we get to Kiev, what do you think is going to be happening in the cities?' Peter asked.

'Why don't you enlighten us, Peter?' Brad said. The atmosphere was uncomfortable.

'People will be stockpiling food and water. The shops and supermarkets will be empty by the time we get there and the petrol stations will have run dry.' He gestured to the seated audience. 'If we try to take these people as one group across Ukraine to one of the borders, we will be captured and shot, or we'll have to hole up and we'll starve to death.'

'I'm sure people will help us,' Kissie said.

'You think they'll embrace a black African while their family is hungry?' Peter sneered. 'You're not even European. We will struggle.

There is no love lost between the Polish and the Ukrainians, and they're not going to risk themselves or their provisions so that a Polish mercenary can survive.'

'You are absolutely right, Peter. We don't have enough vehicles to carry everyone, but I'm absolutely certain that you have no intention of travelling with us and protecting these people anyway, so let's not bullshit each other,' Brad said, shaking his head.

'What are you talking about?' Peter blushed.

Brad stared at the man in the eye. 'You guys seem to think that you're the only people who can speak Polish, but my wife is Polish, and Tom is almost fluent in Polish and Hungarian.' Peter flushed purple and the veins in his neck pulsed. The Polish men exchanged glances with the Hungarians.

'We speak a little Polish too,' Pierre added. 'You guys need to clean up your act.'

'Fuck you, frog eater,' Peter muttered.

'You meet all sorts in the Legion.' The French men laughed.

'Mostly queers, I bet,' Peter said, blushing.

'Wow, how old are you?' Angela said, shaking her head. 'Is this a fucking kindergarten?'

'I've been listening to you for days, weeks actually, and you've made it quite clear that if there was an invasion it will be every man for himself and you would make it to the Polish border by hook or by crook and anyone who gets in your way would feel a bullet between the eyes,' Brad said. You could cut the air with a knife it was so tense. 'Unless you have had a change of heart, you won't be travelling with us.'

'You think you're so clever, Mr American... Mr Navy Seal. You think that we are not the same level as you, but I'm telling you now that one thing I'm sure of is that you will never make it to the border while you're babysitting these people.' He pointed to the people in the room again. 'Look at them. They are teachers and bookworms with absolutely no idea how to survive in a combat situation. None of them are going to last more than a week.'

'I think you're underestimating these very bright people,' Tom said.

'What you're attempting is crazy and we don't get paid enough to die to protect these money grabbers. And that's all they are,' Peter said.

'Money grabbers?' Angela said, shaking her head. 'How dare you?'

'You come here because you get paid five times more money to be in Chernobyl than they do in London or New York. And that's fine when everything is going to plan, and they go out and they collect their little soil samples with their little trowels and their little buckets and then they come back and look at them under the microscope and tell us that everything is radioactive.' He threw his head back and laughed while lighting a cigarette. 'Fucking hell, what a bunch of geniuses they are, coming all the way here to the place where the biggest nuclear disaster of all time happened, and they tell us that the ground and the water is radioactive.' Peter inhaled and gestured to the scientists. 'You people are a fucking waste of space.'

'Why don't you say what you really think?' Levi said sarcastically. 'Stop beating around the bush.'

'Funny, Jewish man,' Peter said, nodding. He glared at him. 'I could stay in Poland and tell you that Chernobyl is fucking radioactive.'

'I wish you had,' Kissie said.

'You are like leeches working for the highest bidder. But now the shit has hit the fan and the money grabbers are stuck here with no way home and you want me to put my life on the line for the same money?'

'Leeches. How dare you?' Angela said. 'You're a mercenary, for fuck's sake. Pot, kettle, black.'

'Fuck you, Mrs American. You walk round here with your head so far up your own arse you can't see what's going on around you,' Peter snarled. 'You need a good fuck, lady.'

'You need to watch your mouth,' Tom said.

'You're disgusting,' Kissie said.

'The clever ones from your team went home when they had the chance, but you greedy fuckers decided to stay and now you're going to have to pay the price.' Peter grinned. 'But the problem is, it doesn't matter how much money you've got right now, lady, because you can't buy your way out of here.'

'If you're planning on going it alone,' Tom said. 'Then I suggest you pack up your vehicle, take whatever water and food you need, and get going while you have the chance. There's no need to get personal and leave on bad terms. You might want a job with Whitewater sometime in the future. Personal protection is a tightknit community, and they don't hire arseholes.' Tom waited for a challenge, but it didn't come. 'Go and pack up your gear, soldier.'

'That's exactly what we intend to do. And we'll be taking these weapons too,' Peter said. He looked nervous as he spoke to Tom. Tom was calm, but the look in his eyes warned the Polish man not to push it too far. 'We'll take the Toyota pickup truck.'

'Those weapons belong to Whitewater, and they'll stay with its employees,' Tom said. 'And you will take the vehicle you arrived in,' Tom said, looking out the window at a rusty old Lada. 'I don't fancy your chances of making it to Warsaw in that heap of junk, but you could probably pick up something newer along the way. There will be plenty of abandoned vehicles on the roads.'

'I don't think so,' Peter said, shaking his head. 'We will keep these weapons and we will be taking the Toyota.'

'There is no negotiation taking place here,' Tom said. His eyes were steely blue and the muscles in his jaw tensed as he spoke. 'We're trying to be reasonable. We are not leaving you unarmed while you try to get home. We know you have some old Polish army weapons in the boot of your car. You can take what you came with and enough supplies to last you for a week and we wish you good luck and a safe journey.'

'Who said I was negotiating?' Peter said. 'We have our weapons in our hands and we won't be giving them up for you or anybody else. I have a wife and children to get back to, so have my colleagues, and we'll make sure that we've got the best chance of making it safely back to the Polish border, which means we'll be taking these weapons and the Toyota.'

'At the moment, those weapons aren't loaded,' Brad said. Peter looked confused. 'The problem with you Eastern European mercs is that you're sloppy. Rule number one during weapon training is to make sure your magazine is full and that you have a spare one to hand. I haven't seen you guys check a weapon or magazine since the day we arrived.'

Peter and his Polish colleagues looked horrified as they removed the clips from their weapons and found them to be empty. The Hungarian men followed suit and were equally embarrassed.

'So, let me reiterate our standpoint for everyone in the room. Whitewater employees are going to try their best to escort all these nice people here to the nearest border along the safest possible routes we can find. And that's not going to be an easy task.' Brad let his words sink in. 'Anyone who no longer wants to be a Whitewater employee is free to leave right now, stock up your vehicle with as much food and water as you need and go in peace. And Godspeed to you,' Brad said. He raised his weapon slightly and pointed it at Peter. 'Having said all that, be under absolutely no illusions that anybody trying to take weapons or supplies that do not belong to them will be dealt with as we would deal with a looter.'

'Looters?' Peter snorted. 'Are you threatening to shoot us?'

'Peter, let me assure you that I have never made a threat in my life. Take your Lada and your supplies and go.' Tom moved his weapon to his hip as Brad spoke. 'Your guns are nothing more than expensive clubs without bullets. Take the magazines out of them and leave your weapons on the table at the back of the room on your way out. If anyone of you wants to remain as a Whitewater employee, you're more than welcome, and I'll make sure that we all stay on the payroll while we deliver these people safely to a neutral country.'

'Fuck your job and fuck you,' Peter said.

'We have important things to discuss and not enough time to fuck about with people who don't want to be here, so I suggest you leave now and let us get on with the job at hand.'

Peter and his colleagues left the room. The Hungarians exchanged a few words between them followed suit, leaving Brad and Tom and the Foreign Legion mercs in the room. Tom took the weapons from the table and carried them to the front of the room, where he leant them against the wall. They waited for the Eastern Europeans to leave the room.

'That was emotional,' Levi said.

'I feel exhausted by the negativity they sucked from the room,' Angela said. 'What's next, guys?'

'Once we've decided our plan of action, any of you who want to know how to use one of these is more than welcome to carry one.' Tom pointed to the returned weapons. 'I will make sure you know which end to point at the Russians and how to make it work,' Tom said, smiling. 'Let's hope that we're far enough ahead of the invasion to make sure that none of you need to shoulder a rifle.' The room remained silent. 'We're not trying to frighten you. It's a precautionary measure, but it may give you some comfort to know that you can defend yourselves and your colleagues if needs be.'

'We have four vehicles, including the Toyota pickup, which our Polish friends are so keen to steal from us, and we need to decide who's travelling with who and why.'

'What do you mean?'

'We're going to try to travel in a convoy of four vehicles with the pickup carrying the majority of our supplies, but we can't risk putting all our eggs into one basket. If we were to lose the pickup, then we would run out of food and water very quickly, so we have to spread the food and water as evenly as possible across the four vehicles. We also need contingency plans in case we are separated, or we lose one or more of the vehicles. Tom will take one group in one of the Fords and I will take another group in the Volkswagen, and we will need two volunteers to learn how to use these weapons. Pierre and Frank will take the pickup, but we need at least one other person who knows how to shoot in each vehicle.'

'I'm more than happy to learn how to use the guns,' Angela said.

'I would like to carry one too,' a Spanish man called Paolo said. He was a quiet man with dark hair and a moustache, who specialised in fungi. 'I used to shoot rabbits on my grandparents' farm near Barcelona when I was a kid,' he said nervously. 'I'm not sure how I would feel about pointing it at another human being, but if push came to shove, and it's us or them, I don't think I have a problem.'

'I've been trained to shoot,' Levi said. 'I grew up in Jerusalem. I carried an M-14 to school.'

'I've seen a lot of guns in my time,' Kissie said, shaking her head. 'And I've never seen any good come from them, but under the circumstances, I will feel much safer if I have a machinegun in my hand. At least I will not feel as helpless as I do right now.'

For the next two hours or so, the team studied maps and tried to work out which routes would be the least used between them and Kiev. They decided to avoid the main roads and use the quieter roads parallel with, or close to, the main arteries. Tom and Brad were adamant that if something went wrong – and it probably would – they would need to be able to get back to the main roads quickly on foot. Both men made a flurry of phone calls, pulling in as many favours as they could. They were trying to gather food, water, and extra munitions to be hidden at points easily located along the way.

It was during one of these calls they were told that thousands of mines were being laid in the region between the Belarus border and the capital, Kiev. They were being laid in wheat fields, and across the farmlands which surrounded the small villages in the rural areas of the country. Ukrainian military couldn't spread itself thin enough to protect every small village and town in that area, which was vast, so they gave the locals the ability to protect themselves by mining as many approaches to their dwellings as possible. This meant that they wouldn't be able to leave their vehicles and track across open land. It was another hurdle and a difficult one to navigate if they had to leave their vehicles behind.

****

Kissie followed Angela onto the steps of the hotel at the rear of the building, where she went when she needed to smoke. Angela smiled at her as she approached and took another cigarette from her packet and handed it to her.

'You know that if we get out of here alive, you're going to kick yourself and blame me for you developing a twenty-a-day habit,' Angela said with a chuckle. 'Although if there was ever a time to start smoking, it's right now.'

'When we get out of here, I'm never going to smoke another cigarette again. And if I ever told my father that I'd had one, he would put me over his knee and beat me with a slipper,' Kissie said, laughing. 'He absolutely hates smoking and despite everything we've been through, if I started, he would probably think it's the worst thing that happened to us.'

'That bad, eh?' Angela said, smiling. 'You've had it pretty rough already, and now this.' She shook her head and took a deep drag on her cigarette. 'We're going to get out of here, don't worry, smoking or not.' She hugged Kissie gently.

'It wouldn't matter what the crisis is, he wouldn't forgive me for smoking,' Kissie said, returning her affection.

'Well, I'm not going to tell him, and I don't think you will, so what he doesn't know can't hurt him,' Angela said.

'That explains everything!'

They heard an engine starting and voices shouting and then a broken bottle smashed on the pavement in front of them. They both stepped back towards the door and looked to their right.

'They're rug munchers!'

Peter and the other men were loading provisions into the boot of two cars. One was the battered old Lada, and the other was a newer model which had four doors and an estate style rear. They were drinking bottles of beer and being lairy. Peter finished another bottle and launched it in their direction. It smashed on the bottom step, showering them in glass.

'Grow up, you Neanderthal,' Angela replied.

'Fuck you, American lady,' Peter said.

'Not for all your money and a gold clock,' Angela said.

'Oh, I think you would like it.'

'Not in this lifetime or the next.'

'Do you want to suck my dick before we go?' Peter asked, grabbing his crotch.

'I'm afraid we're in a bit of a rush and I don't have the time to find it,' Angela said, flicking him the finger.

The other men laughed, but Peter didn't. He was bitter and furious as he'd been made to look foolish several times that day already. Being put down by a female wasn't going to brighten up his day one little bit. He slammed the boot of the vehicle and barked some orders in Polish. The other men stopped laughing, grabbed some weapons out of the boot, and got into their vehicles. Ironically, they all checked that their weapons were loaded before climbing into their seats.

'Wow, you checked if you have bullets in them. You learnt something today.' Angela clapped and gave them a round of applause, which didn't go down very well. A few of them wound their windows down and hurled their best swear words in English in Angela's direction. They pulled out of the car park and onto the main road heading in the direction of Korosten.

'They're going in the wrong direction,' Tom said from behind them. He lit a cigarette and blew smoke rings, poking them with his index finger. 'At any other time, driving through Korosten is the quickest way to the Polish border, maybe an eleven- to twelve-hour drive.' He inhaled deeply.

'But not today?' Kissie asked.

'No. Not today. Korosten is a railway town, and it's much closer to the Belarus border than we are now. The first Russian column that came over the border will use the main roads and will make a beeline for anywhere that has an airport or railway station.'

'Why?' Kissie asked.

'Because to win any battle, you have to set up supply lines. Putin is gonna have to send tens of thousands of men and machines into Ukraine to have a hope of achieving regime change. An army marches on its stomach and tanks can't run on fresh air.'

'It's going to take a lot of food and a lot of diesel, bullets, water, and vodka to keep those columns moving in the right direction,' Angela said.

'Exactly,' Tom said, nodding. 'Taking the train stations and the railways will go a long way to securing the supply lines.' Tom took a deep drag on his cigarette. 'I don't have an awful lot of time for Peter and the other guys. They're cowboys and most of the time, they're a liability. And driving in that direction just reinforces everything that I've ever said about them. They haven't got a fucking Scooby Doo about soldering.'

'Are you saying they're heading straight towards the Russian invasion?' Kissie asked.

'I think if they get a clear run between here and Korosten, they'll probably arrive about the same time as the first Russian tanks.'

CHAPTER 29

Oke & Isime

Oke double-checked what the children had packed into their bags and then she went into the kitchen and gathered up everything that she could carry in one basket. She decided to cram another basket full of dried food, meats, mushrooms, and berries. She had no idea what the facilities would be like when they got to the school, but she could hazard a guess they would be non-existent. It had once been a bustling academy, full of children laughing and learning and positivity. They had access to books and the internet in those days and it sometimes felt like they'd regressed fifty years. She remembered it being a happy place, where the teachers were all smiling, and the children looked forward to being there. Going to school was never a chore; it had always been an absolute pleasure and most of the pupils appreciated the privilege of receiving an education. It was a thing of the past in her world.

She remembered that there was a kitchen at the centre of the building and the staff would make bread and soup on wood-burning ovens and the smells would drift along the corridors. She also remembered how excited everybody was with the introduction of a football pitch and a shower room which had hot water running from the taps. The boys and girls argued about who was playing on each team and they spent hours kicking the ball around. All the boys wanted replica football shirts, and they came from all over the world, but mostly from the UK. The pitch and showers had been installed by a British charity and the water was heated by solar panels on the roof of the school. One thing Nigeria wasn't short of was sunshine. They were happy memories of the town before the extremists arrived and dragged everyone back to a miserable existence. One of their first 'achievements' was to shoot the teachers and close the school for good. A legacy they were proud of and bragged about to this day. Oke couldn't comprehend a society which wanted its future leaders uneducated. There was no sustainability in such a community.

Of course, Oke and her family hadn't been there to witness the atrocities carried out by the extremists but those who survived and remained in the Monguno would sometimes tell tales of the horrors in whispers, always completely aware that the men they were married to, were the men responsible for those atrocities and more. A bang on the door disturbed her thoughts. Surely, they weren't going to move them at such a late hour. She went to the door and opened it and three Boko men were standing there, wearing mirrored sunglasses and smoking cigarettes.

'Why are you wearing those?' Oke asked, waving the smoke from her face. 'It is dark. How can you see where you're going?'

'We need to move you and your family to the hospital,' one of the men said, ignoring her jibe. He was wearing sunglasses, even though it was dark outside, because they looked good. Stupid woman.

'You're taking us to the hospital, you say?' Oke said, placing her hands on her hips.

'Yes.'

'If you are taking Rashid to the hospital, then the doctors will need to isolate him while they investigate,' Oke said. 'Why do you need me and my children to go there too?'

'We are not taking you to the proper hospital. We're taking you to the old school, which is being converted into a hospital.'

'We have a hospital, for what good it does,' Oke said, shaking her head. 'Why do we need another one?'

'We're trying to try to deal with this disease as it's spreading through the town like a wildfire. So, I don't need the wisdom of your spiky tongue, woman. What I need you to do is get your children and your things and take them to the truck.'

'If you're taking us to the school, why not just say we're taking you to school?' Oke grumbled. 'I don't understand why you're calling it the hospital when it has never been a hospital and it is not a hospital now.'

'It will be known as the hospital from now on.'

'It's the school,' Oke insisted. 'If you're trying to make me feel better about taking my family away from their home in the middle of the night, then you are failing miserably. My children are so young they don't know what's going on and they are confused and frightened.'

'We're just following orders, so don't give us a hard time, woman,' he said. 'Hurry up and get your things.'

'My children are asleep. This is cruel. They can see their father is so ill he could die at any moment and yet you're taking them from their beds to a building which has been derelict since I was a child.' Oke waved her hand in the direction of the hill. 'You can call it what you like, but it isn't a hospital.'

'Where we are taking you is a building which will contain sick people who have been blighted by a disease that we don't know anything about, except that it's contagious,' the man said sarcastically. 'It will have doctors and it will have nurses and they'll have beds and medicines, so what the fucking hell should I call it? Because that sounds like a hospital to me.' He growled. 'A building full of sick people and doctors is a fucking hospital. Or do you think I am too stupid to know what a hospital looks like?'

'I don't think that you're stupid. I think you're a liar.' Oke could see the anger on his face. 'You're lying to me so that I don't give you too much earache while you drag my family across town in the middle of the night. If you want to help us, then get my husband a doctor who knows what he's doing and has the right medicine to treat him.

Dragging me and three young children to a deserted old school is not going to solve the problem, it's just going to hide the problem, and that's what this is all about.'

'Enough of this, woman! Go inside and get Rashid,' the man said to his colleagues. 'Pick him up on his mattress and take all the bedding and pillows, too. I suggest you take yours too, woman. There will be no beds there at first until we can get the hospital organised. Make sure you take enough food and water to feed your children for a few days.'

'So, there will be no beds and no bedding and no food and no water to drink?' Oke said, shaking her head. 'What exactly have you done to the old school to turn it into a hospital? Because to me, it sounds like you have an empty building where you're going to dump all the infected people to fend for themselves.'

'Do as you're told, woman, and do it now because if you give me any more trouble, I am under orders to silence objectors with a bullet through the brain,' the man said.

'A bullet is your solution to everything,' Oke argued. 'If you need to shoot me, shoot me. I hope you can look after three young children and a dying husband. Being shot would be less trouble than being alive. Do me a favour and shoot all of us.'

'Shut up, woman.'

'I am nervous and frightened for my family,' Oke said. 'What is wrong with that?'

'I understand. We need to get your things and you and your family moved so, get your children, shut your mouth, and get into the truck and you may have a chance of living through this.'

Oke knew that she'd already pushed the man to his limits. The men of the town did not suffer resistance or argument from the females in the community. It was a totally macho based society where women weren't even important enough to educate. Their opinions were not respected, not heard, and did not matter. They were there to feed their men and service them sexually and ultimately to breed and bring up their children. Any opposition to this process was met with brutality. Rashid was dying. She knew that in her heart and there was nothing she could do about it, and it was clear that the decision had been made to isolate the infected and those who had been close to them from the rest of the community. The school was going to be a hospice for the dying and their families, out of sight and out of mind.

She watched the men put on surgical gloves and masks and they carried Rashid on his mattress; they roughly placed him onto the flatbed of a pickup truck. They dumped his bedding and pillow on top of him as if it was rubbish; he was barely aware of what was going on around him and in one way, that was a blessing. She herded her children like three little sheep to the truck, where they scrambled up and sat on their haunches.

Oke took a long look at her little house, a place where she'd been beaten and raped on more occasions than she could bear to remember. Of course, Rashid wouldn't have classed it as rape but in her mind being forced to have sex with a man she didn't love and was not sexually attracted to was rape. She had once heard a man say that there was no such thing as rape in marriage and it came back to her now. She remembered an item on the BBC World News in the early nineties, when it was made a crime to rape your wife. The world was a fucked-up place, no matter which part of it you live on. As the truck started up and drove away from the home where she'd been so unhappy, in a strange way, she hoped they would never have to return again.

CHAPTER 30

Beb & Amira

Beb and Mohammed walked about two-hundred yards across the sand, using torches to light the way. The sound of camels baying drifted across the dunes. Two torches could be seen coming towards them from the opposite direction, the beams piercing the darkness, reflecting from the sand. Above them, the night sky glimmered with the lights of a million stars, like tiny jewels against black velvet. Beb was frightened that everything he had built around him was about to disintegrate again. He knew how it felt to lose close relatives. His entire family was snatched from him by fate, and now he was faced with the same prospect again but a million times worse. Amira and his daughter were life itself. Without them, he had no future, and the past didn't matter. The pain he felt inside was indescribable, as if his intestines were being twisted by an invisible hand. Although he looked cool on the exterior, inside was a terrified little boy looking through the back window of the Jeep as he was kidnapped and watched his family fading away into the distance, never to see them again. He had lost everything in a few minutes, but it wouldn't happen again.

'My father is Ali, not his real name but the name he chose when he became chief after my grandfather died.' Mohammed spoke, without breaking stride. 'My grandfather was an honourable man and a good chief who had one wife all his life and she gave birth to two children, my father and his older brother. He didn't take multiple

118

wives because he respected my grandmother and her feelings. Unlike my father, who thinks with his dick.'

'Why was his older brother not made chief when your grandfather died?'

'Because he didn't live long enough and my father had a hand in that,' Mohammed said.

'How so?' Beb asked.

'My father and his brother went over the border into Morocco to fetch medical supplies when my grandmother took ill and she needed penicillin. Only one of them returned and we only have my father's version of events. He told the story of being robbed by vagabonds who lived in the Blue Mountains and how he had fought them off bravely but unfortunately his older brother was mortally wounded. We asked him why he didn't bring his body back to his family and he said that the vagabonds must have stolen his corpse as they were rumoured to be cannibals.'

'Cannibals?' Beb asked, shaking his head. 'In all my years in this desert, I have not heard such a thing.'

'Nor I,' Mohammed said.

'Did they go looking for his body?'

'Of course, my grandfather sent several search parties across the border into Morocco and up into the Blue Mountains. They encountered many groups of drifters, thieves, and vagabonds, but none of them had any information about an attack on two Tuareg men.'

'Why would they admit to attacking the Tuareg men if they were guilty?' Beb asked. 'Surely they wouldn't admit to it.'

'No one mentioned that one of the men had been killed and his body stolen. We only asked if news of such an attack had reached them and asked if a Tuareg man, dead or alive, had been spotted or found dead, and was buried as a kindness.' Mohammed turned to Beb and put his hands on his shoulders. 'Listen to me well, Beb. I know how much you love my daughter and my granddaughter, and I know you are a good and honourable man and I'm proud to have you in my family but when we come face-to-face with my father, you must let me do the talking.'

'Okay, Mohammed.'

'You do not know him, and you do not understand what type of man he is because you are an honourable man and honourable men struggle to understand what is going on in the mind of a beast like my father.'

'You have my word that I will say nothing unless I am spoken to,' said Beb.

The men continued in silence, lost in their own thoughts and prayers, hoping for a peaceful outcome to whatever was about to happen. Mohammed's father and two men became visible as they neared and it was clear immediately which one was related to Mohammed. His father was an older version of him but his skin was weathered and deep lines creased his face. It was a face that belonged to a man in his twilight years on this planet, with no years left to waste or play with. If there were things he needed to do before he crossed over, then he needed to do them sooner rather than later.

The men reached the point where there were ten metres between them, and they stopped and faced each other. Beb eyed the men, weighing up their chances. Mohammed didn't look at his father's accomplices. They seemed to be inconsequential so he never took his eyes from his father, not even for a moment. His father had green eyes which twinkled in the torchlight. He recognised the shape and colour of his eyes as they were identical to Amira's and his daughter's. It was obvious that they were genetically related. The other two men were younger than Mohammed and looked strong and fit. One of them carried an old British Army rifle, and the other had a modern 9 mm pistol of some kind. Beb remembered seeing similar weapons on films when they were allowed to watch them at home in Monguno. He was younger then, and watching films was a normal thing to do. How things had changed since those halcyon days and how could he have ever seen the way his life would map out? It was impossible for any man to see what the future held for him, but his had been tumultuous.

Most lives take their twists and turns and have ups and downs, but Beb was beginning to think that his life had been cursed.

'Here you are, Mohammed my son, after all these years of running and hiding like a rat,' Ali said, half smiling, half sneering. 'I am surprised that you had the backbone to look at me face-to-face, when you have wronged me so badly.'

'I did not run and hide from you. I took my daughter away from the danger that you posed to her,' Mohammed said, shaking his head.

'If you didn't fear me, why run away?'

'I did not fear you then, and I do not fear you now,' Mohammed said.

'Then why run?'

'You are an old man with a twisted mind and a liking for young girls, even your own granddaughter,' Mohammed said, bitterness in his voice. 'I would have had to kill you, to stop you from touching her.' Mohammed shrugged. 'Killing the chief carries a death sentence and I have no desire to die yet. Your perversion is the reason we ran.'

'Be careful,' Ali warned. He looked shaken by his son's words. His eyes darted from Beb to Mohammed, as if he wasn't sure who was the biggest threat.

'The time for being careful has gone,' Mohammed said. 'It is time to face the truth.'

'Your truth?'

'No, the truth. There is only one,' Mohammed said. 'If only you could have seen the expressions on the faces of the elders and respected men from our tribe when you announced the decision to marry Amira. If you could have seen them and studied them, you would have seen the revulsion in their eyes.'

'I saw no such thing.'

'You refuse to see anything which is contrary to what you want to see,' Mohammed said. 'I took Amira away from our family to protect her from you, her grandfather, a man who should have been protecting her and surrounding her with love, not planning to take her to his bed.'

'It is love to marry a woman,' Ali argued.

'Yes. A woman. Not a child.' Mohammed let the words strike home. 'You are sick in the head.'

'Hold your tongue!' Ali shouted. The men raised their weapons and Beb raised his.

'Lower your weapons or no one will leave here alive,' Mohammed said, placing his hand on Beb's rifle. 'Lower them now!' he demanded, and the other men lowered their guns. The tension was palpable.

'I think you have forgotten your place in this world.' Ali had anger in his eyes. There was a touch of madness behind them too, and Beb could sense the aggression which oozed from every pore. 'I gave you a life on this planet and I fed you and I protected you and I made you into a man. You are nothing without me and yet you talk to me as if I am a child.'

'I haven't forgotten my place in this world, and you are my father in name only, for we share nothing else of any value,' Mohammed said, shaking his head. 'We may have the same blood running through our veins, but that's where the similarity ends. You beat me and you humiliated me in public.'

'They were lessons in becoming a man,' Ali argued.

'The only lessons I learnt from you were how not to behave as a father and the final lesson you taught me was how not to behave as a grandfather, by trying to take my teenage daughter as a wife.' Mohammed kept his eyes on his father's, and he didn't blink, not even for a second. 'Amira is safe with us, and she will remain with us.'

'Amira will be my wife,' Ali growled.

'I will not allow you to touch her,' Mohammed said, shaking his head. 'Take this opportunity to walk away from the biggest mistake that you have made. I forgive you for making a mistake, but I will not forget it and so we should go our separate ways and live our lives as we choose,' Mohammed said, placing one hand on his heart. 'Go in peace, Father, and leave us be.'

'You dare to speak to me of forgiveness?' Ali laughed, sourly. 'I do not need your forgiveness. You took my wife from me. You stole the woman I had chosen to be my wife and you think that I need your forgiveness?'

'I did not steal a woman from you, Ali,' Mohammed said, standing his ground. His voice was quivering with frustration and anger. 'I did not take a woman from you at all. What I did was take my daughter, my child, a little girl, away from a predator who was fixated on her to the point that he was going to force her into a marriage and ruin her life. You're a dangerous predator, nothing more.'

'What did you call me?' Ali asked, furious. 'Predator? You dare to insult me with a word like this when I have come here to offer you the chance to turn over what you stole from me and walk away with your life, as worthless as it is,' Ali said, spitting in the sand.

'Walk away, father,' Mohammed said. It sounded like a threat. 'Live what life you have left in peace.'

'You have been under the desert sun for too long if you think that you can speak to me, your father, your chief, in this way. I will take Amira from this place and do with her as I will. And you will have nothing more to say about it.' Ali spat again.

'You will not take my daughter,' Mohammed said. 'Not while I have breath in my body.'

'Amira was chosen to be my wife and my wife she will be. I decreed it many years ago and I decree it now and no man will come between me and this marriage,' Ali shouted, raising his hands to the sky.

'Amira is already married,' Beb said.

'Be quiet,' Mohammed said.

'I can be quiet no longer,' Beb said.

'What did he say?' Ali asked, shocked.

'Amira is already married,' Beb said. 'I am her husband and the father of her child, and you will not take her away from me.'

'Is that so?' Ali asked, eyes narrowing. 'She has a child?'

'Yes. You have no claim to Amira as a wife or as a granddaughter. She's a married woman and a mother now,' Beb said.

'Is this true?' Ali asked Mohammed. Mohammed nodded slowly but didn't take his eyes from his father. 'Then this changes everything.'

'It does change everything,' Beb said, nodding his head. 'We were hoping that we could tell you this and you would understand the situation.'

'And what do you think I need to understand?' Ali asked.

'That Amira and I fell in love, and we waited to get married. When it was time and with Mohammed's blessing, we married, and our daughter Heba was born two years later.'

'She has a child to this pauper?' Ali asked Mohammed, shaking his head. Mohammed nodded but didn't speak. Ali looked bitterly disappointed, and Beb thought that was a good thing.

'She is your great-granddaughter. Heba is beautiful,' Beb said. 'I hope that we can put the past aside and you will allow us to live our lives as we have done in peace and harmony with the desert. We wish you no harm. Our daughter is our world.'

'Oh dear,' Ali said, shaking his head. 'You don't understand what you have done, do you?'

'I mean you no disrespect, but my family is the most important thing in this world to me and I ask that you respect the sanctity of our marriage and let us be. Go in peace, Ali.'

Ali rubbed his chin, deep in thought. A few long minutes later, he spoke. 'You speak well, young man, and you speak with confidence and respect unlike my slug of a son, who is nothing but a spineless fool, a wart on my arse, and a waste of fresh air,' Ali said. 'You asked me to respect the sanctity of your marriage and under normal circumstances, I would have no choice as an honourable man but to do so, however Amira was already destined to be my wife long before you met her, therefore your marriage has no sanctity.'

'But we are married, no matter what you think,' Beb insisted.

'Not any longer. Your marriage is void.'

'Our marriage is real,' Beb said, feeling his pulse racing. This wasn't going how he anticipated.

'You insult me, you peasant,' Ali said angrily. 'You have defiled the body of the woman that I honoured to take my hand in marriage.'

'Defiled her body?'

'It was sacrilege. You raped my wife to be,' Ali said. 'Your marriage is an abomination in the eyes of God and therefore deserves no respect from an honourable man like me.'

Ali slid a 9 mm pistol from his sleeve and shot Beb in the chest. Beb felt like he had been hit by a truck and bolts of pain, like white hot lightning, streaked through his body. The bullet cut through him like a knife through butter, leaving an exit wound as big as a walnut on his back. It knocked him backwards three paces before he fell onto the sand. His eyes began to cloud over and the last thing that he saw was a starfilled sky and a figure looming over him. He thought he heard Amira screaming for help and several more gunshots in the distance, and then he fell into the darkness.

CHAPTER 31

Kalu & Damilola

Kalu sat by the bed, his head in his hands. He still had no contact from Kissie, and he was beyond worried about what was happening around her and the people in the town of Pripyat, which was so close to the border with Belarus it was frightening. Watching the news, it appeared that the Russian military had burst across the borders into Ukraine at several points and from several countries with the spearheads pointing straight at the capital Kiev and the other big cities in the east of the country. However, reports on the news were describing resistance on a level which nobody outside of Ukraine had expected, especially Vladimir Putin. Kalu could only have faith in these reports and hope that the resistance would slow down the invasion and buy Kissie and her colleagues enough time to escape the Russian advance and get out of the country. All flights in and out of the country had ceased and despite the danger, he was bitterly disappointed as he felt that he needed to fly to Kiev and help Kissie to get out. He had no idea where she was, but the urge to find her was crippling him emotionally. As if worrying about his daughter in a war zone wasn't enough, he was now facing an emotional conundrum unlike anything he had faced before.

To all intents and purposes, the man lying unconscious in the hospital bed was his son, Beb. The son he had lost to a kidnap in the Sahara Desert many years before, the son who he had given up on, the son who had died and miraculously come back from the dead. The son who had the wrong blood type to be his son. It was the biggest head-fuck of all time.

On that fateful day when he had received a call from the British Embassy in Marrakesh, his world had been flipped upside down and back to front. His son had walked out of the desert and used the only thing he owned to get help, which was a gold Krugerand given to him by his father. When the extremists invaded Monguno, he gave Beb the gold coin to hide and use in the case of extreme danger. Kalu had given each of his children the same coin and told them never to tell anybody that it existed, as people would kill them for gold. It was to be used to pay for a route to safety, to bribe an official, to persuade an obstructive police force, or whatever they deemed necessary to save their lives. That was how he knew that Beb was Beb because he had used the gold coin to access the British Embassy. When the call had come to say Beb was alive, it was like a punch in the guts. There were so many mixed emotions that it was impossible to describe how he felt at that time and in the days and weeks which followed. There was a tornado of guilt raging through his mind because they'd left their son in the desert and headed for the coast without him and all that time, he had been alive. They had spent weeks searching and searching for their son, even persuading the military to engage one of their helicopters in the search for his stolen truck and kidnapped son. The helicopter crew had found the truck burnt out deep in the desert and nomads nearby told of a young boy's body, which had been found burnt. The boy had been buried in the dunes in an unmarked grave. What were they supposed to think except that he had died?

His wife was distraught, as was he, but he had to be the strong one. He had to be the one that made the decision to get in a vehicle and drive north to reach Libya and the port city of Tripoli. It was the only place where they could buy spaces on a boat to cross the Mediterranean in an attempt to reach a safe European haven. She never forgave him for making that decision, and every time she looked at him, he could see resentment in her eyes. Despite exploring every possible avenue available to them to find their son, Kalu had made the

CONRAD JONES

decision to leave him behind, dead or alive. It meant the same thing to
Esse.

If it wasn't for the war following in their footsteps, threatening to
engulf them, she would have made them stay there until doomsday in
an attempt to find their son. Kalu genuinely believed that his son was
dead, and that made the decision to head north easier to bear. He had
three daughters and his wife to consider, and he could not contemplate
risking their lives to linger in the face of such terrible oncoming
danger. There simply was no other choice and yet he beat himself up
every single day since for making the only choice he could.

The phone call from Marrakesh was the stuff of dreams. It was the
prodigal son returning when no one thought it possible. It was his
beloved son returning from the dead. It was impossible to remain calm
and think straight. All he could do was embrace the boy who returned
and show him every day how much he had been missed. He looked
like his son, Beb, but ten years older. He sounded like his son, although
speaking the dialect of the Tuareg for so long had left him with an
unfamiliar accent. His knowledge of the town and his memories of
Monguno could only have come from a boy who had lived there,
grown up there, gone to school there, and had family reaching back
generations. An impostor could not have learnt these things, and yet
his blood type was wrong. It was impossible to be his father.

The only answer which made any sense was that this man wasn't
his son. He was someone who was claiming to be his son, and that led
to some more much disturbing questions. If this man wasn't his son,
then how did he know so much about them and their family and where
they'd lived? How was it possible for a man to appear out of the desert,
the same desert which swallowed his son, and have in his possession
the gold coin, which his father gave him when they first fled from their
home?

The scenarios ran around his mind, turning him inside out. He was
angry; he was sad, he cried, he smiled at the memories his thoughts
invoked. He felt drunk on the cocktail of emotions which coursed
through his veins, but he couldn't come up with a rational explanation.

The hospital had been as patient as they could be with him. The patient had claimed his name was Beb and his identification verified his claims. They had no reason to question whether or not this man was who he said he was. The more Kalu asked questions, the crazier he sounded. At one point, he noticed the ward sister talking in whispers with two of the security guards, gesturing in his direction. He was completely aware of how crazy it must have seemed for a father to come into the hospital to see his son, who was in a critical condition after being stabbed three times, and then cast aspersions whether it was his son at all. He had loved this man unconditionally, and he was in a critical condition, yet he wanted to shake him awake and ask him who he was.

The ward sister had been confused at first and relentless in her questioning. Her thought process was beautifully simple.

Does it look like your son?

Yes.

Then it is your son, and I don't know why you're wasting our time by questioning if it is or not.

It was all well and good that the man in the bed was the man who had returned from Africa all those years ago, but he could not be Beb. He was the man who had been welcomed by his father and his sister with open arms and broken hearts, which needed to mend. Their hearts were broken when he went missing and they were broken again when he returned. This was the man who had lived in their home as a brother and as a son. They had loved, and they had laughed. They had lived their lives as a family in London the best way they knew how. And yet, despite all the guilt and all the memories and all the love they'd shared, this man was not his son. So, who was he and why did he have Beb's gold coin?

And the main question which kept whizzing around in his mind was, where was his son and was he alive or dead?

The sound of the monitor alarm shook him from the dark place of his thoughts. He saw that the monitor had flatlined. Whoever the man in the bed was, his heart had stopped beating.

CHAPTER 32

Kissie, Pripyat

Tom and Brad spent the best part of an hour making sure that their weapons and supplies were spread out between the vehicles, so that if one of them broke down or was damaged, they wouldn't lose everything and could continue. Angela took charge of her team of scientists and they packed their essentials quickly and efficiently with only a few arguments, mostly from Levi. Levi was very reluctant to leave any of the scientific equipment behind and he argued about the cost of each individual item, failing to accept that none of it was any use to a group of people trying to escape a Russian invasion. As disgruntled as he was, he set to with the rest of the team while they packed up the vehicles. Pierre and Frank took particular care in loading up the pickup as most of the heavy weaponry was being stored on the flatbed. They checked each weapon methodically so that it was ready to engage the enemy at a moment's notice. Kissie thought that watching the mercenaries preparing for battle was one of the most frightening things she'd witnessed. Tom sensed the apprehension in the air and stressed that the chances of them needing to use their weapons was slim, however it was better to be prepared. Kissie was reassured by his calm persona, but couldn't shake the nerves and fear she felt deep inside. There was a sense of loathing for the aggressors and a sense of longing for the peace and tranquillity of her life in

London. She wished she could talk into her watch and say, 'beam me up, Scotty,' and be transported far away from the oncoming terror, but there was no option to teleport in this time and place. That was something for the future and in the meantime, they would use two Ford Kugas, a Volkswagen, and a Toyota pickup truck.

Kissie had tried to contact her father on several occasions without success. For a number of reasons, there were no mobile phone signals. She felt the need to speak to him to tell him of the peril she was in, although she knew that he would already be aware of the situation. What she really needed was to hear his voice and him telling her everything would be all right. Part of her thought it was better that she couldn't speak to him for now, as he would be panic stricken by what he was hearing on the news. There was nothing to be gained from making him even more concerned by explaining to him how dire their situation was. They had four civilian vehicles and a detail of four men to protect them and guide them out of the country. She had to put the ache in her guts to one side and concentrate on the job at hand.

The roads around the hotel were quiet. Only the odd military vehicle went by, heading north in the direction of the convoy she'd encountered earlier. There were dozens of plumes of black smoke on the horizon now. It looked like the Ukrainians were putting up a fight. The security man lined up the vehicles in the car park, ready to go. Tom instructed the driver of each vehicle to pop the bonnet and check that there was oil and water in their engines and that they had spare on-board. It seemed a little pedantic at the time but avoiding an overheating engine before they left made perfect sense. While they were on the road, there would be enough to worry about, without watching the temperature gauge climbing into the red or seeing steam coming out of the bonnet. Finally, there was a check of all the tyre pressures, including the spares in the boot of each vehicle. Once that was completed, they were ready to set off on the hazardous journey to Kiev.

The scientists and their security detail took their seats in the vehicles and fastened their seat belts, ready for off. Suddenly, there was shouting and a commotion from somewhere along the main road, at the front of the hotel.

'What on Earth is that noise?' Angela asked, sounding a little concerned.

'I don't know,' Kissie said, shaking her head. 'But it sounds like somebody is shouting for help. But I don't recognise the language.'

'It's Hungarian,' Tom said, climbing out of the Ford. 'Wait here while I go and see what is going on.'

'It sounds to me like someone is pretty desperate,' Levi said, getting out of the vehicle. 'I'm not sitting here while all this commotion is going on. I want to know what is going on.'

'You are such a disagreeable man,' Angela said, following him.

'If I am so disagreeable, why are you following me?'

'Because I'm inquisitive,' Angela said, closing the door behind her.

Kissie didn't want to stay in the vehicle alone as she could see the other members of the team climbing out of their vehicles too. Pierre and Frank remained in the pickup truck but started the engine and followed Tom and Brad, driving slowly behind them. Tom and Brad had shouldered their weapons and moved slowly but surely towards the main road, using the hotel wall as cover. Kissie caught up with Angela and Levi. Angela linked her arm into hers and Kissie could feel that she was shaking. It gave her great comfort to know that she wasn't the only one who was frightened. The commotion from the main road had gone up a notch and Kissie could distinctly hear fear and desperation in the voices. They were shouting words that she didn't understand, yet it was clear that those people were in great distress.

'What do you think is going on?' Kissie asked, whispering. 'Whoever that is, it sounds like they are desperate.'

'I have no idea, but it doesn't sound good to me,' Angela said.

They watched Tom and Brad approaching the corner of the building where they could see what was happening further down the road. Tom turned round and held up his hand in an attempt to halt the team of scientists coming any closer to whatever it was that was happening. The thing he failed to realise about scientists is that being curious and needing to know the facts was all part and parcel of who they were. Angela and Kissie were close enough to see two men staggering down the road. They were a hundred metres or so away from the hotel but heading towards them. Although it was difficult to comprehend at first, it immediately became clear that the two men were missing limbs. One of the men appeared to have no arms, both removed from above the elbow. His left leg was twisted badly at the ankle and the skin on his face was blackened and charred. The second man had lost one arm below the elbow and his right leg was missing above the knee. He was using a rifle to remain upright as he hopped in a desperate attempt to find help. Both men were shouting and desperately trying to attract attention.

'Are they the Hungarian security men?' Levi asked, his mouth open in shock.

'Stay there and don't come any closer,' Tom shouted to the civilians.

He exchanged words with Brad and then they both left their position at the corner of the building and headed towards the injured men. Brad took the man with the missing leg and supported him as he half carried, half dragged him back to the hotel, placing him on the veranda at the front of the building. The man had stopped shouting now, his head was tilted backwards, mouth open, eyes rolling. From where they were standing, Kissie couldn't tell if he was dead or alive but the constant flow of blood from the ruined limb told her that he wasn't going to live long unless something drastic was done quickly. She took off her belt and ran towards the veranda. Brad was frantically waving her away but she couldn't stand there and watch the man in such agony and do nothing to help. When she reached down, she fashioned a tourniquet with the belt, wrapping it around what was left of the thigh. She tightened it as far as she could to try to stem the flow of blood. Brad could see what her intentions were, and he took the strap from her right hand and placed it over what was left of the ravaged limb, pulling as hard as he could. He fastened the buckle and then went to help Tom, who was carrying the second man over his shoulder. Kissie was looking around for more belts or straps to use to stop the bleeding from his missing arms but when they placed him down on the veranda, it became clear that it was already too late. The Hungarian's eyes were dead and lifeless.

'They're the Hungarian men from our security detail, aren't they?' Levi asked, frowning. Although he was looking at their faces, they were so badly burnt, swollen, and bruised it was almost impossible to recognise them. Only the clothing identified them as the men who had left the hotel just an hour before. 'What the hell happened to them?'

'He didn't say much I could understand, but he said that they stopped their vehicles to take a piss and one of them was hit. Peter and the other Poles were still inside the vehicle that was hit and there was nothing left of them. The other men were killed in the blast, and you can see what happened to these two,' Brad said. 'I said that they were heading in the wrong direction, but I thought they might have got further than they did.'

'What does that mean?' Kissie asked.

'It means that the Russians are much closer than we anticipated,' Tom said. 'If it had been a drone strike, we'd have heard the whoosh. I've been listening to the sound of artillery shells falling in the north, but they went west, so they were probably hit by a tank.'

'We need to head west for a few miles before we turn onto the road south to Kiev, but it looks like the Russians have beaten us to it.'

'I don't like the sound of this,' Levi said, shaking his head. 'We can't go north because that's where the Russians are coming from and we can't go west because that's where the Russians are heading to, and we can't go east, or we'll head straight into the forbidden zone around the Chernobyl reactor.'

'If we head directly south, it's nothing but agricultural land with no tracks and no roads crossing them, and from what we've been told today, it will be heavily mined, so we can't walk out of here,' Tom said. 'We don't have any choice but to head east and navigate a route through Chernobyl. Once we get to the other side, we can take the road south which follows the River Pripyat.'

'If we take the road east through the abandoned town, we'll need to wear protective suits and headgear or we might as well wait here for the Russians,' Kissie said.

'Is that not more hassle than it's worth?' Brad asked.

'My field is radiobiology, and the readings I have been taking in the Red Forest are way above anything which has been reported so far. The closer to reactor-4 you are, the more radiation you will absorb.'

'Meaning what exactly?' Brad asked, frowning.

'Meaning that everything we thought we knew about this place is a lie,' Kissie said. 'The Russians have been playing down the level of contamination around Pripyat, Chernobyl, and up to the border with Belarus. If they have been playing down the levels of contamination in the surrounding area, then the situation in the abandoned zone is probably a hundred times worse than we anticipated. We're here because the Ukrainian government wants international recognition of how bad it really is. And it's really bad.'

She could see the confusion on Tom's face as he looked at Brad and shrugged.

'What I am saying to you is that if we drive east and skirt around the reactor area, we could only be exposed to that level of radiation for twenty to thirty minutes before we became so irradiated that it would kill us later on. The effects are not immediate however, once affected, they are unavoidable and very predictable. We would die slowly and painfully as our organs shut down and our delicate tissue matter disintegrates.' Tom looked unimpressed. 'It would be like being inside a huge microwave oven. We would cook from the inside out.'

'I don't like the sound of that,' Tom said, shaking his head.

'We would have more chance against the tanks,' Kissie added.

'You're the expert. How can we avoid being frazzled?' Tom asked, shrugging. 'We're open to ideas.'

'The River Pripyat runs by the reactors and feeds the reactor lake, which was used to cool the reactor cores. I tested the water at the far side and it was off the scale. The sarcophagus is leaking, probably below the waterline.'

'We really don't have time for a science lesson, Kissie,' Brad said. 'Peter and the other men were gone just over an hour ago and these men have staggered back here with missing limbs, which means whatever happened to them happened just a few miles down the road. We need to leave here right now. So, while I understand basically what you're saying, I need you to tell us how we can drive through Chernobyl and come out of the other side without cooking our intestines.'

'We have suits and headgear in the hotel that will give us protection for long enough to get us through, as long as we skirt the ring road on the outer edge of the town. I have been there to get to the reactor lake, it took us thirty minutes to get there and we had to stop at checkpoints every five-hundred metres or so.'

'So, that's long enough,' Tom said. Kissie nodded.

'Yes. We can get to the other side without worrying about driving into a Russian convoy. There will be no one there but us and the insects.'

'Do we have enough suits?' Levi asked.

'Yes. I did a stock take on all the protective equipment last week, and there are enough suits for us all,' Kissie said.

'Okay. Where are they?' Tom asked.

'In a shipping container next to the delivery bays on the car park at the far side of the hotel next to the kitchens,' Angela said.

'I know where they are,' Pierre said. 'I need two volunteers to come with me to get enough equipment for us all.' Two of the scientists held up their hands. One of them, Carrie, was an expert in contamination and safety equipment.

'I know exactly which suits we need,' Carrie said. 'It'll be quicker if I go with you, and I can make sure we get the right equipment.'

'Take Frank with you too,' Brad said. 'The rest of you need to get in your vehicles and wait.'

'Why?' Levi grumbled. 'I don't like being told what to do unless I'm told why I need to do it. And I don't see the point of sitting in a car waiting for whatever I'm waiting for, when I'll be asked to get out of the car again to put on my safety equipment before we leave.'

'I need you to wait in the vehicles because if a Russian tank comes around that corner, we will have seconds to get out of here before we end up looking like these two men here.' Tom gestured to the dead Hungarians. 'So, if you like the idea of keeping all four limbs and your head attached to your body, it will be better to do as I ask and stop trying to look for any reason you can find to be an absolute pain in the arse.'

'Ah, I see where you're coming from. You see my questions as a "pain in the arse",' Levi said, wagging his finger. He walked towards the vehicle, grumbling. 'There is no such thing as a stupid question,' he added.

'It will be safer, Levi,' Brad interrupted.

'If you'd said that in the first place, then there would have been no need for me to ask in the first place. All it takes is a brief explanation as to why I'm doing what I am doing, and there will be no questions to ask.'

'I wish you'd told me that six months ago,' Angela said. 'It would have made life so much simpler.'

Kissie was about to say something sarcastic, but Levi turned and caught her eye, wagging his finger again and shaking his head as if there was no need to say anything at all. He smiled, which was disarming as he didn't do that very often, but when he did, there was real warmth in it. It was difficult to say anything which might insult him, as deep down he was a nice man who enjoyed being disagreeable. He opened the door of the Ford and climbed in, smiling. Kissie heard a whoosh sound. There was a blinding flash and then a devastating boom as the blast wave hit her.

CHAPTER 33

Oke & Isime

Isime looked at her husband and sighed in desperation. The skin on his cheeks had blistered so badly that he looked like he'd been scalded. The whites of his eyes were crisscrossed with broken blood vessels and there was blood coming from his right ear, nostrils, and anus. The inside of his mouth and tongue were covered in white blisters, which were so painful he could no longer take even a sip of water. Breathing hurt him and she could hear thick mucus in his lungs. When he coughed, his body was racked with pain and there were specks of blood in his spittle. He had been sleeping fitfully, drifting in and out of consciousness for hours now, and she wished that he would die, so that he would be at peace.

Kroon was the father of her child, and for that reason only she had some sympathy for him. What was happening to him was horrific, and she wished it on no one. He was suffering excruciating pain and there was no doubt in her mind that he was going to die. His mother had died in similar fashion but quickly and she could only put it down to the fact that she was in her 80s and that her immune system was not as strong as her son's.

Isime had spent the last ten years of her life hating the man and hating his mother even more. It had been a game of cat and mouse, him the cat and her the mouse, trying to avoid being pawed at and mauled and God forbid, letting him have sex with her. The last thing she'd wanted was to have children with him and she did everything to make sure that on the occasions when he had forced her, and she'd fallen pregnant, she'd never carried the child full term. She knew every trick in the book to terminate her pregnancies so that the pig would never be a father, but her son, Mahid had avoided all the odds and was a stubborn baby she could not terminate. As soon as he arrived, she knew why he had survived. It was because she loved him with all her heart from the very first moment she set eyes on him.

Mahid was the only good thing to come out of her forced marriage. Being married to a Boko male was a living hell. It was a cross between being a domestic slave and a prostitute who didn't get paid. All the pain and all the suffering over all those years had manifested itself on his face tonight. The look of pain and suffering in his eyes should have made her feel better, almost revenged for what he had put her through and yet, she could feel no joy in watching him die in such a fashion. Maybe it was because he was the father of her child that she could not enjoy his suffering, the way he had enjoyed hers. Or maybe it was just because she was a decent human being, who could take no pleasure in watching another human being suffer in such an inhuman fashion. Whatever the reason, the situation was untenable and intolerable, and she had no idea what to do.

There had to be something she could do. If only she could reach out to her sister, it might give her some comfort. She went to her son and knelt beside him. His eyes were bloodshot, but not as bad as his father's, and although there was some blistering on his lips and tongue, it was nowhere near as severe. He was lucid, although his fever was running high. It didn't appear to be worsening. Whatever this dreadful disease was, it appeared that the younger the victim, the more able they were to fight it. They had seen similar situations when Covid-19 had come to town. The elderly succumbed to the virus quickly and with catastrophic results. While the young seemed almost unaffected and showed no symptoms, yet they had the ability to carry and pass on the virus.

Whatever it was that had waylaid her husband was not a virus. She couldn't recall any she'd seen or heard of which could cause such devastation in a human so quickly. Her sister had said as much, but then her sister was a very clever woman and had spent time working in the hospital as a nurse. She said it was something to do with the patrol the men had been on the day before they became sick, and she was probably right. This sickness had never been seen before, which meant they had brought it back from wherever they'd been. They had come into contact with something insidious.

A loud banging on the front door snapped her back to reality. She covered her face and went to the door, hoping it might be someone who could help.

'Hello, Isime,' the man at the door said. She recognised him as one of her husband's friends, Tariq. He lived in the same street in a house just like theirs, but he was a widow. 'How is your husband?'

'He is not well at all, Tariq,' she said. 'I have never seen such a painful disease as this.'

'Yes, I have seen some of the other men who succumbed.'

'I think he will be dead very soon,' Isime said, shaking her head. 'He won't last the night.'

'That bad?'

'Yes. I have never seen a man so sick in all my days. He is blistered and burnt from head to toe, and I can't even give him water any more as he can't keep anything down and he is in so much pain, he cries like a child.'

'This is terrible news. He has been my friend for many years. Don't worry about what will happen when he dies, as I will look after you and your son,' he said.

'Thank you,' Isime said, wondering what he meant by that.

'What about his mother? How is she, the old crone?'

'She is dead,' Isime said.

'Oh, dear. And there I am making fun of him.'

'She must have contracted the disease while talking to her son before the symptoms showed. Once he started coughing, I kept her out of the bedroom, so that she didn't catch it. And I stayed away from her so as not to carry it and infect her, but she died, anyway.'

'Where is her body?'

'She is in her bedroom at the front of the house. I haven't moved her because they said I couldn't leave the house and I didn't know what to do with her body.'

'You did the right thing,' Tariq said.

'My husband and my son are so sick I didn't want to leave them.' Isime sobbed, the stress overwhelming her.

'Okay, okay, calm down now and don't worry about a thing,' he said, touching her shoulder. She took his hand away as politely as she could. He frowned, and she saw a change in his manner. 'You need to get your things together.'

'What things?'

'We are going to take you to the school, which has been turned into a makeshift hospital, while we deal with this crisis,' he said.

'But they can't be moved,' Isime said, sniffling.

'They must be moved tonight.' Tariq changed his tone. 'Your sister and her family are already there, and you can be together and try to help your children.'

'My son is very sick, and I don't want to move him,' Isime said, shaking her head. 'The doctor needs to come here.'

'The doctor is dead,' Tariq said. 'He fell ill while treating the first men who became sick.' Isime looked shocked. 'Everything will be okay if you do as I ask. There's nothing to worry about. They are fetching doctors and nurses to the hospital as we speak and they'll bring the right medicine to treat this illness,' he said, stepping inside the door. Isime could see that there were more men outside. He turned to them and barked orders. 'Take her husband and his mother to the truck and put Isime and her son into the back of the pickup.' He turned to face Isime. 'Pack some baskets with some food and water, enough to last you and your son for a few days. And take some blankets and bedding.'

'But what about my husband?' Isime asked. 'Why are you not taking him to the hospital?'

'None of the men who have contracted this disease have survived. If your husband is as bad as you say he is, then we need to take him to the main hospital where they can care for him humanely and give him painkillers to ease his suffering.'

'But don't you think I should be with him when he dies?' Isime asked.

'He will be on an isolation ward,' Tariq explained. 'At the moment, you don't look ill at all, and I think it's best if we keep it that way.'

'But…'

'Enough. You need to pack your things and care for your boy while we take you to the school. If there is any change in your husband's condition, then we will let you know.'

'And you say that my sister and her family have already been taken to the school?' Isime asked, unsure as to whether to believe him or not. 'It seems a bit odd to take us to the school and not to take my husband.'

They walked into the bedroom as the other men bundled her mother-in-law out, one holding her wrists, the other her ankles. The men were wearing gloves and surgical masks. Blood dripped from her body and left a trail through the house. Tariq looked at Kroon and shook his head.

'I think you are right. Your husband will not be here for very long, but you do not have to worry because when he's gone, I will look after you,' he said with a sly grin. Suddenly, it dawned on Isime that this man was not as kind-hearted as he was pretending to be. She had seen the way he looked at her when he came to visit in the past and his eyes gave away the devil in his soul. His ambitions went beyond looking after her, as he said. She knew what *looking after* her meant. 'Once your husband is dead, you will need a new husband immediately to look after you and your boy and to give you more children.'

'Tariq, do not presume the worst yet, please,' Isime said, frightened. It was traditional for another male to take the widow of a friend or relative and she couldn't think of anything worse. 'He might live and if not, I will be in mourning for a long time.'

'You will be in mourning until another man makes an offer. Not everyone would be good enough to take on a widow and her brat. But I will do that and look after you and you can look after me,' he said, still grinning. 'Enough chatter. Now get your things and get in the truck.'

Isime turned away from the door without saying a word. She didn't want to let him know that she understood completely what he was saying. He was a violent man with a violent temper and his first wife had died in a mysterious accident when she fell down the cellar steps. Since then, she'd felt his eyes on her and had seen the desire in them. The fact that her husband was at death's door had not invoked feelings of sadness or sympathy for her loss. He'd seen it as an opportunity to get his hands on his friend's widow before he was even dead in the ground. The kind of man with those priorities was not the kind of man she wanted around her or her son. The problem was, if that was what he wanted, then there would be little to nothing she could do about it.

CHAPTER 34

Beb

Beb cried out in pain and frustration, knowing he had been badly wounded. He felt the world was moving in slow motion as he fell. The sand felt soft and cool against his burning skin, and then his feelings faded to nothing. As soon as Beb hit the sand, Mohammed shot Ali in the chest, knocking him off balance, and he staggered backwards. His father stared at the bullet hole in his chest, his eyes wide and startled, as if he couldn't understand how a bullet could pierce his flesh. Mohammed fired again, this time hitting his father in the shoulder, spinning him around like a top before he fell face first onto the desert. Mohammed barely had time to enjoy watching his father fall before a 9 mm bullet smashed into his cheekbone, tearing a ragged hole in his face. The bullet crumpled against the bone before it ricocheted downwards, ripping his lower jawbone away, exposing his teeth and tongue.

Mohammed fell to his knees. The injury was catastrophic, and he hardly had time to feel the pain before his body stopped working and his brain switched off. Death was almost instantaneous. He collapsed backwards and his lifeblood seeped away into the sand. The quiet was deafening. Ali's men approached Mohammed and Beb with their weapons raised staring at their bodies in shock and horror that their chief had been shot by his son, and his son had been killed by them. This wasn't how it was supposed to play out.

'Ali said his son was a coward and would give up his daughter without a fight,' Wakim said, his hands shaking.

'Well, he got that wrong,' his companion said. 'The entire mission was a mistake from day one. I didn't want to come to begin with.'

It was clear that Mohammed and Beb were mortally wounded. They were no longer a threat, but they did not know how many more men were travelling with them. They knew there was at least one more, and in the darkness, they had no idea where he was, but they had a good idea he would be armed and pointing his weapon in their direction.

'We must get him back before he bleeds to death,' Wakim said.

Their priority was to pick up their chief and take him back to where the rest of the raiding party were stationed. Ali was an old man with a failing body and a weak immune system and he wouldn't survive losing a lot of blood. He had two bullet wounds, which were bleeding profusely. They turned him over onto his back, and his eyes blinked, sightlessly staring at the stars above them.

'Ali, can you hear me?' Wakim asked. 'He's not responding. There's a hole in his chest and another in his shoulder. If he dies, you know that the rest of the tribe will blame us for not protecting him.'

'We are not to blame for this madness. He brought this on himself and now his son is dead and bleeding into the desert and for what?'

'Stop bleating and grab a hold of him around the waist. We need to get him out of here and stop the bleeding before it's too late.'

'Don't shoot,' a familiar voice called out from the darkness.

'Who is that?' Wakim asked, aiming his gun at nothing in particular.

'It's Malik.' Four men came from the dunes behind them. 'Put your gun down before you have an accident.' They carried a bundle of bedding like a rolled-up carpet between them. The bundle was thrashing about, and they could hear the muffled cries of a female.

'Who is that?'

'We have the girl, Amira.' One of the men gasped, out of breath. 'But there was no sign of his brother Katouh.' He pointed at the chief. 'Is he shot?'

'Yes, twice.'

'Who are they?' Malik asked, pointing to Beb and Mohammed.

'Mohammed, his eldest son and that one claimed he was Amira's husband.'

'What a mess.'

'That means Katouh isn't far away and when he realises his brother is dead, he will be looking for us.'

'This is terrible. Ali has been shot and his son is dead.'

'Yes, he has been shot and all because of his stubborn pride.' The man pointed out Mohammed's body. 'This is his eldest son, Mohammed, an honourable man who I remember before he took his daughter and left the caravan. Now he is lying dead in the sand because he wanted to protect his daughter. There is no justice in this.'

'You need to hold your tongue, stupid man,' Malik said. 'Ali is not dead and is still our chief. If he hears you, it will not go well when he recovers from his injuries.'

Two more Tuareg arrived and began treating Ali.

'Who is this one?' one of the men asked, pointing out Beb's body.

'That is her husband, and he said that the girl has a child?'

'Yes. There is a child in the tent.'

'You left the child?'

'Yes, a little girl.'

'Why did you leave her?'

'Ali said there may be children but was very clear that we were only to bring the girl and no one else,' Malik said. 'I didn't have it in me to kill the child, but I am not going to risk bringing her when I have been told to do otherwise.'

'What are you going to do, leave it for the desert to decide her fate?'

'I'm going to do what Ali told me to do, which is capture the girl and bring her back to the caravan unharmed and untouched.' Malik started walking, and the bundle continued to struggle, her muffled cries becoming more desperate as she realised what they'd done with Heba.

'We must move Ali quickly. I cannot tell how many were travelling with Mohammed, but we need to get away from this chaos as quickly as possible in case anyone has heard the gunshots.'

'What are you worried about?'

'I'm worried about trying to explain this nonsense,' Wakim said. 'Explaining this to any rational man would be impossible.'

'I agree,' Malik said. 'What we have done here this night will not be repeated to anyone when we return to the caravan. And I only hope that if Ali survives this, he retains the wisdom to do the right thing for Amira and her child.'

'Her child will not last twenty-four hours alone in the dunes,' one of the men said. 'I did not come here to kidnap one child leaving anther to die. This is wrong. We must go back for the child.'

A shot rang out and the back of Malik's head exploded.

CHAPTER 35

Kalu, London

The crash team entered the room, and Kalu was ushered out by the ward sister. The door was closed unceremoniously behind him, and he was left standing in the corridor, looking through the window. He was flanked by two uniformed police officers. He watched as the doctor set up the defibrillator and prepped Damilola to be shocked. It was like watching an episode of casualty except through a window rather than on a plasma screen, and yet it was no less dramatic. Kalu felt almost completely numb, and his mind was in turmoil. Did he love this man any less than he had the day before or was the fact that his blood type was wrong enough for him to switch off his emotions and try to rationalise what had actually happened to his son. Whatever the answer was, it eluded him now.

'It looks like his heart has stopped,' one of the officers said. Kalu looked at him as if he was from another planet and the officer realised that what he had said was not just painfully obvious, it was verging on stupidity. 'Sorry. That was a stupid thing to say.'

'Sometimes, when we can't think of the right thing to say, it's best to say nothing at all,' Kalu said, staring through the window as the crash team tried for a third time to defibrillate Damilola. 'At least, that's what I've found. Saying the wrong thing at the wrong time is something we're all guilty of, I'm sure.'

'I believe there's some issue whether that's actually your son?' the second officer said. Kalu frowned but didn't look at him. He focused on what the doctor was doing. He shocked Damilola again, but there was no response.

'I think you have just pipped your colleague at the post,' Kalu said, shaking his head without looking away from the traumatic scene in front of him. The policeman looked confused. 'Congratulations, you've just won the most stupid line of the day award.'

Kalu looked at the police officer, who turned a shade of pink with embarrassment. 'I'm not sure if you've noticed, but the man in that room who has pretended to be my son and who I thought was my son has had a cardiac arrest. So, at this point, whether he is or isn't my son is neither here nor there in the grand scheme of things.' Kalu shrugged. 'Even if he isn't my son, I don't think this is the time for me to be answering questions, however stupid they may be.'

'I'm sorry, doctor,' the officer said, looking sheepish. 'But a serious crime has been committed and we're not even sure who the victim is. It's our job to ask questions, even if sometimes they're difficult to answer.'

'What I find as I've gone through life is a lot of things are to do with timing. Get the timing right and nobody notices as it's just expected but get the timing wrong and everyone thinks you're a wanker,' Kalu said, patting the officer on the shoulder. 'So, please do me a favour, and fuck off until we know if the man in that room is alive or dead.'

'I'm not sure there's any need for that attitude...' the officer began, but the scene beyond the glass caught his attention and he thought better of it.

The doctor leading the crash team was looking at Kalu through the window and shaking his head apologetically. His eyes said how sorry he was. Kalu watched him record the time of death as he spoke to the team, their expressions solemn and disappointed. There was sadness in their eyes that they'd failed to save the life of another young male stabbed to death on the streets of London.

CHAPTER 36

Kissie

Kissie felt like she'd been hit by a bus. Her hands and face were numb and her eyes gritty and sore. Her chest felt tight, and her breathing was shallow. It was difficult to open her eyes and when she did, her vision was blurry. She tried to blink to clear her vision, but it didn't work. She was dizzy and felt as if the world was spinning around her in a whirl of sights and sounds that she didn't understand. Her brain wasn't computing the information it was being given. There was a high-pitched whine in her ears, which was almost painful. She shook her head as if to try to shake it out, but it persisted, even when she put her fingers in her ears. She could hear raised voices but didn't recognise them. There were male voices and there were female voices; all of them were anxious, urgency in their words and in their tone and yet she couldn't understand what they were saying, let alone respond. She remembered from her training that, in an incident where consciousness has been lost, it's important to connect with the body's extremities to make sure that everything is where it should be. She wiggled her toes in her shoes, feeling the friction between her skin and her socks and the tightness of the boots fastened around her feet and ankles. Everything felt normal. The image of the limbless Hungarians flickered across her mind, like a scene from an old movie filmed in black and white. She wriggled her fingers, opening, closing, making a fist, and straightening them out. They felt numb, but they were attached. She tried to sit up, but her body refused. The dizziness was overwhelming.

Kissie tried to control her breathing, sucking the scorched air in deeply and then releasing it slowly. The spinning sensation was making her feel nauseous as she tried to lie on her side in case she vomited. She felt dust and debris falling onto her skin like warm snowflakes. The smell of spent ordinance filled the air, tainted with the odours of burning hair and flesh. They were familiar smells to her, and they invoked memories which she'd tried for many years to forget. She didn't want to hold on to the past, but the past wasn't ready to let go of her.

The voices were becoming clearer, their meaning beginning to make sense. She identified Tom's voice. It was clear and calm as he went from one person to another to assess their condition. She could hear him asking if they were okay and if they had any injuries that weren't obvious. She heard him talking to five or six people, who sounded okay but shaken and shocked. She could hear several people crying. Then she heard Tom speaking to Levi, calling his name a dozen times or more, but she didn't hear any response.

'Levi, can you hear me?'

'Levi, can you hear me?'

'Levi, can you hear me?'

'Levi, can you hear me?'

'Levi, can you hear me?'

It seemed to go on and on, echoing through her mind and all the time her brain was telling her the reason Levi wasn't answering wasn't because he was being disagreeable or argumentative, it was because he was dead. There was an explosion, and he wasn't replying. What else could it be?

He's dead, so deal with it. Others will be dead too, probably lots of them, and we haven't left the hotel yet. What chance do we have of reaching Kiev?

She began to panic and tried to open her eyes again, but her vision was blurry. She closed them and rubbed them gently with the back of her hands and it felt like she was sandpapering her eyeballs.

'Don't rub your eyes, Kissie,' Tom said, kneeling next to her. He took her right hand in his. 'Squeeze my hand.' Kissie squeezed. 'Good. Are you hurt?'

'I don't think so,' Kissie mumbled. Her lips felt swollen. 'I feel like I've been run over.'

'That's natural. You may have grit or broken glass in your eyes, so rubbing them won't do you any good at all. Put your head back.'

'Okay,' Kissie said, tipping her head back. Tom poured water in her eyes. 'That feels good.'

'Blink the water away. Don't rub them. Are you injured anywhere else at all?' Tom asked.

'I don't think so,' Kissie said. 'I heard you talking to Levi. Is he okay?'

'No,' Tom said. 'He didn't make it.'

'What do you mean?'

'He's dead.'

'Oh no.' Kissie sighed. 'Can't we get an ambulance?'

'It's too late for that, I'm afraid,' Tom said. 'He didn't feel any pain, Kissie. He took the blast full on his back and his ribs are shattered. I think the shock wave ruptured his lungs.'

'What was it?' Kissie asked, trying to sit up straight.

'A drone strike, most probably,' Tom said matter-of-factly. 'The missile hit the far side of the hotel. We were protected from the blast by the bedrooms and the gable end at this side of the hotel.'

'But that's where Pierre and the others went to fetch the radiation suits,' Kissie said, as her jumbled thoughts tried to make sense of what happened prior to the explosion. 'Are they all okay?'

'I'm going to pour some more water in your eyes. It will help to clear the grit out of them,' Tom said, ignoring her question.

Kissie felt cold water being poured into her eyes, running down her face, and it felt good. She ran through a thousand facts in her mind as she tried to fathom why Tom wasn't answering her questions, but in her heart of hearts, she already knew the answers. She didn't want to open her eyes because she didn't want to see what had happened. Levi hadn't replied because he was dead, and she couldn't recall hearing Angela speaking since the explosion. Where was she?

'I'm going to leave you for a few minutes while you wash your eyes and let the dizziness pass.'

'Why do I feel so sluggish if I'm not hurt?'

'You've been hit by the blast wave, and it will disorientate you to the extreme, but it will settle down if you don't panic and take your time before trying to stand up,' he explained. 'Do you understand me?'

'Yes.'

'Good. I need to check on the others,' Tom said. 'Take your time and don't stand up until the dizziness has gone.'

'Okay,' Kissie said. 'Have you found Angela yet?'

'Keep rinsing your eyes with water and take deep breaths until you feel strong enough to stand,' Tom said. 'Concentrate on getting back to your feet and supporting your own weight.'

Kissie was badly shaken and disorientated, but her mind was sharp enough to notice the clever deflections Tom had made by avoiding her questions. She could understand completely what he was doing and why he was doing it. He was a veteran of several theatres of war, and he was putting into practice the things he'd learnt in those terrible places. Human beings panic when exposed to dangerous situations and panic achieves nothing but creating more panic. It made sense not to give distressing news to people who are already distressed. Tom was moving methodically from person to person, assessing their condition, making sure they weren't critically injured, and then moving on to the next, reassuring each person as he went.

Kissie could hear voices coming from beyond the car park. There were several languages being spoken. The Ukrainian voices seemed to be trying to organise the survivors, and she realised that the residents and staff of the hotel were making their way from the ruins at the far end of the building onto the relative safety of the car park to the rear and the road to the front. She poured more water into her eyes and then took a long swig from the bottle, swilling the water around her mouth before spitting it onto the tarmac. She blinked, trying to clear her vision once more and this time it improved, so that she could actually see what was going on around her.

There were thirty or so people wandering from the hotel in varying degrees of distress. Many of them bloody and bruised and she could only guess the state of the injured who remained in the building. It appeared that the far side of the hotel had been reduced to the first-floor walls and the roof, and the upper floors had collapsed into the building itself. Anyone who'd been inside the building to the east of the reception area would now be beneath tons of smoking rubble. Without heavy lifting equipment, they had zero chance of being rescued. The absence of screaming and panic surprised her. People were trying their best to help the dazed and injured while maintaining a level of calm, which didn't belong in such a scene of devastation. It should have been chaos, but it was eerily calm.

Kissie felt the dizziness fading away, and she had pins and needles in her legs. Turning onto her side, she pushed herself up onto her knees, using the door handle of the Ford to support her. She looked around to see how many of her team were around, but she couldn't see any of them. Many of the residents and staff were making their way past their vehicles and onto the main road at the front of the hotel. She could hear sirens in the distance and wondered if the fire brigade, police, and ambulance services were still operational. As if to answer her question, a fire engine approached from the east, lights flashing and sirens blaring. It came to a halt outside the main entrance and the firefighters exited the vehicle and went into the well-practiced routine of attaching their hoses ready to extinguish the pockets of fire which were beginning to climb from the debris of the hotel. A plume of flame was dancing from between collapsed rafters where the kitchen had been, and she thought the gas pipe had been severed. The firemen aimed their hoses on it while others searched for the supply cut-off point.

Kissie watched them for a few minutes and then walked around the Ford to the pavement. There were four bodies laid out on the grass, their faces covered with coats and jackets. She wanted to lift them to see if they were her colleagues, but she didn't recognise their clothing and leaving them with a sense of dignity was more important than her own curiosity. There was no sign of Tom, Brad, or Angela.

She wandered along the pavement towards the back of the hotel, walking against the tide of injured and dazed people who were heading in the opposite direction. She looked where the kitchens had been and saw that the shipping container was still intact, although some of the roof had collapsed onto it. It was a metal box, designed to be banged around, and had withstood the impact. There was a group of people ferrying equipment from inside the container, placing it in piles on the car park. They had tied masks over their noses and mouths to combat the acrid smoke. As she neared, she could see Angela was there giving instructions, and she recognised Brad and Tom. There was no sign of Pierre or Frank or Carrie. She wondered if they'd gone through the hotel to fetch safety equipment, and she shuddered at the thought. She walked across the car park to where her colleagues had gathered the safety equipment, and Angela smiled as she approached.

'Finally, she arrives,' she joked. 'How are you feeling?' Angela asked, opening her arms to give her a hug. Kissie closed her eyes and held her as tightly as she could, craving the affection and support, and the tears burst from her eyes as the shock hit her. 'That's okay. You let it all out.'

'Levi didn't make it,' Kissie said, sobbing.

'I know. I will miss him, the grumpy old bugger,' Angela said. 'We need to concentrate on getting the rest of us out of this place before we all end up in the same boat as Levi.'

'I think Pierre and the others went through the hotel,' Kissie said, gesturing towards smoking rubble at the far end of the hotel.

'Oh no we didn't. We went around the outside of the building, so that we could have a cheeky smoke on the way,' a voice said from behind them. Kissie turned around to see Pierre and Frank approaching with Carrie and the other scientists. 'Were you worried about us?' Pierre asked, smiling.

'Not really,' Kissie said, sniffling.

'You can't get rid of us that easily,' he added.

'We thought you were in there underneath all that rubble,' Tom said, smiling. He shook hands with the Frenchman and patted him on the back enthusiastically. 'I'm glad you're here, as you can help us carry the suits over to the vehicles. Like you were supposed to before you buggered off for a sneaky cigarette.'

'Smoking is supposed to be bad for you, but on this occasion,' Carrie said, shaking her head. 'It nearly blew me off my feet.'

'We just went a long way around and what is it you English say?' Pierre said. 'We were in the right place at the right time.'

'We have a saying in the states,' Brad said. 'Lucky bastard.'

CHAPTER 38

Oke & Isime

When Oke arrived at the school, it was a chaotic scene. Women and children were being unloaded from trucks and lorries and herded in through the main doors, encouraged with horse whips and electric cattle prods as if they were animals being bundled into the slaughterhouse.

There were sick and dying men being carried into the building with little care or concern about the pain they were in. Their skin was burnt and blistered and painful to the touch, but there was no pity or empathy shown. There was no morphine available in the town and the real hospital had limited supplies, which they used for surgery only. Some of the women were very angry and refused to go inside, but they were dealt with in a brutal fashion and as usual, the punishment did not fit the crime. Screaming fits and outbursts of abuse were silenced quickly with five-thousand volts. The cattle prods were a very unpleasant means of encouraging a human being to move in a certain direction. The shock was painful and could leave nasty bruises on the body of the victims and it silenced them instantly. Protesting was futile.

The pickup truck they were riding in pulled up at the bottom of the steps and the tailgate was dropped by one man, while two others dragged Rashid and his bedding off the truck. They carried him by the wrists and ankles, and although he was barely conscious, they caused him so much pain he cried out in agony.

Oke got the children off the flat bed one at a time and shared their supplies between them to lighten the load and they followed the men into the makeshift hospital. It was a similar scene inside, like something from a horror film; moaning and screams of agony echoed along the corridors. The lights had been rigged to a series of generators and she could hear the engines droning from somewhere outside and the smell of diesel tainted the air. Voices were raised and angry exchanges seemed to be happening in every part of the old school.

Oke decided to keep her thoughts to herself for now and she concentrated on getting the children settled without causing them any more distress than necessary. They were terrified as it was without seeing their mother arguing or beaten by the Boko men.

Her husband was taken upstairs to the first floor where they turned right and carried him into a large classroom, which she remembered had been used to teach art, something which was now forbidden. The walls had been painted over with a thin coat of whitewash, but some of the old murals were still visible through the paint, and she was sure that one of them had been painted by Beb and his friend. His face appeared in her mind and a twinge of pain stabbed her heart. Not a day went by when she didn't think of her little brother. He loved going to school, but that was in a time when all the children were educated, no matter what sex or religion they were, and art was actively encouraged. They were such happy times.

Rashid was dumped in the corner of the room. There were already four families in there and space was at a premium. Considering the concern about the spread of this terrible disease, social distancing and spatial awareness had been forgotten, and further infections would be unavoidable. The Boko men left her husband lying on the crumpled pile of bedding and walked out without a single word about what would be happening next. They said the sick men would be treated, but she didn't see any evidence of it. Oke knelt and pulled the mattress flat beneath him and straightened his sheet and blankets, putting his pillow beneath his head to make him more comfortable. Luckily, his eyes were only half-open, and he was semiconscious, drifting in and out of a delirious state. He wasn't aware of the terrible conditions that they had been put into.

The school was a big building with wide corridors, tiled floors, and high ceilings, which meant the acoustics were similar to that of a large cavern or public swimming baths. She could hear a dozen conversations going on at the same time, and the wailing and groaning of the sick and dying drifted to them from the other parts of the school. It was nightmarish. She took some bedding from one of their baskets and made a makeshift camp for the children, who were shocked into a silent and clingy mood. The oldest tried to comfort her younger siblings, but Kareem was so frightened he could barely let go of her leg. Oke got them settled on their bed and gave them some bread and a drink of water. It was pointless telling them to go to sleep, as the noise in the school was deafening.

'Thank the heavens, you're here.' She heard a familiar voice. Oke turned around to see her sister and her nephew. They were carrying several baskets, the boy struggling to keep hold of his. Oke ran to them and took one of the baskets from Mahid. He looked very unwell. She ushered them over to the corner where she had set up their belongings. 'Mahid is sick, but they wouldn't help me to carry my things.' The sisters hugged and looked at each other. 'Are you still well?' she asked.

'I haven't got any symptoms yet,' Oke said. 'And the kids are okay, but how are we going to protect them in this place?'

'I have been at my wit's end,' Isime said. 'Kroon was so sick that I thought he was going to die at any minute, and I went to get help from his mother, but she was already dead in her bedroom.'

'Oh, my poor Isime,' Oke said, hugging her and kissing her on the cheek. 'And where is Kroon?'

'They said they were taking him to the real hospital, where they have set up an isolation ward for those in a critical condition,' Isime said. 'They said they would be able to make him comfortable for his final few hours,' Isime said, wiping tears from the corner of the eye. 'You know how much I hate that man but seeing him in that state was terrible. My son will be traumatised by what he has seen over the last few days.' Mahid coughed and Isime went to him, sitting him down on a thin mattress. 'Rest.' She gave him a drink of water and he lay down and closed his eyes, exhausted. 'He's so ill, Oke,' she said. 'He needs medicine or I'm afraid he'll go like his father.'

'Don't panic,' Oke said. 'We'll speak to whoever is in charge and ask them when the doctors are going to be here. Did you go to the hospital with Kroon?'

'No. They wouldn't let me,' Isime said.

'Who wouldn't let you?' Oke said.

'Tariq Omar,' Isime said, shaking her head. 'He's such a letch. I hate the way that man looks at me. I don't believe they are taking him to the hospital, but what could I do?'

'I don't believe they have, either,' Oke said, agreeing with her sister. 'And I don't believe for one minute that there is an isolation ward in the hospital. It's all lies. General Bassi is behind them.'

'But why would they lie?'

'I think they have brought all the infected to this place to avoid the disease spreading to the hospital employees or anywhere else in the town. They told me to bring bedding and supplies enough to last for a few days, but I think they are quarantining the sick men and their families, and they will leave us here until we either die or we don't,' Oke said. 'Out of sight, out of mind.'

CHAPTER 38

Beb & Amira

The rifle bullet passed through Malik's head spraying the men near him with blood and brain matter. He collapsed onto the sand with a thump. His eyes rolled into the back of his head and his tongue lolling from the side of his mouth. Before the men had time to react, another shot rang out, and one of the men treating Ali cried out and fell onto his back, killed instantly.

'Run! We must get the chief and the girl out of here before we're all shot dead.'

'What about the child?'

'You can go if you want to.'

'Fuck that.'

The Tuareg men crouched low and ran as fast as they could, hampered by the struggling Amira and the unconscious Ali. The sound of bullet shots rang out across the dunes and fountains of sand exploded into the air to the left and right as they ran. After a few minutes, they'd faded into the darkness and there was nothing more to shoot at. Katouh circled back on himself to the tents where they'd been camped before the raiding party found them. He approached slowly from the east, cautious that this may be a trap and the Tuareg may have left a sniper waiting for him to return. He couldn't see anything moving in the tents and there were no lights, which worried him.

'Amira,' he hissed from behind the dunes. There was no reply, and he peered over the top of the dune, looking down on the tents. He could hear Heba crying, but she sounded far away. The sound of her in distress was impossible to listen to, and despite the obvious danger, he had to come out of his hiding place and find her. When he reached Amira's tent, he found it was empty. The bedding had been taken, and the light was smashed into pieces on the floor. There had been an epic struggle.

'Amira,' he shouted into the wind, but there was no reply. The sound of Heba crying drifted to him again, this time from the west. He ran fifty yards, wishing that he could switch on his torch, but it was too dangerous. 'Heba,' he shouted, and the little girl called out for her mother. Her voice carried on the breeze and ripped at his heart.

'Heba,' he shouted again. This time, he held his breath and waited for the toddler to call out again. She called for her mother once more and he knew that she wasn't far away, but it was still too risky to switch on the light. 'Heba,' he called once more, moving in a zigzag pattern to confuse any possible marksman that might be lying in the dunes trying to get a bead on him. Heba cried for her mother again, but this time her voice was thick with mucus and tears.

'Heba!' he shouted. 'Heba, call to me, darling.'

'Mum!' she called. 'Mum!'

Katouh focused on her voice and this time, he had the direction right. She sounded like she was no more than twenty yards to his left. Katouh made his way across the sand and found her sitting on a blanket with a bottle of cold tea in her hand. Her cheeks were streaked with tears and her nose was snotty, but apart from that she looked to be in one piece.

'Heba, Heba, Heba, don't cry, darling,' he said, scooping her up in his arms. 'You're safe now.' He looked around for Amira. 'Where is your mother?'

'Gone,' the little girl said, sniffling. She pointed her tiny finger at the infinite darkness.

CHAPTER 39

Kalu

Kalu sat beside the bed, his chin resting on his hands as he looked at the face of the man who had claimed to be his son. Beb looked to be at peace, as if he was sleeping. But it wasn't Beb. He wasn't sure how he was supposed to feel. On one hand, he had believed that the man was his son, returned from the dead and he had accepted him as such, only to have him snatched away again in this cruel twist of fate. First, he had discovered his blood type wasn't right, and before he could wrap his head around that fact, he was dead.

The police were waiting outside the room, and they were running out of patience. This was now a murder investigation and the uniformed police officers had been replaced by plainclothes detectives who looked like they'd been around the block and back again a few times. One of them had a nose which was bent and flattened against his face, which meant he'd either been involved in a lot of fistfights or had pursued a particularly unsuccessful career in amateur boxing. The other had his hair shaved to the bone and the craggy complexion that belongs to someone who spent a lot of time out of the sun, drinking and smoking heavily. Neither of them looked friendly, nor did they look the patient type. They were sitting on a bench outside the room, each nursing a cup of lukewarm liquid which was pretending to be coffee.

Kalu ran through the scenarios in his mind, but each one led back to the same place. Whoever this man was, he had finished his days on Earth in a hospital bed, bleeding internally because he'd been stabbed in the back three times. His wallet had been in his pocket, which contained money and credit cards, and Kalu had been surprised to see that two of the credit cards were actually his. They were ones he didn't use on a daily basis, and he only kept them as a back-up in his spare wallet, which he kept in the bedside drawer upstairs at home. He hadn't touched it since before lockdown. A quick balance check on his mobile phone informed him that both cards had been maxed out in the last seven days. Most of the transactions were cash withdrawals or the purchase of items which could be sold on quickly. This information further muddied the waters. If his son ever needed money, which he often did, then Kalu gave it to him.

His son had liked to socialise and had expensive tastes in watches, designer clothes, and shoes, but he did not like to work for it. Kalu had lost count of the number of jobs he'd started and then finished within a month or so. In fact, two months was probably the longest he'd lasted in any employment, much to the annoyance of his sister Kissie.

Kissie spent many hours trying to talk to her brother, giving him forceful advice about standing on his own two feet and not being a drain on his father's finances. Kissie rarely asked for any money, much preferring to go out and earn her own and pay for her own things without borrowing or running up debts on loans and credit cards. Kalu was certain she didn't even own a credit card until she planned her research trip and even then, it was purely as a back-up, yet her brother had stolen two of his father's credit cards and maxed them out in the space of a week. It was difficult to imagine a scenario where his son would need a large amount of cash so quickly and so desperately that he was prepared to take it rather than ask for it. There was nothing at home to show for it. He had not come home with bags full of Prada or Gucci and he hadn't seen a Rolex or Hublot on his wrist.

The only scenario Kalu could think of which would require such an amount of cash gained illegitimately was crime. The only situation he could imagine where a lot of money was required to generate even more money in return was to purchase and distribute a large amount of class-A drugs. It wasn't a great jump to carry on that scenario and come up with the reason he'd been stabbed in a public toilet in a Tube station in the middle of the afternoon. The wallet and cash in his pocket were evidence that it wasn't a common street robbery gone wrong. He hadn't fought back against his attacker because he hadn't had the opportunity to. The attack had been executed from behind, with the intent of disabling and debilitating the victim quickly and to ensure they didn't fight back or try to pursue the attacker.

Drugs, drugs, drugs, drugs, what else could explain this situation?

Another problem Kalu had was that his experience of communicating with detectives in a hospital environment usually went the same way. It was a common pattern when a victim had been stabbed or shot in a drug-related incident. The distribution of class-A drugs was a dangerous occupation but a very lucrative one with a lot of competition. And the competition tended to be armed and dangerous. It's a violent world to step into, but the rewards are high for those who are good at it. All this leading to a much-held perception by both the police and the public that violence within the drug trade is both accepted and expected. There is little sympathy within the police community for distributors and their dealers and if they get hurt, it was tough titty. Getting stabbed was just an occupational hazard in the world of drug distribution, and most investigations are closed as quickly as possible.

Was the murder drug-related?

If the answer is yes, write it on the file and put that file into the cabinet marked *drug related.*

If the answer is no, go back to the beginning and try to find the links which will indicate that it is, in fact, drug related. Then read question one again.

London is a big city with all the glitz and glamour that a European capital requires but look beneath the surface and there's a bubbling, writhing underworld of drug trafficking, sex trafficking, and people trafficking, and if you get involved with any of those industries, you're not going to get a lot of sympathy from law enforcement when things go wrong. So, the dilemma was, did he mention the credit cards to them, or did he give the police as little as possible and let them investigate properly, rather than making assumptions? He leant forward and held the victim's hand. Squeezing it gently with his own.

'I don't know who you are, but I know who I thought you were, and I loved you very much,' Kalu said, wiping away a tear. 'I wish you could tell me who you are and what happened to my son, because whatever happened to him, you must have been there. You must have spent a lot of time with him, and I want to ask you all about it.'

The door opened and the ward sister poked her head around.

'Sorry to disturb you, Dr Sammi. I've got two detectives here who are desperate to talk to you. Are you up to it as I don't think they're going to go away anytime soon?' she said, shaking her head and biting her lip. 'I've put some fresh drinks in the relatives' room, which is next to the nurses' station.' She smiled. 'Shall I tell them you'll meet them in there in five minutes, so that you can go to the loo and gather your thoughts?'

'Yes, please,' Kalu said, standing up. He bent over and kissed the dead man on the forehead. 'Travel safely, whoever you are.'

CHAPTER 40

Oke & Isime

Oke and Isime fashioned their area as best as they could with the bedding and supplies they'd brought with them. Rashid was deteriorating rapidly, and so was Mahid. The sisters tried to keep the other children away from them, especially as their coughing was becoming more persistent. They were both covered in sweat but couldn't keep any liquids down.

Oke could see her younger sister was struggling not to panic. It was a wonder they weren't screaming the place down, begging for help from someone, but there was no help forthcoming. The other women in the room were all in the same position.

The women shared their experiences, and it was clear that everyone was telling a similar story. They were married to Boko men who had gone on the same patrol, which was an overnight raid across the border into Chad, but that was all they knew. Oke knew they went over the border now and again, but what the mission was or where, nobody was saying. Everyone was of the same opinion that wherever the patrol went to that night, they were infected by an invisible enemy, far more deadly than any enemy they'd encountered so far. This enemy was threatening to wipe out the entire community and there didn't seem to be any fresh ideas as to how to combat this sickness.

The best thing General Bassi and the leaders of the community could come up with was to dump the dead, the dying, and their families into a derelict school to let the illness run its course. It was a case of kill or cure. Some of the women they spoke to had worked in the hospital with Oke over the years. Many of them had friends or family who still worked there and there were whispers that it had been decreed by the general that none of the infected people were allowed in the hospital, as the doctor and several nurses had been infected and succumbed to the disease very quickly. He had come up with the idea of quarantining the infected into one building to stem the spread.

The men who'd been brought to the school were in varying stages, ranging from very ill to nearly dead. The symptoms were identical. A persistent cough which became increasingly more painful as the disease progressed until, eventually, the victim was coughing up blood and lung tissue. Their skin became red and blistered and as the cells broke down, it became tissue-thin, tearing when they moved, creating agonising rents in the flesh. Some of the men were developing infections in their lesions and with no antibiotics to treat them, they would die of sepsis if untreated. Many of the children were displaying milder versions of the symptoms, but some were slipping into the next level, experiencing dreadful pain. A lot of them had developed the cough and their eyes were bloodshot but the effects on their skin didn't appear to be as severe in all the cases.

Isime's son, Mahid, was displaying signs that he was deteriorating into the next phase of the illness. His body was limp, and he had no energy at all, barely able to open his eyes or take a sip of water. He had gone through a short period of crying and being distressed, which had lasted several hours, but now he was so exhausted, all he could do was sleep, which was a blessed relief. So far, the sisters were symptom free, and every few hours, they checked each other and Oke's children to see if they were showing any signs of the illness.

As dawn broke and the sun started to rise, the generators were turned off. While that wasn't a huge shock to most people in the building, what it meant to Oke was that there were people outside who were monitoring what was going on inside. Someone outside gave the order to kill the generators, which meant someone was in charge.

'They turned the generators off to save diesel fuel,' Oke said, keeping her voice down to whisper.

'The sun is coming up, that's why,' Isime said, yawning. She patted a damp cloth on her son's forehead, and he winced in pain. 'His skin is becoming so painful he can't bear me to touch him. He's going downhill fast.'

'I know the sun is coming up, but whoever gave the order to kill the generators must be in charge of this circus,' Oke said, standing up. 'And if he's in charge of the generators, then he should be in charge of everything else.'

'Like what?' Isime asked, exhausted. She was at her wit's end.

'He will know when the doctors are going to arrive and when the nurses are going to arrive, and what medicine they are going to bring to help us.'

'Don't hold your breath on anyone coming to help us,' a woman said from the opposite corner.

'What do you mean?' Oke asked.

'I can hear what you're saying from over here,' the lady said. She was very thin. Oke had seen her at the markets but didn't know her name. She could tell from her features that she wasn't from Monguno and probably not even from Nigeria. She had probably been captured in one of the raids across the borders and forced to marry a Boko man, as the sisters had. 'I think we need to be very careful what we ask for and what we say between us. They are listening to everything that is going on and they don't want the truth to get out of this building. That is why they put us in here in the first place.'

'What is your name?' Oke asked.

'My name is Fanna,' the woman said.

'I recognise that name,' Oke said. 'Am I right in saying that you are from the Gambia or Senegal?'

'Yes. I am from Banjul. My father is from Gambia, and my mother is from Senegal,' Fanna said, smiling. 'We had to leave Banjul and were trying to get to Morocco to catch a ship across the Mediterranean to be with family who have gained citizenship in Germany, but we were ambushed near the desert and sold to traffickers. I ended up here and I ask every day what I did to deserve this hell.'

'We hear you, Fanna,' Oke said. 'This is my sister, Isime. We are from this town, and we tried to leave to reach Europe when Boko first attacked but the traffickers double-crossed my father and the boat we were put on wasn't seaworthy.'

'That's terrible,' Fanna said. 'What happened?'

'All my family drowned, and we were pulled from the sea by fishermen and taken back to Tripoli, where we were sold to these animals. It's a long story but a familiar one,' Oke said, taking a drink of water. 'None of the women here want to be here. We are all slaves to these pigs,' she added. The temperature was rising as the sun climbed above the school. 'What happened to the rest of your family?'

'My father and my brother tried to defend us when we were attacked, but they were unarmed and they were shot and left at the side of the road like dogs,' Fanna said, shaking her head. 'My mother and my sisters were sold to traffickers, and I haven't seen them since. God only knows where they were taken or what happened to them. My mother was old and of no use to traffickers, but my sisters were young and unmarried with no children and the traffickers love young women. I hate to think what they did to them. Part of me hopes they're dead.'

'I'm so sorry for you,' Isime said.

'I'm so sorry for all of us,' Fanna said.

'How many children do you have?' Oke asked. There were four children lying close to the Gambian, but it was obvious by their ages that they weren't all hers.

'Only one of them is mine. This is my daughter, Aish,' she said, pointing to the youngest. 'She's just over two. The other three belong to my husband from his previous marriage. His wife died from malaria some years ago. That is him there,' she said, pointing to a bundle of rags in the corner. It was just possible to make out the head and the feet sticking out of the covers. The man's face was pink and raw in places where the blisters had grown and then burst. His mouth was open and Oke could see that his tongue was swollen and almost filled

170

his mouth. 'I don't think he will live for much longer and I pray to God every minute that he is suffering. I want him to suffer the most painful death that is possible,' she whispered. 'I know that's cruel, but I hate the bastard.'

'We understand,' Oke said, lowering her voice. 'I do know how you feel, sister.' They hugged. 'Tell me, have you ever seen a sickness like this where you come from?'

'Not in Banjul. I have seen something similar but not in real life, on the television,' she said, keeping her voice to a whisper.

'On television?'

'Yes. Not long before we left home, I saw a programme about the nuclear disaster at Chernobyl in Ukraine. It happened in 1986 and it was hushed up by the Russians at first. They made a drama out of it, and I saw it on Netflix.'

'Oh, my goodness me, Netflix,' Isime said sadly. 'I remember we used to spend hours watching film after film after film with my mother and father, and our little brother was absolutely crazy about superhero films. He would run round the house with a towel as a cape and his underpants over his trousers, one fist in the air,' Isime said, managing a smile. 'Do you remember how he used to run around like a lunatic, shouting "to infinity and beyond", and "Hulk smash"?'

'Yes. I remember. Of course, I do.' Oke looked confused, but excited. 'Shush a minute, Isime. Tell me about this drama that you saw and what the similarity is to this disease?'

'There were thousands of people who were exposed to the radiation when the reactor exploded at Chernobyl, but most of them didn't know that they were being exposed until it was too late,' Fanna said. 'The symptoms were similar in many ways. Their skin began to redden and look as if they'd been burnt, blisters formed, and then the skin itself began to break down and split just like them. In the film, they said that the internal organs begin to break down, but you can't see it obviously, which causes them an immense amount of pain, and that might explain the level of suffering that we are seeing here.'

'What about the cough?' Oke asked.

'Some of them developed a cough quickly and some of them developed a cough later on, sometimes years, because the radiation affected the DNA so much that it caused cancer in a lot of the infected people.'

'I can remember reading about it at school years ago. I asked my father about it while we were eating our supper and he told me that radiation sickness is a very deadly thing, and it displays itself as if the victims have been burnt from the inside out,' Oke said, whispering now. She nodded and looked from her sister to Fanna, and clapped her hands. 'I didn't put the two things together until now. That is it. That must be it. I have been racking my brains since the moment they brought my husband back to my door because I could not fathom how a man could leave the house completely healthy and then return in such a damaged condition as he was.'

'I have been thinking it is the same, but doubting how it could be?' Fanna said. 'There are no power stations like that near here.'

'No, but other things are radioactive, aren't they?' Oke said, nodding. 'Even an X-ray at a hospital is a type of radiation. Wherever they went to on that patrol, they have come into contact with something they didn't understand. This explains everything.'

'It does,' Fanna said. 'They couldn't see the danger because you can't see radiation and they came back to the village none the wiser, but their clothes and their bodies were contaminated and it can make anybody who comes into contact with them contaminated too.'

'Their clothes?' Isime asked.

'Yes. I took his from him and burnt them. We are guessing at radiation poisoning because the symptoms are similar,' Fanna said, shaking her head. 'But we mustn't let anybody else hear what we are saying. Can you imagine what would happen if the general found out that we are talking about radiation sickness?'

'The general thinks that all women are as thick as pig shit and he treats us as if we are,' Oke said, her face darkening. 'It makes me so angry that he thinks the people in this town are so stupid that they won't realise what has happened. At some point, the truth will come out but by then it will be too late to do anything about it.'

'So, if you think that they have been contaminated by radiation, and that my husband brought it back from the patrol and infected my son, how can the sickness be treated?' Isime asked, excited. 'My son is very sick, and he's getting worse by the hour, but if we know what it is, surely we can find out how to treat him.'

'I'm not a doctor, but I don't think it's as easy as giving someone a tablet or an injection,' Fanna said, shaking her head. 'I remember that some of the people on the film were taking iodine tablets, but that was as a prevention rather than a cure. I think it stops the absorption of radiation into the body, but I can't remember properly. The thyroid gland, I think, but that was before they were sick. It stopped them from becoming as sick as they would be.'

'But how did they treat them once they were sick?' Isime asked, again.

'They couldn't,' Fanna said.

'What do you mean?' Isime said, shaking her head. 'They must have done something?'

'No. Once the radiation has been absorbed, it's too late,' Fanna said.

'That can't be right.'

'From what I can remember, all the doctors can do is assess how much radiation a person has absorbed,' Fanna said, shrugging.

'Okay, I understand that, but once they have assessed them, what did they do?' Isime pushed.

'Nothing.'

'Nothing?'

'I remember that with limited resources their main objective was to lessen the chances of further radiation contamination and they did that by removing the clothes that the infected person was wearing and disposing of them.' Fanna recalled. 'They threw them where humans couldn't come into contact with them. And then they made them shower using soap and water to remove any loose radiation particles that were on the surface of the skin but that didn't help to remove any contamination from within the body,' Fanna said. 'They used something called the disseminator and I think the other one was called a Geiger counter and they indicated whether or not items of clothing or parts of the body had been infected with radiation, but we have to assume they are.'

'Okay. So, now we know that to stop ourselves or the other children becoming infected we need to remove their clothes and dispose of them, then wash the children in the shower?' Oke suggested.

'Yes. Can we do that here?' Fanna asked.

'When I was a child here they built the washrooms and the football field. The showers are downstairs to the right of the main doors, and I remember them putting water tanks on the roof to collect the rain and then the sun was magnified through prism glass to heat the water. Even though this place has been empty for years, the showers should still work,' Oke said, standing up. 'We need to move fast. Right, kids, take off your clothes and let's get you down to the shower room.'

'I'm tired, Mummy,' Kareem moaned.

'Don't argue with your mother,' Oke said. 'Get up and do as you're told.'

'But, Mummy…'

'Now, Kareem,' Oke said. Giving him the stare. 'I suggest you do the same with Mahid,' she said, turning to Isime. 'We'll throw their clothes out of the window and get them showered, and then we'll do the same with our own clothes.'

'I think that is the best we can do for now,' Fanna said, nodding. 'I'm sure that once a person has been contaminated, it is too late to do anything but wait to see how badly they'll be affected by it.'

'So, that's why they have dumped us here,' Oke said. 'Because there is nothing that they can do to help us.'

CHAPTER 41

Kissie & Pripyat

Kissie and the rest of the group retrieved as much of the safety equipment as they could find. They had a full complement of suits and helmets, three Geiger counters, and an assortment of gloves, boots, and breathing apparatus. They also retrieved some concentrated detergent, brushes, sponges, and clean towels. Carrie said they had everything they needed to make them safe on the drive through Chernobyl, and they headed back across the car park to where their vehicles were loaded and waiting, surrounded by debris. Some of the hotel staff had laid out more bodies on the grass and Kissie counted up to twenty-five before she decided she didn't want to count any more.

Levi's body had been moved and laid next to the other victims and covered with a blanket from one of the bedrooms, but Kissie recognised his boots poking out. She felt a pang of sadness pierce her soul as she thought about Levi moaning and groaning and asking unnecessary questions. He was a good man with a dark sense of humour and in the blink of an eye, was gone.

Her anxiety was going through the roof. The journey from Monguno to London had come at such an emotional price, she was still paying. The fragility of life was magnified in the corridors of war, and she was feeling vulnerable and mentally unstable. Curling up in a ball was all she wanted to do. Close her eyes and wake up when it was over.

'Kissie, are you with us?' Tom asked, looking concerned. 'You look a little spaced out.'

'I'm coping the best way I know how,' she said, nodding.

'Good girl,' he said. 'We're all trying to keep our shit together, so you're not alone in your struggle, okay?'

'Okay,' Kissie said, saluting. 'I'm back in the room.'

Tom made everybody stand by the vehicles they'd been assigned to travel in. Brad and Tom briefed each group again and checked around the vehicles for any obvious damage and then moved on to the next and repeated the process. There were no punctured tyres or pierced radiators, and all the glass was intact.

'How far is it from here to the unauthorised zone?' Brad asked.

'It's about twenty-five kilometres,' Angela said. 'But if we're heading directly towards Chernobyl town, then we need to suit up sooner rather than later. It's better to be safe than sorry where radiation is concerned.'

'Okay, everybody suit up but leave the helmets off until the very last minute,' Tom said, turning to Kissie. 'If there are sympathisers on the ground or spotter drones in the air above us and they see us wearing full decontamination gear, they will assume we're legitimate military targets.'

'That makes sense,' Kissie agreed.

'I know they are not discriminating between one or the other at the moment, but let's not give them any more reasons to fire a missile in our direction than they already have,' he added.

'If there are any sympathisers on the ground around Chernobyl town, they'll be wearing the same suits as us, or they'll be charcoaled and crispy in no time,' Kissie said. 'We will be able to spot them easily, especially in the dark.'

'Listen up!' Brad shouted. 'Once everybody is ready and suited up, we're going to follow Pierre and Frank, who will be driving the pickup truck,' Brad said making sure that everybody could hear him.

'Any problems or any issues, you flash your lights, sound your horn, and pull your vehicle to a halt. Do not, under any circumstances, exit your vehicle unless myself or Tom instruct you to do so. We know the Ukrainians are in the process of deploying mines but we have no way of knowing where they're putting them or what types they're using. We have no mine detectors available, so the best thing to do is stay in the car until we reach the other side of the town. I'm going to ask Kissie, Angela, and Carrie to advise us on the safety levels and where we can stop and when.' He looked around the anxious faces. 'Does anybody need to go to the toilet because you're not going to have the chance until we get to the other side of Chernobyl. We're going to navigate the ring road and all the checkpoints, which we're assuming will be unmanned, which means that we'll probably have to get out of the vehicles and open the barriers ourselves, which is going to slow us down. So, please, if you need to pee or do a number two then do it now.'

Kissie and several of the other scientists walked across the car park and entered the section of the hotel which was undamaged, and they found that all the doors had been left open, which meant they could use any toilets they wanted to. She wasn't sure if she wanted to urinate or not but the fact that she might not be able to for several hours made the decision to try a simple one. It was difficult to describe how nervous she felt taking down her jeans and underwear and sitting on the toilet seat with the thought that another missile could strike the building at any time.

Witnessing several drone strikes had made her incredibly nervous, and her sense of vulnerability was off the scale. She had been frightened many times in her life. She had been terrified more times than she cared to remember, but never had she felt such a sense of inevitability. It was an absolute certainty that more missiles would be fired at Ukraine. There would definitely be tank shells, mortar shells, artillery shells, and rocket-propelled grenades being fired in their direction. Therefore, it was inevitable that more people would die and the odds of them making it out of the country unharmed were increasing with every minute that ticked by. She finished and went to the sink to wash her hands, looking at her reflection in the mirror. Kissie was surprised by her reflection. Her hair was full of dust and debris, making it look grey and ageing her by twenty years. She had always wondered what she would look like when she got old, but she hadn't expected to find out so quickly.

She went outside and made her way to the Ford, trying not to look at the victims again. When she reached the car, Tom gave her a weapon, which she now knew how to fire, and without further ado, they were all in their vehicles, engines started, and ready to set off on the first part of their journey back. She felt both relief and fear, but the overwhelming sensation was that she had been here before.

CHAPTER 42

Beb & Amira

Katouh took Heba and held her safely to his chest while he retraced his steps back to the tents, praying that Amira had made her way there too. He was hoping she had hidden Heba in the dunes in case the raiders attacked, but there was no sign of her or anyone else. The tents were empty, and the material flapped gently in the breeze. He looked inside and instantly ascertained they'd been ransacked. Each tent had been searched, their belongings spilled onto the sand and their valuables stolen. It didn't look good. His stomach felt tight, and he couldn't help but think the worst had happened. Using his torch, he spotted multiple tracks in the sand. They had entered the camp from behind their position, but where they left the camp, their footsteps were deeper and the strides shorter. Ali and his men had distracted them, coming from the north, and led Mohammed and Beb away from the tents and away from Amira and their child. The footprints were concentrated around Amira's tent, which indicated they were struggling to walk normally and were probably burdened with weight. Something like a struggling human.

It became obvious to him that they'd kidnapped Amira. The footprints were deeper still as they led away from their camp towards where Ali had met with Mohammed. That must have been part of the plan from the beginning, to engage Mohammed in conversation while bushwhacking him from behind and kidnapping his daughter. There was no intention of entering into negotiations and making peace or coming up with a reasonable solution, which both parties could agree to. Ali had come here to take Amira with or without her father's permission.

Katouh knew that Mohammed and Beb had engaged Ali and his men in a gun battle, but he had no idea what the outcome had been. He had seen the muzzle flashes and heard men cry out in pain, but he couldn't approach without putting the entire family in jeopardy. There was no sign of Mohammed and Beb when he had fired into the Tuareg men from a distance. The fact that they hadn't returned to the tents didn't bode well, and he feared for their safety. He took a harness from Amira's tent and sat the toddler inside it, feeding her arms through the straps, so that she was safely fastened on his chest, while leaving his hands free. With Heba safe, he set off across the sand to see what had become of his brother and Beb. The scent of cordite drifted on the breeze, a lingering memory of a deadly gunfight on the dunes, where there had been more than life at stake.

Their family and their entire way of life had been threatened by a crazy old man, driven by greed, lust, and his insane interpretation of authority. He deemed he could take whatever he wanted, no matter what morality said. They had had no choice but to try to negotiate their way out of the position which they found themselves in, even though they knew there was very little chance of making progress with their father. Despite growing up as significant members of their tribe, the tribe was directed by their leader, and they couldn't ask them for help. They were the old fool's offspring, yet he showed them no consideration of that fact. He didn't care about anything but getting his hands on his granddaughter.

Katouh felt anxious from the tip of his tongue to the deepest pit of his stomach, not knowing what he was going to find in the desert. He was certain Amira had been kidnapped, which left her child without a mother and possibly without her father and grandfather. In his mind, he wondered if he would be able to bring up the little girl in the desert on his own in the lifestyle that they'd chosen. He doubted very much if that was possible, and he also doubted if it would be fair to expose such a young child to the loneliness and desolation of the Sahara Desert with no family and no companions but her uncle. Playtime would be limited and not much fun. His heart yearned for his missing family.

When he reached the site of the confrontation, he illuminated it with his torch and immediately identified the body of his brother Mohammed. And Beb was just a few yards away. He studied the scene for what seemed like forever, hoping beyond all hope that one of them would cry out for help but everything was still. He approached and saw the bodies of two Tuareg men, one shot through the head and the second to the centre of his chest. Both men lay still with sightless eyes staring up at the myriad of stars that twinkled in the desert sky above them. He was impressed by his accuracy with the rifle, even in the dark. He wondered if the dead men were already walking among the stars above them and he could only hope that they were, for if there was nothing after this life, then what was the struggle all for?

He knelt beside Mohammed and shone his torch on his ruined face. His teeth were showing in a macabre smile, and it broke his heart to look upon his brother's face in such a terrible state. He had been such a handsome man. They had been brothers and best friends since their childhood and when Mohammed had told him that he was going to leave the caravan, Katouh hadn't hesitated for even a second. He insisted that he was going too. Katouh said that he would rather spend the rest of his days walking the desert with his brother than spend a single day in the company of his father alone. He couldn't tolerate the decision to marry Amira any more than his brother had, and he was willing to lay down his life to protect her and join his brother in exile from the rest of the tribe. He used his index and middle fingers to close the lids on Mohammed's eyes and he placed his arms across his chest. It would be difficult, but he would wash his body and bury him where he lay.

Katouh crossed the few yards to Beb on his knees. He had been shot twice, once to the left side of his chest, and another bullet had gone through his right shoulder. His eyes were closed, and his mouth was open as if he was surprised that the bullet had hit him. In the darkness with just torchlight to guide them, he could have been shot before he had even realised the bullet had been fired, and he probably hadn't even heard the gunshots before he felt the pain. It was obvious that Ali hadn't come to talk about peace and reconciliation; he had come to gloat and to antagonise and ultimately kill his own son, in the process of kidnapping his own flesh and blood, his granddaughter, with a view to taking her into his bed. The sick fuck.

Katouh looked up at the stars and made a promise that he would take Heba out of the desert and find somewhere safe where she could grow up in peace and become a woman who had her own mind and could make her own choices. Once he had found that safe place for Heba, he vowed to go back into the desert and travel it broad and wide until he found his father. And when he found him, he would kill him and what would be, would be. Sadness overwhelmed him and his eyes filled with tears before they were running down his cheeks and dripping from his chin. They dropped onto Heba's forehead, shocking her for a moment and making her cry. Her cries echoed across the dunes.

'Katouh,' Beb whispered, his voice cracked. His throat was dry as a bone and he could barely swallow. 'I can hear my daughter crying,' he gasped. 'What is wrong with her?'

CHAPTER 43

Kalu opened the door and stepped into the corridor, closing the door behind him. He felt like he was leaving behind much more than just the room. What would happen to the body? Was it his responsibility to arrange the funeral, when he didn't know who it was they were burying? It wasn't Beb, so who was it and what would go on the death certificate? The situation made his head spin. Leaving that room was like walking away from the answers when all you have are questions. If only he had had the time to ask him some of those questions before he had to pass over to the other side. Had he known what was about to happen, they could have talked man to man. Maybe things would have been clearer and maybe not. The fact was, he would probably never know the truth of what happened to his son. He hadn't died from stab wounds in a Tube station in London, that was a fact. He took a deep breath, closed his eyes, and steeled himself to have a conversation with the detectives, who had been impatiently waiting to speak to him for over an hour.

'Hello, Dr Sammi,' the detective with the broken nose said. 'I'm Detective Sergeant Alfred and this is Detective Constable Coop. I know this is a very difficult time for you, but we need to ask you some questions,' the DS said.

'That's fine,' Kalu mumbled.

'The ward sister has saved the relatives' room for us, and she's even brought three cups of the sludge from the coffee machine.' The detective half-smiled at his joke, but Kalu was expressionless. 'Dr Sammi. Is that okay with you?'

'Yes.' Kalu said, nodding. 'Call me Kalu,' he said, trying to act normally. Although there was nothing he would rather not do, he agreed to answer their questions. He still wasn't certain what he was going to tell them. If he didn't know the truth himself, then how was he supposed to explain it to the police? 'I realise you must have a lot of questions to ask, but I'm not sure I'm going to be much help to you. There's so much I don't understand myself.'

'On the contrary, Kalu, I'm sure you'll be able to throw some light on the issue of identification.'

'I doubt that,' Kalu muttered. 'As far as that goes, we're all in the dark, me more than anyone.'

'Let's see, shall we, as we're struggling at the moment? We have a murder victim, and we can't positively identify him,' the sergeant explained politely. 'We were led to believe the victim was your son, but now there may be some doubt about that?'

'Yes. I understand the issue,' Kalu said, stepping out of the way as a gaggle of nurses walked by, following a doctor in a line, like ducklings following their mother. 'Shall we go somewhere more private?'

The three men walked into the relatives' room and sat down. The detectives took single chairs each while Kalu perched on the edge of a two-seater settee. He picked up a plastic cup of coffee and sipped the lukewarm liquid. He wondered how the manufacturers could get away with calling it coffee. *Surely it was a breach of a trade descriptions act*, he thought. His mind felt like it had been emptied by a giant vacuum cleaner, leaving only banal thoughts behind. All sense and reason had vanished. Normality had been dismantled, leaving him empty and numb, void of all emotions.

'We've been told by the hospital that you're disputing the stab victim is your son, Beb Sammi?' the DS said. Kalu didn't look up from his coffee cup. 'Is that the case, Kalu?'

'It's not a dispute,' Kalu said, shaking his head. 'A dispute is something that can be discussed or argued for and against. The possibility of the victim being my biological son is zero.'

'Can you explain that to us?' the detective said, frowning. This was complicated and complicated meant paperwork and paperwork was shit.

'I'm not sure how to explain it, but I'll put this into simple words as I'm struggling with it myself.' Kalu took off his glasses and cleaned them on his tie. 'The victim has different blood to me and his mother. He has A-negative blood. I know that from the notes, as he needed a transfusion while he was in theatre.'

'He's A-negative and you're...?' the DC asked, making notes.

'The rest of the family is O-positive,' Kalu said, shaking his head.

'His mother?' the constable asked, looking up.

'She's dead,' Kalu said. 'But she was O-positive, as I've said.'

'And parents with that blood type cannot have a child with A-negative?' the detective sergeant said.

'Absolutely impossible. You see this fact cannot be mistaken and it cannot be disputed or argued against.' Kalu tapped the table to reinforce his point. 'Because of the blood type, I can categorically tell you that I did not father the man who is lying dead in that room. He is not my son, Beb.'

'But you thought he was this morning?' the DS said, shrugging.

'Yes.'

'And he has a driver's licence, national insurance number, and bank cards in the name of Beb Sammi?' the detective asked. 'So, he was living his life as Beb Sammi?'

'Yes.' Kalu felt exhausted.

'We get this kind of thing happening all the time,' DC Coop said, shaking his head. A faint smile touched his lips. Kalu felt his hackles rising. The implication was barely disguised.

'You get what kind of thing happening all the time?' Kalu asked, suddenly looking up from his coffee, as if he'd been slapped. 'I'm interested to hear your theory on this?'

'Fathers who think they are the father of their children and then something happens and they find out that actually they're not the father,' the DC said, 'and they realise the missus has played away and got caught pregnant but kept her mouth shut, hoping no one would notice,' Coop explained, matter-of-factly. His superior glared at him.

'Subtle,' the DS said, shaking his head.

'It happens all the time,' the DC added, shrugging.

'What my colleague is trying to say is that sometimes the paternity of a person is not in dispute until that person is injured or deceased,' the DS explained, trying to take the sting out of the scenario. 'It's only when medical evidence is discovered in hospital that these things are uncovered. Obviously, in this situation, it has come to light because the victim needed a blood transfusion, and that alerted you to the fact you're not his father.'

'Yes,' Kalu said. 'But your theory is both incorrect and insulting.'

'The truth hurts,' the DC said, shrugging.

'So, you're suggesting that the mother of my children –and we had four, just for your information,' Kalu said calmly, but there was a steely look in his eyes. 'At some point in Nigeria, decided to have sex with another man, who is unknown to me, fell pregnant, and then took it upon herself not to tell me that the child wasn't mine?'

'Basically, yes,' DC Coop said, nodding. Kalu closed his eyes and squeezed the bridge of his nose between his finger and thumb. 'It happens all the time,' Coop added.

'In that case, I think you should probably fuck off and investigate your crime somewhere else,' Kalu said, sitting back on the settee, closing his eyes. He rubbed at his temples with his fingers, trying to relieve the tension. 'Why have they sent idiots to investigate this?'

'There's no need to be abusive, Dr Sammi,' DS Alfred said, frowning. 'We don't appreciate being told to fuck off.'

'I'm sure you don't, no one does but I bet it happens all the time?' Kalu said, repeating the DC's words to them. 'Being told to fuck off, I mean.'

'Yes. It does,' DC Coop said, nodding. DS Alfred stared at him, shaking his head. The DC blushed when the penny dropped. 'I'm just saying it does happen. We do get told to fuck off all the time.'

'I can't understand that,' Kalu said. 'Fancy that.'

'Listen, Kalu,' the DS said, lowering his voice. He sat on the edge of his seat, his eyes narrowed angrily. 'We've got a job to do, and we have to do it and sometimes during these investigations, secrets come to light and they're not always pleasant ones, but the facts are the facts and we have to investigate them.'

'Secrets come to light?' Kalu repeated.

'Yes. Secrets like the paternity of a child.'

'Okay, now you listen to me,' Kalu said, pointing his index finger. 'I don't have a problem answering your questions or helping you with your investigation. Obviously, a man has been stabbed and lost his life and you need to investigate the crime.'

'Absolutely.'

'However, your first instinct is to ask me if my wife was sleeping with anybody else, when what you should have asked me, is did it come as a surprise to me that his blood type was different and how could I be certain that his blood type was the same as mine at some point in his life?' Kalu said. 'Jumping to the conclusion that my wife, who I loved very much, was fucking someone else, is the best you can come up with.'

'I'm not sure I follow your argument,' DC Coop said, frowning. 'She might have been.'

'Let me explain. The fact that I am a doctor should indicate to you that I probably know more about blood types than you do?' The detectives nodded but looked confused. 'In Nigeria, we do regular blood tests because disease is so prevalent and isn't always visible before it becomes contagious.'

'Okay.'

'My son, Beb, was tested at birth and was O-positive, the same as the rest of the family,' Kalu said. 'So, he *was* my son.'

'Ah, I see,' the DS said nodding.

'Which means that it's very unlikely my wife was fucking around behind my back and gave birth to another man's son,' he added, feeling his blood pressure rising. 'Maybe you could find a training course on tact and not jumping to conclusions?'

'I don't think there is one of those,' DC Coop said, frowning and looking at his superior.

'There's a gap in the market then,' Kalu said, shaking his head. 'Maybe you should put it in the suggestions box?'

'Good idea,' DC Coop agreed.

'Apologies if we've been a little clumsy,' the DS said, holding up a hand in apology. 'If that's the case, then it's obvious that the victim is not your son.'

'Exactly.'

'So, how is it possible that you believed that he was your son until today?' the detective asked.

'That, I can explain,' Kalu said. He took a deep breath and a sip of coffee. 'We were migrants, refugees escaping a civil war. Our town was attacked by extremists, and we had to flee for our lives,' Kalu said, closing his eyes. The images of that traumatic journey flashed in his mind causing his emotions to seesaw. 'To cut a long story short, we tried to make it across the sub-Saharan continent to Tripoli, where we planned to take a ferry across the Mediterranean to Europe. Before we reached the Sahara, our truck was taken by thieves and my son was in the back of the vehicle.'

'So, he was kidnapped?' the DS asked, shocked.

'Yes.' Kalu stood up and walked to the window. He looked out over a grey city, which he didn't belong in. London was the polar opposite of Monguno, and it never felt like home and probably never would. 'Of course, we searched for him with the help of the police and the military. We even had a helicopter searching the desert. We found some nomads who had heard about the body of a young boy found burnt to death. His body had been buried in the dunes, but no one knew exactly where,' Kalu explained. 'It's a long story, but we thought that he was dead, and we had to continue north. Somehow, we made it to

Tripoli but were ripped off by traffickers and forced onto a wreck which sank, with the loss of my wife and two eldest daughters.' He choked on the memory and sat down, head in his hands.

'I had no idea about any of this,' DS Alfred said, shaking his head. 'I'm so sorry for your loss. Please take a minute to compose yourself.'

Kalu waited for the wave of emotions to wash over him. 'Only my daughter, Kissie, and I made it and we settled in London. Ten years later, my son walked into the British Embassy in Marrakesh, using a gold coin which I had given to him when we left Monguno. He told us that he had been trafficked and was sold to a Tuareg tribe. He was enslaved and travelled the Sahara for nearly ten years until the opportunity came to run away. When he did, obviously, he came to London to live with us.'

'So, your son was kidnapped in Africa and then ten years later, he miraculously appears, and you think that your son is back from the dead?' DC Coop asked, astounded.

'Yes.'

'Except, he isn't your son because he has the wrong blood type?' The DS added. 'But you didn't know until today?'

'Yes.' Kalu rubbed his eyes with the back of his hands and smiled. He shrugged. 'When I tell the story, it sounds like the craziest situation I can think of, but at the time, we were so happy to think that he was still alive. We didn't challenge it.' Kalu shook his head and sat back again. 'He looked like my son, but older. He knew everything about our family, and he knew everything about growing up in Monguno. His mannerisms were the same: the way he walked, the way he talked, the way he moved, the way he laughed, but the overriding fact that he had the gold coin too. Everything told me that it was my son, and I had no reason to question it, until now.'

'And now you know he can't be your son who do you think it is?' DC Coop asked.

'How could I possibly know the answer to that question, when this morning I had no reason to doubt that he wasn't my son?'

189

'Sorry, I'm struggling to work this out,' DC Coop said, making a whistling sound. 'This is enough to bend your head,' he added. 'So, this man has been living in your home, pretending to be your son for years?'

'Yes,' Kalu said, nodding. 'And I don't know who he is and I don't know what happened to my real son,' he added, shrugging. 'I feel like he's been stolen from me and murdered for the second time. How can that happen twice in one lifetime?'

'I'm dumbfounded,' the DS said. 'No wonder you're confused about his identity. It isn't often that I agree with DC Coop, but it is enough to bend your head.' He paused to think of his next question. 'I think we came at this from the wrong angle, and I'm sorry about that. Let's start this again.'

'Okay,' Kalu agreed. 'Although the facts remain the same.'

'Yes. Of course,' the DS said, nodding. 'The victim slept at your home last night?'

'Yes. I left for work about six a.m., and he was still in bed.'

'Did you speak to him?'

'No,' Kalu said, wishing he had. 'I didn't want to wake him. He was late getting in last night.'

'We've had a chance to look at his belongings,' the DS said. 'Everything looks kosher except he has two credit cards, which belong to you, in his wallet?' He frowned. 'Did you know he had them?'

'Not until today,' Kalu said, shaking his head. He was almost surprised they'd noticed, but now they had, he had to be forthcoming. 'I checked my accounts and they're both maxed out.' The detectives exchanged glances. 'Today has been a day for revelations,' he added.

'How much has he taken from them?'

'Over ten thousand,' Kalu said. 'Over about eight days from what I can see.'

'Can you think of any reason he would need that amount of cash in a hurry?'

'I can only guess,' Kalu said, shaking his head.

'Guess what?'

'It's obviously something he's got himself involved in,' Kalu said. 'Gambling debts, loan sharks...'

'Does he have a gambling problem?' the DC asked.

'Not that I'm aware of,' Kalu said, sighing.

'Could it be drugs?' DC Coop asked, tactlessly.

'I'm not aware of any drug habits,' Kalu said. 'He certainly didn't show any symptoms of addiction and I know them like the back of my hand.'

'Why do you think he was at Kennington Tube Station?' the DS asked.

'I have no idea,' Kalu said. 'I can't think of any reason why he would be south of the river.'

'Where did he socialise?' the DS asked.

'In the city,' Kalu said. 'Covent Garden, Soho. He had expensive tastes.'

'Did he mention the names of friends he went out with?'

'No, not really,' Kalu said, thinking. His mind was blank. 'I didn't even know what his real name was. The entire thing was a charade, but I didn't see it.'

'We found a membership card for Whispers nightclub in Soho,' the DS said. 'Have you been there?'

'To a nightclub in Soho?' Kalu laughed. 'I'm not a nightclub type of man, but I know he frequented the area.'

'It's a busy place, popular with footballers and actors, pop stars and like,' the DS added. Kalu shrugged. 'He never mentioned the place to you?'

'No. I've never heard of it.'

'It's renowned for high-class hookers, celebrities, and class-A drugs,' the DS said. 'It's twenty-five pounds for a gin and tonic.'

'I bet you don't have many at that price,' Kalu said, wondering where this was going. 'My son didn't have that kind of money.'

'Neither have I,' the DS said. 'Maybe he was trying to move up into that league?'

'Oh, I see,' Kalu said. 'You think he took the money from my cards to purchase drugs to sell on at this club?'

'No,' the DS said confidently.

'You sound sure about that?' Kalu asked.

'Most of Soho is sewn up by a particularly ruthless dealer called Jet,' the detective explained. 'If he had tried to set up shop in that part of town, we wouldn't have found the body.'

'I see,' Kalu said. 'I don't know what to tell you that would be of any use.' He shrugged. 'I'm speculating.'

'We're exploring the possibilities,' the DS said. 'You may know something that we don't.'

'I have no idea what he was doing, but I never saw any evidence of drug taking,' Kalu said.

'Are you okay if we search his room?'

'Yes,' Kalu said. 'No problem.' He paused and thought about his lock-up where Beb had stored his restoration project. They didn't need to know about that for now.

CHAPTER 44

Oke & Isime

An hour later, the entire school had become a hive of activity. Whispers passed from one room to the next that the infected could be reinfecting themselves and others via their clothes and bedding. They had to be removed and thrown out, somewhere they couldn't infect other humans. It had been discussed and decided that they shouldn't be disposed of in the building, and they should be thrown outside from a window. They didn't want the guards to see, so a window on the ground floor was chosen as it was hidden by undergrowth, brambles, and thicket. The Boko men wouldn't see them disposing of the items unless they were on top of them, and if they couldn't see them, they wouldn't ask awkward questions. The women in the school had solidarity that they needed to work as one, and that General Bassi and his horde were the enemy. Their sick husbands didn't matter and there was no love lost. Most of the women despised their husbands, and some hated them even more than that. The men were beyond being aware of what was happening around them. They could neither understand what had happened to them, nor do anything about it. It was down to the women to band together and try to combat the illness and ride out its effects on their families.

The infected were moved away from the children and their bedding was disposed of and replaced with new.

They took their children to the showers, room by room, family by family. They used the soap their mothers had packed and washed every inch of their skin and hair. There were tears and tantrums, but generally, it ran smoothly.

Oke took charge of the first floor and a woman called Kubra organised the ground floor. There were fifteen families upstairs and twelve down. No one mentioned radiation, just the fact that the disease could be spread via clothing and touch. One of the women downstairs asked to speak to Fanna and Oke. They met on the landing and introduced themselves.

'I'm Elke,' the woman said. Her cheekbones were high, and her eyes were green. 'I'm from Ghana,' she said. 'I was captured in Libya two years ago and sold to these men.'

'I'm Oke. This is Fanna from Gambia, and this is my sister, Isime,' she said. 'We grew up in this town but left when Boko invaded. Our father tried to get us out of here, but our family was drowned. We all have one thing in common. We were all kidnapped and trafficked here.'

'I have a child with my husband and they're both very sick,' Elke said. 'I don't think they'll survive the day, but you're doing the right thing showering your families. You must do it daily.'

'We can't do anything else but wash them and watch them suffering,' Isime said.

'I heard someone whispering about radiation sickness?' Elke said. The women shushed her. 'Sorry. I am asking because I was a scientist in my country.'

'A scientist?' Oke asked, lowering her voice to a whisper. 'What type of scientist?'

'I was a chemist specialising in the use of nerve agents,' Elke said. The women looked at each other. 'I studied the long-term effects of organophosphates on our farmland,' she said. 'And the use of pesticides and novichok agents in war zones.'

'I have heard of those,' Oke said, nodding. 'The Russians used it to poison people in Britain.'

'Yes. And they have sold it to rebels in Africa,' Elke said, whispering now. 'I studied a case in Somalia, where over forty members of an armed political group were wiped out. The cases were identical to what we're seeing here. I think this sickness is being caused by something similar to those agents. The symptoms are identical.'

'That patrol came into contact with a poisonous chemical?' Isime asked.

'Or General Bassi has bought it and doesn't know how to handle it,' Elke whispered. 'These agents are deadly. Just taking the seal off its container could infect the entire building in minutes. The closer the victim to the original source, the faster the infection and the worse the impact will be.' She paused to look around. 'I saw pictures of men who look like they were boiled and skinned alive. The effects are dreadful, as we can see here. Poison isn't a strong enough word for it,' Elke said. 'They're far worse than a poison and they kill over ninety per cent of the people they come into contact with. I think it is more likely to be one of these agents, rather than radiation.'

'But if they were poisoned by one of them, how is it spreading to other people?' Oke asked.

'It can pass by respiratory contact or through the skin,' Elke said. 'Once infected, there is little that can be done.'

'There must be something?' Isime said.

'Atropine helps in some patients, but it has to be injected frequently and it kills as many as it saves,' Elke said. 'I might be wrong, but I think it is either a novichok agent or organophosphate poisoning, but that takes much longer for the symptoms to show.'

'This sickness has come on very quickly,' Oke said.

'The nerve agents are almost immediately visible on the initial victims, but the secondary infections can take between eighteen to thirty-six hours to surface.'

'So, we could be infected, but don't know it yet?' Oke asked. Elke nodded.

Oke began counting backwards in her mind. Tick tock. Her guts twisted in knots. 'I need to go and check my children again,' she said.

CHAPTER 45

Kissie, Chernobyl

Kissie watched the pickup truck pulling out of the car park onto the main road and resisted the urge not to open the door and run across the fields. Being on the roads, trapped in a vehicle at the mercy of airborne enemies, which you couldn't see until it was too late was making her anxiety boil into sheer panic. She closed her eyes and gathered her thoughts. The pickup turned left, heading east towards Chernobyl. Kissie had been into the abandoned zone a dozen times, and it was eerily exciting the first few times. A city frozen in time, overgrown now as Mother Nature claimed back the space. The tower blocks were once home to tens of thousands of families, now only a few thrill-seekers and drifters occupied them. Security guards frequently took pot shots at trespassers, but they couldn't deter them completely. Despite the danger of contamination, curiosity drove thousands to covertly visit, and their photographs were internet gold. There was something fascinating about abandoned buildings, but an entire city is mind-blowing. She knew the quickest route, using the ring roads to skirt the town to the south and onto the road to Kiev, following the River Pripyat. There was nothing else on the road as they navigated their route out of Pripyat and drove in the convoy, surrounded by dense woodland. They could hear bombs dropping in the distance, a deep resounding 'boom' sound. Her imagination made each one sound closer, as if the bombers were stalking them.

Pierre and Frank kept their speed steady, and they covered the twenty kilometres in as many minutes. The pickup slowed as they approached the first roadblock. They stopped their vehicle, leaving enough room to U-turn if they needed to. There were two guard huts, one either side of the road, which were painted with red and white chevrons, and a metal barrier blocked their path. An army Jeep was parked to the left of the road but there was no one in it.

'Why are they stopping?' Carrie asked. Kissie thought her Irish accent was beautiful. Her long black hair was shiny and tied up in a ponytail. 'What's going on?'

'There's a checkpoint here,' Kissie said, turning in her seat.

'Is it a military checkpoint?' Angela asked.

'No,' Kissie said. 'It's usually security guards manning it.'

'I can't see anyone there it at all,' Angela said, craning her neck to see around.

In the pickup, Frank and Pierre used field glasses to search for signs of the guards, but the checkpoint appeared to be abandoned. Pierre sounded the horn, but there was no response.

'What do you think?' Pierre asked.

'I think you should stop honking the horn.'

'That's debatable.' Frank shrugged and smiled. 'Don't worry. Kissie said this is a civilian checkpoint, manned by unarmed security guards,' Frank said. 'I think they've scarpered home when they heard about the invasion.'

'I agree. So, what do you think now?'

'I think I need to go and lift that barrier because it won't do it on its own,' Frank said. He opened the door.

'Put your helmet on,' Pierre said.

'I'm going to be two minutes,' Frank protested. He climbed out and ran towards the guard hut to the left, where the counterweight for the barrier was. It was fifty metres away, and he stooped low and moved quickly, weapon tight to his shoulder, ready to fight if necessary.

'Frank is getting out,' Angela said. 'I think he's going to lift the barrier.'

'Why hasn't he got his helmet on?' Carrie asked. 'Don't they ever listen?'

'He'll be okay here,' Kissie said. 'We'll need to put them on when we reach the next checkpoint. That one is manned by the military, as it's much closer to the power station reactors.'

Automatic fire punctured the air. The women ducked instinctively, and Angela inhaled loudly. 'Who's shooting, for fuck's sake?'

Shots rang out again and Frank ducked into the sentry box. Another burst of fire shattered the windows and splinters of wood exploded in all directions.

'They're shooting at Frank!' Angela shouted. 'We're civilians!' she called out of the window. 'We're fucking civilians!'

Brad, Tom, and Pierre were out of their vehicles in seconds, moving in a well-practiced formation to the driver's side of the pickup.

'Where's it coming from?' Tom asked, aiming his weapon at the trees, scanning for the attackers. He couldn't see an immediate target. 'Where are you, you fuckers?' he whispered, looking through a telescopic sight. 'Come to your uncle Tom,' he muttered. 'I won't hurt you.'

Another burst of fire sent bullets smashing into Frank's hiding place.

'To our right, behind the other sentry box,' Pierre said, crouching. 'Are you hit?' he called to Frank in French.

'No, but this box is made of fucking balsa wood,' Frank shouted. 'I may as well be out there,' he added.

Another prolonged burst of fire erupted. The top half of the sentry box disintegrated into fragments and Tom broke cover, returning fire. Brad flanked to the right and Pierre broke left. All three concentrated their fire on the trees behind the other sentry box and within seconds, the guns fell quiet. They moved swiftly and silently towards the barrier.

'Are you hit?' Pierre shouted.

'No, but I'm covered in fucking glass and splinters, and I'm very pissed off,' Frank replied. He appeared from the remains of the box and lifted the barrier. 'Let's find out who the fuck tried to blow my head off,' he added, running across the road, taking cover behind the Jeep. The men moved behind the intact sentry box and entered the trees. The scientists lost sight of them for a few nervous minutes.

Each step was made cautiously. Every twig that snapped was a giveaway for an enemy sniper. They spread out, ten metres between them, and moved painfully slowly through the trees.

'Look out for mines,' Brad said. 'Avoid any newly dug soil.'

'Are you trying to cheer me up?' Frank asked.

'Just keep your eyes peeled,' Brad said, smiling.

'Over here,' Tom called.

'What is it?'

'I've found the security guards.' The men converged on Tom's position. 'There are four of them, tied up and shot in the back of the head.' He pointed further into the trees, where the bodies lay in a ditch.

'They're civilians,' Brad said. 'They could have let them go home. How were they a threat to the Russians?'

'They weren't,' Pierre said.

They moved on and found the bodies of their attackers. 'We hit two of them, but I think I saw two more running to the south. They're wearing combats but no uniforms,' Pierre said.

The men walked to where the attackers lay. They had been hit multiple times. They checked the bodies for ID.

'This is a Ukrainian driving licence,' Pierre said, checking a dead man's wallet. 'They're Russian sympathisers.'

'Doing what?' Brad asked.

'Making sure this checkpoint is open when the Russians arrive,' Tom said. They searched the immediate area.

'Over here,' Brad called. He held an object that was twice the size of the average digital camera. 'This is a GS205-XRZ. US Special Forces were testing this last year.'

'Is it a laser sighter?' Pierre asked.

'A laser designating gimbal,' Brad said. 'It communicates directly with the drone pilot.'

'How have Ukrainian sympathisers got their hands on a piece of kit like this?' Tom asked.

'Russian money,' Brad said.

They heard a whooshing sound and the ruined sentry box exploded in a blinding flash of light. The men hit the ground and covered their heads. Tom jumped into the ditch where the dead security guards had been dumped. Concrete, branches, and glass rained down on them as they cowered on the forest floor. Pierre looked up as the second whooshing sound grew louder.

'Incoming!' he shouted as the pickup truck exploded. A white flash engulfed it and a deafening boom hit them.

CHAPTER 45

Beb & Amira

Katouh plugged Beb's wounds and disinfected them, but he couldn't stop the bleeding. If he didn't find someone with medical knowledge and equipment, Beb wouldn't last twenty-four hours. One of the wounds was a through-and-through but it needed to be cauterised and there was a bullet still in his chest, although it didn't seem to be deep in the cavity. He could see it. Beb didn't stand a chance of surviving unless he moved him immediately.

He knew that they were at least three weeks' ride from the nearest town, which had a general practitioner in residency and if he was sober, he may be an option, but he rarely was. The nearest hospital was at least three days' drive by car from the doctor's surgery. He knew he didn't have the time or resources to get Beb to either of those locations. There was also the issue of his father and the Tuareg caravan, because he had no idea where they were when they attacked them, or where they would be going. From what he had seen from the dunes, Ali had been shot twice, the same as Beb, and they would be looking for professional medical help too. The last thing he needed to do was run into them while looking after Heba and her father.

Once he had done as much as he could to stop the bleeding and make Beb comfortable, he fashioned a hammock and put him on one of the camels. He took another with Heba sitting in front of him. He packed up their camp, loaded it onto the other camels and headed north, deeper into the desert. It might have seemed like a foolish thing to do, but many years ago, they'd traded medicine with a tribe of Bedouins who spent most of their time cruising the centre of the Sahara, avoiding the less nomadic tribes and the migrants who were crossing the desert in their thousands. They had a route, which they adhered to for decades. It was basically a huge circle, thousands of miles round. He remembered that one of their tribe had been educated in Egypt and went to university to study medicine. She was a surgeon for a while, before returning to her nomadic roots. Civilisation hadn't been for her, and she yearned for the freedom of the Bedouin life. If he could get Beb to someone with that type of training, he may have a chance of survival, but the odds were not good.

As he set off north, his mind drifted to Amira, and he couldn't help but feel guilty for not trying to rescue her. If he did, it would be a suicide mission, leaving Beb mortally wounded and bleeding to death and her daughter alone in the desert with no one to fend for her. It was an impossible situation and he had to prioritise, which wasn't difficult in this situation. Beb's wounds were fatal unless he received treatment soon. Heba was safe with him for now and he could take it for granted that his father would be in no condition to organise a wedding, even if it was his own. Amira would be looked after by the rest of the tribe as one of their own. She had been loved and would be welcomed back into the fold. He knew she would be fed, and she'd be given a comfortable bed to sleep in at night and her grandfather's wounds were bad enough to incapacitate him for a few weeks at least, if he survived at all. With that in mind, he would try to find the Bedouin, access medical treatment for Beb, ask them to look after the girl for a while, and then he would search for Amira. First of all, he had to find the Bedouin and that would be like trying to find a specific grain of sand in a mountain of it.

CHAPTER 47

London

Detective Sergeant Alfred and DC Coop were waiting on the results from the lab, while the team trawled through hundreds of hours of CCTV tapes. They were gathered in the operations room, which had been assigned to the Metropolitan murder squad. They were heading up the investigation into the victim they'd called Beb Sammi. Although they knew that wasn't his real identity, it was the best they had at the time. He'd been Beb Sammi for over ten years. There was nothing worse than calling the victim John Doe. It smacked of desperation and having an investigation that didn't even have a starting line. They'd picked up footage of Beb stepping off the train at Kennington where he loitered on the platform for longer than necessary. He appeared to be nervous and constantly looking around to see if he had been followed. When he left the platform and headed up the stairs towards the toilets, he was followed by a woman just a couple of minutes behind him. Her head and the side of her face were captured.

'See there, pause it there,' the DS said, loosening his tie. His shirt collar was opened at the neck and his sleeves rolled up. The sweat patches beneath his arms were visible and spreading. 'Try to clear up that image of her there.'

The tech adjusted the focus, and the head and shoulders of the woman became clearer. 'Okay, we have a young black female mid to late 20s, short hair style with spiky dreadlocks,' the DS said.

'Bangs,' one of his detectives said. He was Jamaican. 'They're called bangs.'

'Why?' the DS asked.

'What?'

'Why are they called bangs?'

'The origin of dreadlocks goes back two thousand years before Christ, in Egypt and the Celts were said to have hair like rope and snakes,' the tech said, without looking up. Her name was Emily, and she was a brainbox. 'The followers of the Ethiopian emperor, Ras Tafari, made an oath not to cut their hair until he was returned to power, and so dreadlocks became associated with Rastafarianism in modern day culture,' she added.

'No way,' DC Coop said, frowning. 'There was a bloke called Ras Tafari?' Emily looked up and nodded. 'And that is where the name Rastas comes from?'

'Yes,' Emily said. 'Dreadlocks are associated with that tranche of African history, but the dreadlock was worn by the Celts, Vikings, Egyptians...I could go on and on. It wasn't monopolised by Africans,' she added. 'It's become a stereotype.'

'I'm sorry I asked,' the DS said. 'Can we get back to the job at hand?'

'It's interesting though, isn't it?' Coop said, nodding. He eyed Emily and wondered what it would be like to fuck a brainy bird. 'Maybe we could have a chat about it sometime,' he added.

'I don't have any spare time,' Emily said. 'Sorry.' She worked on the image. 'That's the best I can do.'

'Okay, does anybody recognise this woman?' the DS asked.

'She looks like a younger version of Jet Unganu,' DC Coop said.

'I thought that straight away,' another detective agreed.

'And a lot of her meatheads are sporting that very same hairstyle at the moment,' he added.

'Yes. I agree with Coop,' one of the other detectives said, nodding. 'Most of her crew are wearing bangs like this. Now, it could be a coincidence that someone with this hairstyle is following our victim or we could have just stumbled on our motive and the perpetrator.'

'We all know that there's no such thing as a coincidence when we're investigating a murder, especially a drug-related murder,' the DS said. 'I recognised that hairstyle as soon as I saw it on screen and Coop is right, that woman looks like a younger version of Jet. That could be her daughter or if not, I'm betting a pound to a penny that she's a blood relation of some kind.' The DS turned to the tech. 'Okay, let that run and let's see where our friend with the bangs goes.'

The recording ran on fast-forward, making the people look like extras on a Benny Hill episode. It showed Beb reaching the top of the escalator and then he went out of view as he headed towards the gents' toilet. The woman could be seen reaching the top of the escalator no more than ten seconds later.

'There she is, the little beauty, right behind him. She must have picked up the pace to have closed the gap between them, but it clearly shows her close behind him and where we lose Beb, we also lose her.'

'She's our killer,' Coop said.

'Let it run on and see when she comes back into view.'

The recording showed the woman coming back onto the screen and heading towards the next set of escalators, which led up to the ticket hall and the exits. As she reached the bottom of the moving staircase, she changed direction momentarily to drop something into a cleaner's trolley. Then she was on the escalator again, but carrying a holdall.

'Bingo,' the DS said, clapping his hands together. 'We have her following him into the toilets and then we have her going up the escalators with his bag. The only thing that's missing is the murder weapon and I've got a feeling it'll be in that cleaner's trolley.'

'We've got her, guv,' Coop said.

'Not yet,' the DS said. 'Get onto Kennington Tube Station, and find out what happened to that trolley, where they keep it, and where they put the rubbish when their bags are full. I think she dumped the knife into that trolley, and if you look carefully at the footage there, she doesn't have any gloves on. We find that knife, we find her, and we nail her.'

****

Suzette Unganu was sitting in the lounge of the Lord Rodney, a big old-fashioned pub decorated with dark-stained oak, brandy barrels, and brass rails that looked like they'd been polished for a week. The pub was reasonably busy, with diners sitting at most of the wooden tables. Office workers were scattered about, wearing suits and ties and talking politics about the price of oil and what that silly fucker Putin was up to. She was growing impatient, but then patience wasn't her strong point. This had been her golden opportunity to step out of the shadow of her auntie Jet and create her own light.

Jet had been good to her over the years. She had paid for her private education at a boarding school in Surrey, and she paid the rent on a flat in one of the nicer parts of Kensington. She had also lined her up with four decent jobs, all of which she had lasted no more than a week at. Suzette had her own ideals and aspirations as to where she wanted to be and how she would get there. Suzette knew her auntie looked after her because of her own sense of guilt, as her sister, Suzette's mother, had died from an overdose of crack cocaine and diazepam. Both of which she'd got from Jet herself.

Suzette's mother was a beautiful woman, with a beautiful soul, easily distracted and abused by the bad boys she was attracted to. Her love affair with drugs had begun when she was a teenager, when she and Jet would dance the night away on ecstasy and amphetamine. Over the years, recreational use turned into habitual abuse and the drugs took a grip on her heart and soul. Suzette didn't know who her father was because her mother couldn't remember the men she'd had sex with during the period of conception. There were a few to pick from, but she didn't know what their names were. That period of her life was a series of one-night stands, fuelled by cocaine and alcohol and when she woke up in the mornings, she was covered in vomit, penniless, and eventually pregnant. Things didn't get any better for her and Suzette was passed from pillar to post while her mother continued to party her life away, bouncing from one man to the next, never truly finding what she was looking for, because in reality it was the drugs high that she craved, not love.

Suzette wasn't surprised when she found her mother dead, but she was surprised by how much her death impacted Auntie Jet. Jet was devastated and spent thousands of pounds on a funeral that hardly anyone attended, overcompensating because of her guilt. To this day, she still felt guilty, and Suzette was wrapped in cotton wool and spoilt, but her auntie's kindness wasn't as appreciated as it should be. Jet had tried her level best to keep Suzette away from the family business, but it was an impossible task. Everyone who was anyone knew who Jet was and what she did for a living and Suzette was determined to become involved and eventually help in the running of the family's distribution network. Jet resisted at first, but Suzette was persistent to the point of distraction and eventually it was easier to give her cameo roles in some of the operations, rather than listen to her wittering on day and night. Her auntie Jet set her up as an employee and paid her as an admin assistant and bookkeeper. She was registered as being employed by a string of bookmakers in east London called Bet Jet. Of course, Suzette knew nothing about bookkeeping or the betting industry but that was fine as the entire thing was simply a cover, so that Suzette had a legitimate explanation as to where her income came from. The problem was that Suzette enjoyed consuming her auntie's products just as much as their customers did, which led to a very expensive cocaine habit.

As soon as she heard that her auntie Jet was considering doing a deal for the African goat boy to purchase some products wholesale, she saw a glaring opportunity to steal it from him and make a killing on the products herself. She knew everyone there was to know, and she knew that she would be able to move a sports holdall full of cocaine quickly and easily and without her auntie knowing anything about it.

'Where the fuck have you been?' Suzette asked when she saw Harry Trainor approaching the booth which she was sitting in. Harry didn't look very happy, and she frowned as he sat down and glared at her. 'What's wrong with your face? It looks like a smacked arse?'

'That's because I don't like people who waste my time or try to take the piss out of me,' Harry said, squeezing her knee painfully hard.

'Ow, that hurts,' she snapped. She punched his arm away and bared her teeth at him like a rat ready to bite. 'Don't you ever fucking touch me again or I will stab you up so bad that you have more perforations than a teabag,' she snarled, trying to avoid attracting the attention of the diners nearby.

Two elderly ladies looked over and whispered to each other, their shopping bags surround their feet.

'What are you looking at?' Suzette challenged them and they looked away quickly. 'Nosey old fuckers,' she added. 'Now, what is your problem, or have I got to straighten your face?'

'Big words and big threats from a little girl,' Harry said, his voice almost a whisper. 'If you weren't Jet's niece, you'd already be at the bottom of the Thames, so before you start banging around threats, you need to remember who it is you're fucking talking to.' Harry leant closer to her; a gun clearly visible inside his waistband. 'Now you listen to me, little girl, I could shoot you right here and not one of these fucking snowflakes would turn up in court, so less of the hard-case act.' Harry grinned and there was madness in his eyes. 'I don't know what kind of fucking game you think you're playing or who you're playing with, but you're messing with the wrong people.'

'What the fuck is your problem?' Suzette asked, shaking her head. The urge to have a cigarette was overwhelming. Her nerves were jangling. 'I've just given you a bag of top-quality beak, at three-quarters of the wholesale price and you come in here throwing your weight around like you're Jonny Concrete?'

'I don't know where you got your bag of "top-quality beak", as you so eloquently put it,' Harry said. 'But what I've just taken to our friends on the other side of the river is a bag full of baking soda.' Harry stared at her, his face like thunder.

'What the fuck?' she muttered, blushing.

'I've been doing business with them for over twenty-five years now and as much as there is mutual trust between us, all transactions are double-checked to ensure the integrity of the products. So, you can imagine how embarrassed I was when the litmus paper turned the wrong colour?'

'You are shitting me?' Suzette said, astonished. Her face went pale, and she looked like she was about to vomit. 'I have absolutely no fucking idea how that could happen.' She shook her head, her mouth open in surprise, while she tried to explain to herself how it could have gone so wrong. 'I followed the gear from start to finish. There is no way this could have happened.'

'I don't give a fuck about who you followed, where you followed them to, or where you followed them from, but I do give a fuck about the fact it looks like *I* was trying to pull a fast one on people I've done business with for decades,' Harry said, angrily. 'I suggest you keep your head down for a while, as my associates are a bit miffed they haven't got as much product today as they thought they would have. You see, this business is all about profit and loss, sales projections, and the estimated return on investment. It takes time and effort to set up a deal like this, and as the old saying goes, time is money.'

'Harry, I'm so sorry. I can't understand how it happened,' Suzette said, shaking her head and realising how much trouble she was in.

'Suzette, my dear, being sorry in this business gets you absolutely nowhere except the bottom of the river or sharing a hole in a Victorian graveyard, where no one has been for years, with someone you've never heard of. Either way, you can vanish from the face of Earth in the blink of an eye, and no one will care whether you're sorry or not,' Harry said. A narrow smile touched his lips. 'My business partners were expecting to make twenty-five grand on that product over the next two days. You see, when a shipment is scheduled, the dealers and distributors have to be in place to move the products as quickly and efficiently as possible before the old Bill start sniffing around, understand?'

'Yes. Of course. I know how it works, Harry.'

'Good. So, we now have a supply chain ready to spring into action like a well-oiled machine and no fucking product to sell.' He shrugged and shook his head, frowning, his bottom lip drooping like a child sulking. 'Can you see how upset I am?' he teased.

'Yes, I can fix this, Harry.'

'How can you fix it?' he asked. 'Your product is in the fucking bin where it belongs, and my friends have no gear and people waiting to sell it. Not only is that disappointing, it's also very bad for the reputation of the business, and as your auntie Jet will tell you, reputation is everything.'

'Of course, I understand that you're pissed off, but I had no idea that the gear in the bag wasn't real,' Suzette said, her eyes becoming watery. 'I'm very sorry.'

'You're sorry?'

'Yes.'

'You're sorry, I'm sorry, every fucker is sorry, but that doesn't matter,' Harry snapped. 'I'm beginning to think that you're not listening to me,' Harry said, turning away as if he had become disinterested in the conversation. 'You see, what you're failing to understand is that you entered into business agreements and failed to deliver on your side of the bargain. No number of apologies or excuses will change the fact that my associates are now out-of-pocket by twenty-five grand. They're seeking that amount in compensation, plus another twenty-five to smooth out the ripples in the business.'

'But, Harry…'

'Shut up and listen,' Harry said, slapping her face. The elderly women looked shocked. 'Do you want to take a fucking picture?' Harry asked them. They grabbed their purchases and put on their coats to leave. 'There is layer upon layer of people involved in the supply chain and they will all be left hanging, with their dicks in the wind because you fucked up.'

'Harry, help me out here please,' Suzette pleaded. 'If I had that kind of money, I wouldn't be doing what I did today.'

'Then I suggest you make a few calls and say goodbye to the people who mean anything to you,' Harry said, standing up. 'What are your favourite flowers, by the way?' he asked as he walked away. 'I'll have some sent to your funeral.'

CHAPTER 48

Oke, Isime, & Fanna

Oke went back to the children. They were sleeping, which was a blessing, as they'd seen so much trauma in such a short space of time. Their father wasn't the most loving man on the planet, but he was still their father and they looked up to him, respected him, and loved him. Seeing him deteriorate as fast as he had, turning from a man into a monster in the space of just hours, was probably one of the most traumatic experiences any child could endure.

She decided to let them sleep rather than wake them to ask them if they felt okay. She had been asking them if they felt okay all day, and it could wait until they'd slept a little longer. She decided to check on her husband, and as she stood up and turned around to cross the room, she coughed. It wasn't the type of cough which starts as a tickle, or a bit of an irritation which you need to clear from the back of your throat, it was the type of cough which comes from absolutely nowhere and is uncomfortable, almost painful. She wiped away spittle from the corner of her mouth with the back of her hand and was horrified when she saw the pink flecks of blood on her skin.

'Oh, please no, don't let me get sick when I need to look after my babies,' she said, her voice a whisper, so that nobody else could hear. She wiped her hand on her smock and crossed the room to where her husband lay. He was barely recognisable from the man he had been yesterday. She didn't go too close. She kept her distance and watched him for a few seconds. His eyes were open but focused on nothing, his mouth open, tongue lolling to his cheek. The blisters looked so painful she couldn't understand how he wasn't screaming the place down. Without touching him, she sensed that he had passed on. She watched his chest for long minutes, looking for the rise and fall, no matter how insignificant it was, but there was nothing at all. Rashid was dead.

Isime filled up a jug with cold water and made her way back up the stairs. As she climbed to the first floor, the temperature increased and the smell of the dead and dying became more intense, cloying at her senses like fingernails on a chalkboard. The hallways and stairwell echoed with the sound of hushed chatter, sobbing, and the crying of young children. The school had become a hospice, a place where people were waiting for death, either for themselves or for their loved ones, and the atmosphere was tinged with fear and frustration. As she walked into their classroom, two men were walking out wearing aprons, rubber gloves, and makeshift masks around their faces. Between them, they carried the lifeless body of Rashid. She put her hand to her mouth in shock and nearly dropped the jug, not because she had any emotional ties to the man, he'd been a pig, but simply because she found death shocking, no matter who it was. She saw Oke across the room, sitting a few metres away from her sleeping children.

'Are you okay?' Izzy asked. 'I saw them taking Rashid's body out.'

'Good riddance to bad rubbish,' Oke said. 'I am glad to see the back of the bastard and I hope he rots in hell. The children are sleeping, and they don't know yet, so when they wake up, don't tell them anything. I'll tell them that their father has been taken away to another hospital. They don't need to know the truth.'

'Don't worry, I won't say a thing,' Isime said, approaching her son. She knelt by his mattress and looked at his skinny body, ravaged by blisters and sores. His head was turned away from her and she leant over to see his face. She could see the whites of his eyes were crisscrossed with dark black lines and he was staring sightlessly at the wall behind him. She placed her fingers to the pulse in his neck, and when she realised he was dead, she let out the most unholy scream Oke had heard in her life.

CHAPTER 49

Kissie

When the smoke cleared, there was nothing left of the pickup truck but a smouldering twisted chassis. The rest of the convoy reversed at high speed and stopped about a hundred metres away, where the passengers opened the doors and ran into the trees for cover. Brad, Tom, and the two Frenchmen made their way around the explosion site, remaining beneath the cover of the woods until they reached the others. The scientists were clearly shaken by the missile strike, as were their protectors, although the military men did a much better job at hiding their fear. Brad used his field glasses to check the skies around them. There was no sign of the drone which fired the missile.

'What the fuck just happened?' Angela said, angrily shaking her head.

'Someone broke the pickup truck,' Pierre said.

'Why is it funny?' she fumed. 'You could have been in it when the silly fuckers fired a missile!'

'We could have been, but we weren't,' Pierre said, smiling. 'The luck of the French, you see,' he added with a wink.

'How did Waterloo work out for you?' Tom asked with a wink. 'Not so lucky there.'

'Or Agincourt,' Brad said. 'Another unlucky one.'

'Can you please stop being so jolly?' Kissie said, wiping a tear from her eye. 'I've just pissed my pants and you're doing war jokes.'

'Okay,' Tom said. 'That was a close call. We're all shocked and people deal with shock in different ways.'

'Are they just firing at anything that's moving?' Angela asked, clearly shaken.

'The men that were firing at Frank were Russian sympathisers.'

'Meaning what exactly?'

'So, they were Ukrainians who were already here, waiting for the invasion to happen. Their orders were to go to this checkpoint and make sure it was unmanned when the Russian tanks arrive,' Tom explained. 'They had a laser designator on them, which they used to point at the sentry box, and then the pickup truck. A drone picked up the message and fired its missiles in our direction. It could have been fired from a drone, which is a long way away from here. So don't panic and think that it's flying directly above us waiting to take another pot-shot. Without the designator, it doesn't know we're here.'

'That's a relief,' Kissie said.

'The barrier is open now, so we need to get into the vehicles, skirt around the bomb crater, and get out of here quick smart,' Tom said. No one moved. 'Snap out of it, people!' he shouted, clapping his hands. 'I need you to listen to me and do exactly as I'm asking. We need to get back into the vehicles, skirt the missile crater, and get out of here as fast as we can. Does everybody understand what I am saying?'

Most of the gathering nodded that they understood, and they each moved at a different pace. Slowly but surely, the group made its way back to the vehicles. Some of them were visibly upset and crying, and others looked shocked.

'When I said I pissed my pants, I wasn't joking,' Kissie said. 'I'm going to go behind a bush and try to sort myself out. I'll be with you as soon as I can. Can you get me a pair of knickers? They're at the top of my bag,' she said to Angela as quietly as she could, embarrassed by her situation.

'Of course, I can,' Angela said, jogging towards the Ford.

'Okay, Kissie,' Tom said, nodding. 'I need you to be as quick as you possibly can. Everybody else, get the engines started, and as soon as Kissie is ready, we'll be on our way.'

Kissie tried to shake off the overwhelming feeling of dread that had settled over her since the strike at the hotel. She looked for the best place to offer her some privacy and she stepped behind a tree and began to undo her belt. The protective suit she was wearing was bulky and cumbersome and uncomfortable at the best of times, but now her underwear and pants were wet she felt ten times worse. She needed to take it off. It was making her claustrophobic. She glanced around the tree and saw that all her colleagues were in the vehicles. Pierre and Frank were standing beside the Fords and Angela was rummaging around in the boots of the vehicle, looking for a fresh pair of pants. Angela found what she was looking for, and she waved a pair of blue lacy knickers in the air as if they were a trophy. Kissie saw Frank and Pierre giggling like schoolchildren and Frank gave her a cheeky wink, just as an ear-piercing whistling sound became audible and quickly became deafening. The missile exploded fifty metres in the air above the vehicles, spraying thousands of razor-sharp metal cassettes designed to wipe out as many humans as possible with one explosion. Kissie fell backwards, tripping over her own trousers. She heard the sound of thousands of pieces of metal whizzing through the trees, cutting through branches and embedding themselves in tree trunks. The noise was terrifying, and she lay on her back until the silence of the forest reigned again. She was about to sit up when a second missile hit the convoy.

CHAPTER 50

Beb

Katouh set off and rode for hours until Heba couldn't go any further without needing the toilet. He used the opportunity to check his compass and make sure that they were heading in the right direction. At that time of year, the huge Bedouin caravan would be moving west to east on the northernmost point of the circle, which they travelled. He was hoping that if he headed north, at some point he would come across them or find their tracks, which he could then follow.

The caravan was several hundred people in number, with huge numbers of goats and camels. They left a trail that even the worst tracker could follow and Katouh had been trained to track things in the desert since he could walk. Being able to track in the desolate dunes could mean the difference between life and death if you're separated from the tribe which you are travelling with.

He checked on Beb and was pleased to see that the blood around the wounds was beginning to coagulate, and the bleeding had slowed, but he knew that what he could see was going on on the outside of the body was not a fair reflection of what was going on inside it. Internal bleeding would kill a victim one hundred per cent of the time if it isn't stemmed. His biggest fear now was an infection. He had one small bottle of penicillin tablets and a strip of amoxicillin which might hold off infection for a few days but was not a permanent solution to the problem. He took the top from a flask and put it to Beb's lips to allow him to sip from it. The fact that he could sip and swallow and move his head slightly gave him hope that if he could get him to a medical practitioner, he might be able to save his life. Beb's eyes flickered open for a few seconds. His pupils were dilated, and it took a few seconds for him to focus on Katouh's face. A smile touched his lips.

'Katouh,' he whispered.

'Yes. It's me.'

'Where is Amira?'

'She has gone to relieve herself.'

'What about Heba?' Beb asked, his voice hoarse and barely audible.

'She is here riding in front of me. You don't have to worry about her,' Katouh said, giving him some more water.

'Can I see her?' Beb whispered.

Katouh went away and picked up Heba. She was more than happy to be lifted up to see her father, but when they got back to his hammock, he had passed out again. He made Beb comfortable, mounted his camel, and set off north. There was no time to think about cooking food. He needed to cross as many miles of the desolate sands as he could if he was to have any chance of intercepting the Bedouin caravan.

CHAPTER 51

Kalu

The bin room at the Tube station was situated at the rear of the building but couldn't be accessed from inside. Access could only be made by a backstreet behind it. The amount of litter generated by a London Tube station was immense, and the rubbish storage room was the size of an Olympic swimming pool, tiled, floor to ceiling with dazzling strip-lights, which buzzed as they started up and hummed while they were on. DC Coop was pissed off that he'd been assigned lead officer in the search for the murder weapon. The DS had made it sound like a vital role, but he had a knack for giving people shit and telling them it was caviar. Coop had been sent to trawl through the bins, full stop.

The station manager was a portly man, wearing a suit which was too small for him. His shirt was open at the neck, exposing a grimy collar, and the odour which emanated from him indicated it needed changing. His name badge was faded by the washing machine because his wife couldn't be bothered taking it off his shirt when she did the laundry. Winston Hill, it read, barely legible. His ruddy complexion was exasperated by physical exertion and walking around the narrow alleyways and backstreets to escort the search team to the bin room was the most exercise he had undertaken for years.

Once they were inside, they walked down a corridor until they reached a door covered with a metal shield and locked with three huge padlocks that could have belonged on a castle.

'That's a lot of security for a room full of rubbish, Mr Hill,' Coop said, shaking his head. 'Isn't it a bit overkill?'

'Call me Winston. You have no idea what the tramps around here are like,' Winston said. 'They'll break into anything and anywhere. They can chew through locks. These skips are like a goldmine to them, full of half-eaten food and drinks bottles. And it's warm and dry,' he added. 'The problem is the claim culture we live in.' Winston looked around as if someone was listening who shouldn't be. 'They got the lock off one night and one of them sticked himself on a used syringe a junkie had thrown in the bin and then contracted hepatitis-C. The cheeky fucker sued us.' He shrugged. 'Another time, one of them ate everything he could find and ended up in hospital with pathogen poisoning. That's no joke. He snuffed it and guess what his family did?'

'Let me guess,' Coop said. 'Did they sue you?'

'Yup. Hence the place is locked up like a bank.'

He opened the door, and they were met by a wall of yellow skips on wheels. Coop stood on tiptoe and tried to look over the first one.

'Fucking hell,' he moaned. 'How many of them are there?'

'Twelve,' Winston said. 'But the ones you want are the closest to the door. All yesterday's rubbish is in the first three skips.'

'Right, let's get them wheeled out here and emptied,' Coop ordered. 'We are not leaving here until we find our murder weapon.'

'What are you looking for?' Winston asked.

'A fucking big knife,' Coop said.

****

Back in the murder team office, the techs were still running through CCTV footage. DS Alfred was on the phone arguing with a CHIS handler about gleaning information about Jet Unganu and her relatives who worked in her operation. It wasn't going well, and the handler told him there was nothing doing as his informers were in vulnerable situations, and if they started asking questions about Jet's relatives, they would shine a spotlight on themselves. They might as well wear a badge saying, *I'm a Grass*.

Jet Unganu was as sharp as a tack, and she trusted no one. Anyone asking questions was dealt with quickly and harshly, no matter how innocent the questions were. Anyone who worked in the organisation knew better than to stick their nose in any part of the business which they didn't belong in. There were several informers in play, some closer to Jet than others, but they all had one thing in common. Their information was gleaned by listening to the conversations going on around them. They never asked any questions or pried into the mechanics of the business. What DC Alfred was asking for would put the informers into perilous situations. The CHIS handler was an experienced detective with decades of service under his belt. He had seen superintendents like Alfred come and go many times. Most of them were of the same ilk, full of piss and wind. His job was to ensure the safety of his informers and the officers that handled them. There was no way DS Alfred or anybody else was going to change that.

DS Alfred ended the call mumbling, fuck you very much for nothing. He felt that they had the perpetrator at their fingertips and all they had to do was grasp her and they could lock her up.

'Have you got a minute?' one of the techs asked, poking her head around the door frame. 'If you're not too busy.'

'I'm always too fucking busy, but as it happens, I have just ended a phone call with a particularly unhelpful colleague, who doesn't give a shit if we arrest our suspect or not.'

'Oh dear.'

'He cares more about the criminals he pays for information than he does about locking up the murderer,' Alfred moaned.

'That must be frustrating.'

'Yes, it is, a tad.' Alfred sighed. 'Anyway, let's look on the bright side. I hope you've got something useful to tell me, as we need a break on this one and then we can get it wrapped up and get down the pub to celebrate.'

'I found some footage around Waterloo Tube Station,' she said. 'And I think you should see it because it throws a new light on where the victim went before he reached Kennington station.'

'If it throws any light at all on where the victim went, I need to see it,' Alfred said, getting up from his chair. 'Okay, let's see what you've got.'

'We've got this footage taken from the station, showing Sammi walking up the steps onto the street, then we pick him up around the corner on footage from a passing bus, heading in the direction of this car park, which is about two-hundred metres down this road here.' She pulled up Google Maps on one screen and pointed out where the footage was relating to on the map, as she explained the victim's movements. 'He goes off camera for approximately twelve minutes, and then we see him coming back, taking exactly the same route back to the station,' she said. 'That makes me think that he did something on or around this car park here.'

'Like what?' Alfred asked, nodding.

'If we zoom in closely on Google Maps, we can see there's a row of lock-ups.'

'Excellent work. Bloody hell, you little beauty,' Alfred said, clapping his hands. He slapped her on the back as if she was an old pal. But she didn't look very happy about it. 'Well done.'

'Thank you, sir,' she muttered.

'So, he has a lock-up.'

'I think so. Why else would he have gone there?'

'Why indeed?' DS Alfred took out his phone. 'Get me a car and a search team and I want Dr Kalu Sammi on the phone, and let's see if he knew anything about this lock-up, because if he does and he failed to tell us about it, then I'm going to be a bit pissed off that he hasn't mentioned it.'

CHAPTER 52

Oke, Isime, & Fanna

Isime had to be restrained as a Boko guard came in to remove her son's body from the building. They were ruthless when dealing with the dead. As soon as any of the victims passed, they were removed within minutes, leaving the families no time to grieve over their loved ones before their bodies were taken away for disposal. And they were not disclosing where the bodies were being taken to, or what was going to happen to them. For a grieving mother, not knowing where her dead child was being taken, was almost as distressing as the death itself. Isime couldn't be consoled; no matter how her sister tried, she just couldn't calm her down. It was distressing enough that her nephew had passed away without seeing her sister hysterical and uncontrollable. It was soul destroying listening to her. She lay curled up in the foetal position and cried for her son. It was just heartbreaking. Oke had never felt so helpless.

The same scene was being acted out throughout the building. The victims of the sickness were falling fast; not a single one had shown any signs of improvement before they died. There were no signs of any doctors being brought to the school, or nurses, or medicines, or anything that the general had promised before they were taken from their homes and dumped into the derelict building.

Isime lay on her mattress and cried for what felt like hours. Oke was beginning to feel disorientated, and she was coughing harder and with more frequency. She made a point of keeping her distance from her children, although thankfully they were still drifting in and out of sleep. They were exhausted. She dreaded them waking up, as they would ask what had happened to their father and their cousin. Seeing Isime so distraught would answer their questions. As young as they were, they weren't stupid.

Oke felt ill. Very ill. She needed to use the toilet, so she left Isime and headed down the corridor. There were toilets just on the other side of the stairwell and the stench from them became worse as she approached. The sickness was giving people uncontrollable diarrhoea. It was quieter on the first floor and one of the stalls was empty. She did what she needed to do, which was incredibly unpleasant. When the cramps had finished, she stood up, adjusting her clothing. She turned to flush the toilet and was horrified to see blood in the pan. It wasn't menstrual. It wasn't time for her period, and she was as regular as clockwork. She wondered if it could be because Rashid had wanted sex the morning he arrived home, although her brain searched for any reason for why she was bleeding. She was grasping at straws, trying to think of any reason except the sickness. She coughed again, bringing up phlegm this time. She spat into the toilet and was disturbed to see that it was flecked with blood too. There was no way that she could avoid the fact that she'd been contaminated. All she could do now was to try to make sure that she didn't infect her children or her sister.

CHAPTER 53

Kissie, Chernobyl

Kissie was lying on her back, staring up at the sky through the remaining skeletal branches. Their leaves and limbs had been shredded by shrapnel. The clouds were grey and tinged bluish at the edges, and they skittled across the sky at a dizzying rate. She wondered if there were more drones above them, where she couldn't see, waiting and watching for the opportunity to kill the innocents below. The dust had settled, but there was still ringing in her ears, and she felt dizzy from the thundering impact and the shock wave which followed. She had no idea of exactly how long she stayed there, but she was in no rush to stand up. If she did, she'd have to look around and see what had happened to her friends and colleagues who had been sitting in the vehicles, terrified and waiting to leave. It had been her fault the convoy hadn't moved off. It had been she who sent Angela to fetch her dry underwear. She saw her waving them in the air, smiling. No, she didn't want to see the aftermath, not now, not ever.

Since the explosion, there had been no noise at all from the direction of the road. No voices, no shouting, no screaming for help, just a deathly silence. Even the birds had stopped singing. Apart from the whistling in her ears, there was nothing but silence. Kissie turned onto her knees and tried to rise. She clung to the tree and waited for the dizziness to pass. How long that was, she wasn't sure. She stretched her legs and lifted her arms up, steepling her fingers together and squeezing the palms of her hands to make sure that everything was working as it should be. She turned and leant against the trunk, glad that it blocked her view of the road. Part of her needed to look, but the other part forbade it. She looked at the trees around her and saw that they'd been cut to ribbons by the shrapnel from the airburst. Shards of metal glinted from every trunk for as far as she could see. There were not hundreds of pieces of metal, there were thousands, maybe even more than that. It was almost incomprehensible to imagine what would happen to a human body if it was hit by such a torrent of deadly flying metal. The thought of what had happened to Angela, and the others made her feel nauseous.

She needed to look at the vehicles to see if any of them had survived, yet she knew in her heart and soul that nothing could have survived the two explosions. The fear of seeing her friends dead was almost as powerful as the fear of being alone. Her mind raced as she realised that if they'd all died, she would be truly alone. She considered the prospect of being the only survivor, and it was terrifying. If there was no one left, how could she make her way through the forest to the other side of Chernobyl? On foot with armed militia men crawling everywhere, she didn't stand a chance. Panic set in and she could feel her chest tightening and her breath becoming shallow and fast. She knew she had to retake control of her mind and body, or she wouldn't make it through the day. She wondered if it would have been better to have been killed in the explosion. At least she'd no longer have to worry about being alone or how she was going to get out of this hopeless situation.

'Come on, Kissie,' she said to herself. 'You need to get a grip because if you start to panic, you're going to make a mistake and you can't afford to make a mistake right here, right now.'

She took a deep breath, closed her eyes, and counted to ten.

One

Two

Three

Four

Five

Six

Seven

Eight

Nine

Ten

She breathed out and did it again. Her breathing slowed, and she opened her eyes and looked around. She was feeling calmer, despite being surrounded by the evidence of the dreadful thing which had just happened. She steeled herself and stepped from behind the tree, looking towards the road.

The scene was utter devastation, like something from an apocalyptic movie. There was a bomb crater ten feet deep and twenty yards wide and metal debris strewn across the road in all directions. She could make out the chassis of one vehicle, stripped of its structure and completely unrecognisable as a car, but the rest were nowhere to be seen. Thankfully, there was no sign of the remainder of the convoy or the poor souls who'd been sitting in the vehicles when the first missile struck. There was nothing but a hole in the road and twisted remnants strewn everywhere. The shrapnel from the airburst combined with the explosive power of the second strike had completely destroyed everything they touched. She knew that her friends were dead before she'd looked at the scene, yet it didn't make it any easier to look at it. They were gone. Vaporised in a few moments of hell-like conflagration. None of those people deserved to die. No one in this world deserved to die like that, cut to shreds by razor-sharp shrapnel, blown to bits by the explosions, and their remains burnt to cinders in the inferno which followed. Except Putin. He deserved it.

Who thought up those weapons? she thought, and who said they should be used against civilians? All those people had been wiped off the planet in seconds. They were gone, and she was still here, alone.

It was difficult to take her eyes off the scene or to think straight. But that was exactly what she needed to do. She had to think about her next move because her life depended on it. If she got it wrong, then the results could be catastrophic and fatal. If she got it right, she still had the chance to make it out of this hellhole. She forced herself to look left, the way they'd come from, and she considered heading back that way, but it made no sense, whatsoever. She looked for anything which might help her. She scanned the debris and carnage, looking for inspiration, but none was forthcoming. She looked to her right at the remnants of the pickup truck. It was over a hundred metres away, and then she saw the bomb crater and the spot where the sentry box had once stood. Beyond them, she saw her one and only opportunity to make it out of there. The army Jeep, which they'd spotted near the barrier, appeared to be in one piece, protected from the blasts by the trees between it and the impact zone. Kissie didn't need to see anything else. She jogged through the trees as fast as her shaking legs could carry her until she came level with the point where the barrier had been. The smell of burning wood was heavy on the air.

She made her way through the trees to the edge of the road and hid behind a smoking trunk, looking in both directions to make sure that there were no more sympathisers around. No one in their right mind would have hung around that checkpoint. It was a smouldering wasteland. She bent lower and jogged across the road to the Jeep and looked inside. She tried the handle, but it was locked and there were no signs of any keys in the ignition. She turned round and leant against the door, banging her head in frustration against the glass.

'Where are the fucking keys?' she asked herself, desperately trying to think where they could be. It came to her in a flash. The men who manned the sentry boxes and the barrier had probably arrived for their shift in the Jeep. They had been captured and executed in the trees. One of those men would have the keys in his pocket, or at least, she hoped they did.

Kissie crossed the road and made her way back into the trees until she came to the ditch where the dead men had been disposed of. They were beginning to smell already. The ditch was deep and partially flooded. The banks were too steep to slide down slowly. She jumped into it and the mud came up to her knees. Dirty water seeped into her boots and socks. Kissie waded to the nearest corpse and tried not to look at his face, but it was impossible. He was in his early twenties, clean-shaven, with pale-blue eyes. The wedding ring on his finger sent a pang of pain through her. He had a wife at home; wherever that was. She would be frightened and waiting for her husband to come home. Her mobile wouldn't be working, and she would be out of her mind.

How many other wives would be waiting to hear from their husbands? she wondered. Too many.

Kissie patted his pockets but found nothing. She moved on to the next body. He was older, fifties probably, with a grey beard and stained teeth. She could smell excrement and cigarette tobacco. He might have asked for a last cigarette before they shot him. She had seen that on a film, and it stuck with her. The smell of cigarettes made her think of Angela, and tears filled her eyes. She wondered if she had felt any pain, or would it have been instantaneous?

She patted him down but couldn't find the keys. Kissie moved onto the third body. He was face down in the mud. She grabbed his shoulder and tugged at him, turning him over. His face was missing, and insects were already entrenched in the gaping maw. She retched, but nothing came up. It took all her effort to feel in his pockets. She moved from one to the next, repeating the process. Sure enough, in the next pocket she searched, she found a bunch of keys with a Jeep fob attached.

Kissie moved away from the bodies and waded through the mud, scrambling up the bank. At the top, she stopped to get her breath, shaking the mud from her legs and ankles. She couldn't hang around and she made her way back to the Jeep, unlocking it with the remote. It beeped, and the lights flashed. She climbed into the driver's seat and took a deep breath to calm her nerves. Being inside the vehicle made her feel a little safer, but not much. She checked her phone, desperately wanting to speak to her father. There was no signal. She inserted the key and was relieved to see it had a full tank of diesel. It was relatively new and should be mechanically sound. It would take forty minutes to reach the reactor lake and then another thirty minutes from there to the river itself. Once she reached the river, she could join the main road which led south to the River Dnipro, Ukraine's biggest river, which would eventually take her to Kiev.

The ring road around Chernobyl was empty. She saw no security guards, no military personnel, and more concerning, no other people trying to escape. The second checkpoint she came to was normally manned by Ukrainian soldiers, but when she arrived, it had been abandoned and the barrier was left open. Although the Ukrainians were the innocent party in this invasion, she was glad there were no soldiers there. If she never saw another military uniform again, it would be too soon. She had had her fill of macho men and their machines, and their machineguns and their missiles, to last for ten lifetimes.

It was the same story at the third and final checkpoint. They were unmanned, and she didn't slow the Jeep down as she passed through them and turned onto a legitimate road. As she left the woodland behind, the scenery turned to flat farmland, irrigated by hundreds of miles of canals and dams. Behind her in the mirror, she could see towers of black smoke dominating the skyline. The fighting was intensifying.

A few miles on, she reached the steel grey waters of the reactor lake, a man-made body of water diverted from the River Pripyat, built to cool down the reactors to keep the core temperature stable. She had studied it regularly. When reactor four suffered the meltdown, seepage was inevitable, and the reactor lake was now contaminated. It looked innocent enough, but it was far from it. She kept a steady speed as she drove the length of the lake, and then she followed alongside the Pripyat River until it joined the Dnipro River, which was a vast expanse of water that flowed through Kiev to the Black Sea.

The minor road met a major road and as she approached it, she could see vehicles backed up, bumper to bumper. Hundreds of them. She was relieved to see human beings, but anxious at the speed the traffic was moving. It was barely a crawl. Kissie needed a drink of water and she needed to use the toilet. She knew that there was a small boathouse next to the river about twenty miles further down the road. The company she worked for had hired a small cabin cruiser from them to test the waters of the Dnipro, which supplied seventy per cent of the nation's water. She decided that when she reached it, she would stop there and use the toilets. She had the access code to the door lock and the kitchen area, where there was a small fridge stocked with bottled water and soft drinks. She looked at the vehicle in front of her, which was a Lada crammed full of people, with cases strapped to the roof. The driver was using his mobile.

His phone is working, she thought.

Kissie checked the mirror and saw a blue Toyota behind her. The driver was having a heated conversation on his phone. She grabbed at her Samsung. It was showing three bars. At last, she had a signal.

CHAPTER 54

Beb

Katouh had stopped to tend to Beb and Heba. Heba was tired and moody and crying for her mother most of the time. She couldn't understand why she wasn't there and her father was bleeding in a hammock. It was too much for her to comprehend. Katouh felt hopeless. They had been trekking for nearly twenty-four hours without sleep. He was reaching the limits of his physical capabilities, and Beb was becoming more delirious by the hour. He sniffed at the wounds and there was no sign of infection yet, but it was only a matter of time. The combination of heat and open wounds was deadly, and he needed to get Beb to someone who could close them.

He checked the compass and set his direction to north-northwest, hoping beyond all hope that they could intercept the Bedouin caravan. He gauged that he may have another twenty-four hours before it would become too much for Beb and he would lose him. They rode beneath the glaring sun of the Sahara. The horizon blurred into an unrecognisable heat haze as the temperature soared. He thought about the tragic loss of his brother Mohammed, and he wondered what his mother would have made of it all. She had been a good woman, proud but not arrogant, unlike his father. His mother respected his father because of his position as the head of the tribe, but she seldom agreed with his decisions, and she had no qualms about telling him when he was making a mistake. His father would sulk for days when she told him he was wrong. It was a running joke within the family. Whenever he had that familiar pained expression on his face, everyone knew that he had been scolded by his wife. It was a shame that she was no longer with them. If she had been, none of this would have come to pass. The old fool would never have dared to claim his granddaughter as another wife, and Mohammed and his brother would never have been parted from their friends and family in the caravan. Mohammed would be alive today, Beb would be riding his camel, not being carried by one, and his wife would be caring for their daughter.

Katouh watched the shimmering horizon and recognised the change immediately. He made out the colours and shades first and then he made out the patterns which he had been familiar with all his life. They were the shapes of goats and camels and the men and women who rode them. At first, he thought it was just a few and wondered if it was a small group of Tuareg or Bedouin but as the seconds ticked by more and more of them came into view over the horizon. There were five or six, then ten, then twenty, and then many more. He closed his eyes and said a prayer of thanks. There were no caravans this size in the Sahara apart from the Bedouin goat herders. Katouh took his stick and tapped the camel on the shoulder, and it instinctively began to trot. The others followed to keep pace with them.

'We have found them, Heba,' he said. 'Let's go ask them to help make your father well again.'

CHAPTER 55

Kalu

Suzette couldn't get her head around what had gone wrong with her plan. It was as simple as simple could be. Goat boy picks up a bag of drugs and Suzette takes it off him. Simple as simple ever was, yet it had fucked up beyond all recognition and now she was in danger of winding up at the bottom of Thames. It was all so fucked up. The fact that her aunt had decided to invite the goat boy into her operation had been ridiculous from the start. Jet said she felt a connection with him because he had come from Africa, been kidnapped, lost all his family, and then been reunited with his father and sister. Suzette wasn't sure when her aunt developed a conscience, but the 'feeling a connection' nonsense didn't fly. He was a fucking goat boy. There were people far more capable than him, champing at the bit to be given the chance to deal on her behalf. The queue went around the block and back again.

Suzette had decided she was going to push her way to the front of the queue, but it'd gone badly wrong. She had assumed that the goods she'd taken from the goat boy were kosher. And that assumption had placed her in dire straits. There was no way that she could come up with £50,000 in way of compensation. Harry Trainor could go and fuck himself. She thought it was grossly unfair that they were demanding that amount, but then drug gangs were rarely fair. They couldn't even spell fair. They wanted compensation, and she didn't have it, so she needed to find the next best thing, which was the real bag of cocaine.

If she could come up with the goods, she may have a shot at living long enough to try again. It was clear that the goat boy had stashed it somewhere between picking it up at Great Portland Street and her taking it from him at Kennington. She had no idea where he could have hidden it, but he had clearly switched the bags at some point during the handover. There wasn't time to second-guess where it was or ask his friends and family, because as far as she was aware, he didn't have many of either. He lived with his father north of the river and if anybody knew where his hiding place may be, it was him, and she intended to ask him.

She knew he was a doctor at Great Ormond Street, and that he worked in private practice here and there, so she waited in the car park beneath their apartment block. Doctors work long shifts, but he would have to come home at some point, and when he did, she would be waiting.

****

Kalu parked his car and turned off the engine. Two police vehicles and a CSI unit were already there. He could see DS Alfred leaning against the boot of an unmarked BMW, smoking a cigarette. His expression didn't give much away, but he had sounded pissed off when he spoke to him on the telephone. The detective was red-faced and looked like he was sweating. Kalu thought he was a heart attack waiting to happen. The DS took another deep drag, flicked the stump onto the floor, and crushed it with his foot. Kalu opened the door and climbed out, still numb, angry, and frustrated at being duped for so many years, and at the same time, he was terrified about what was happening to Kissie. He still hadn't been able to make contact, and he wasn't sure what he would say when he did.

How are you doing in that war zone and by the way, your brother is dead, but don't worry because he isn't your brother, anyway?

'Dr Sammi,' the DS, greeted him, frowning. 'Does one of these lock-ups belong to you?'

'Yes. I told you that on the telephone.'

'I have to follow procedure,' the DS said. 'Which one is it?'

'That one there,' Kalu said. 'Number three.'

'You didn't mention that you had a lock-up when we asked to search Beb's things?'

'You asked if you could search his bedroom. Why would I?'

'We asked you if we could search Beb's bedroom, obviously looking for the reason he was stabbed,' the detective said. 'It didn't cross you mind he might have stored something here?'

'What, am I supposed to be psychic now?' Kalu asked, losing his temper. 'I'm here voluntarily, detective. I suggest you don't piss me off or you can come back with a search warrant.'

'Oh, sore subject, is it?' the DS mumbled beneath his breath. 'Do you have the key to the lock, please?'

'Yes,' Kalu said, marching to the door. 'I do have the fucking key because it's my lock-up, not my son's, and you need to change your tone with me or you'll get zero cooperation, understand?'

'One hundred per cent, doctor,' the DS said, smirking. 'And we have your permission to search the place?'

'Yes, you do,' Kalu said, struggling with the lock. The key didn't fit into the hole. 'I'm certain it was this key.' He read the brand on the padlock. It was a Yale, but the key was for a Smiths.

'Is there a problem?'

'The lock has been changed,' Kalu said, shaking his head.

'Oops,' the DS, said, frowning. 'Now then, why would someone do that, do you think?'

'I have no idea,' Kalu said. His mobile rang. It was Kissie. He turned and walked away.

'Do not answer that phone,' the DS said.

'It's my daughter, and she's in Ukraine,' Kalu said. He answered it. 'Kissie, can you hear me?'

'I don't care who it is,' the DS said angrily. He stood in front of Kalu.

'Fuck off, detective,' Kalu snapped, pushing past him. He glared at him as he walked away. 'Not you,' he said to Kissie. 'Tell me you're safe.'

'I can't,' Kissie said. Her voice broke, and she tried hard not to break down. 'I'm not safe, Dad.'

'Where are you?'

'South of Chernobyl.'

'So, you got out of Pripyat,' Kalu said, relieved. 'I was so worried. It's so close to the border.'

'We got out, but we lost a few colleagues before we even set off,' Kissie explained. 'They bombed the hotel.'

'Oh no,' Kalu said. 'Tell me where you are and what you're doing?'

'I'm trying to get to Kiev, but it's been horrific, Dad.' She sniffled.

'Who are you with?'

'No one. My colleagues are all dead. Their vehicles were hit by a missile at a checkpoint near Chernobyl. They all died.'

'Are you on your own?'

'Yes.'

'Exactly where are you?'

'I'm on the banks of the River Dnipro, heading south, but the traffic is gridlocked. It's bumper to bumper, crawling at the moment.'

'But you're moving in the right direction.'

'Yes, but I don't want to be here anymore.' She sniffled again.

'Be strong, Kissie.'

'I'm trying.'

'I'm so glad you're okay, Kissie,' Kalu said. 'I've been watching the news. All the roads to Kiev are jammed and the roads south are gridlocked too,' he said. 'It's taking people ten hours to cross to Poland and Moldova.'

'What do you think I should do?'

'You need to get to Kiev and go to the British Embassy. They will put you on a train,' he added. Kissie sniffled. 'Are you listening to me?'

'Yes,' she said. 'I just want to come home,' she cried. 'I don't want to be here anymore.'

'Listen to me, Kissie,' Kalu said. 'The invasion has stuttered. Ukrainian fighters are giving the Russians more than they bargained for. You have time, but you need to get to Kiev.' Kalu racked his brain. 'What are you driving?'

'A Jeep,' she said. 'It was at the checkpoint, but the guards were all murdered. There were sympathisers there, targeting for drones.'

'Is it four-wheel drive?'

'Yes.'

'Can you go off-road and bypass the traffic?'

'The security men said the Ukrainians were planting landmines on the agricultural land.' Kissie sobbed. 'They said we couldn't use the fields.'

'I've seen reports on the news,' Kalu said. 'They're saying that for the benefit of the Russians. They want them to think everywhere is mined, it will slow them down while they sweep for them. They're laying them around small towns where they can't spare troops to defend them. Are you near a small town?'

'No. The nearest town is Selo, about thirty miles south of here,' Kissie said.

'Try to get off-road, Kissie,' Kalu said. 'Use the fields. Jump the queue and don't stop for anything or anyone,' he said, thinking about his next words carefully. 'You remember leaving Monguno, don't you?'

'Yes, a little,' Kissie said.

'You can't trust anyone.'

'I know, Dad,' Kissie sobbed, feeling more alone than ever.

'The Russians are not your biggest concern right now,' he said. 'The people around you are desperate. They will do anything to help their family survive. Don't stop for anyone….' The signal failed. 'Kissie?'

'We're cutting the lock from the door,' the DS shouted.

'Kissie, can you hear me?' Kalu said, panicking. He redialled her number, but the line was dead. 'Kissie?' he said, closing his eyes, but she was gone. He crouched down, sitting on his haunches.

'Fuck, fuck, fuck, fuck, fuck,' he said to himself. 'Be safe, little girl,' he said, biting his lip. 'Be safe and come home to me,' he whispered to the sky above him.

He heard footsteps approaching and looked up to see a uniformed officer. She looked embarrassed to be there.

'The DS is asking if you could come to the lock-up,' she said. 'Sorry, but he needs to speak to you.'

'My daughter is in Ukraine,' Kalu said, gesturing to his phone. 'We haven't been able to communicate since the invasion started. That was the first time we have spoken.'

'I'm sorry to hear that,' the constable said. 'Is she near the frontline?'

'She was,' Kalu said. 'She's trying to drive south to Kiev, but the roads are blocked.'

'That must be worrying for you,' she said.

'Worrying?' Kalu repeated. 'You could say that.' He stood up and put his mobile away. 'Let's go and see what your sergeant wants, shall we?'

'Thank you, doctor,' she said, looking relieved.

'We don't want him having a heart attack,' Kalu said quietly. They approached the lock-up, and the search was underway. The Beetle had been pushed out onto the car park.

'Do you have the key to this toolbox?' the DS asked curtly. Kalu shook his head. 'Is this your toolbox?'

'Nope,' Kalu said.

'Cut it off,' Alfred ordered.

The lock was removed with bolt cutters and a detective opened the lid. Inside was a locker key and a bag of white powder. It was weighed, and the bag pierced. A minute amount was taken and put into a plastic vial and shaken. The liquid remained clear.

'It's not cocaine,' the detective said. 'It's probably benzocaine or lidocaine.'

'They're pharmaceutical drugs used as cutting agents to increase the profit on cocaine,' the DS said.

'Really?' Kalu said sarcastically.

'Yes.'

'You do realise I have a PhD in medicine?' Kalu asked, shaking his head. 'I do know what they are and what they're used for.'

'So, we have cutting agent but no cocaine,' the DS said. 'Where is the cocaine?'

'Fuck off,' Kalu said, walking away. 'The next time you talk to me, get a warrant and my solicitor will be there,' he added over his shoulder. 'You're a fucking idiot.'

'I'm an idiot?' the DS called after him. 'I'm not the man who lived with an impostor for ten years thinking it was my son.'

Kalu paused, his temper frayed. He wanted to run at the police officer and punch him in the face until it was mush. Anger bubbled to the surface, oozing from every pore. He wanted to scream.

'I'll wager the cocaine is in the locker that this key fits?' the DS called. 'And when we find it, you'll have some questions to answer and you'll answer them, like it or not.'

'I'm shaking in my boots,' Kalu said, opening his car door.

'You should be,' the detective said, smiling. 'Your credit cards, your money, your lock-up, which you failed to mention.' He winked. 'Can you see where this is going?'

Kalu started the engine and reversed out of the car park. His mind raced with what the police officer had said. *Your credit cards, your money, your lock-up, and a dead man who was your son but isn't?*

The drive back home was slow and painstaking, but he reached the underground car park safely. He turned off the engine and climbed out of the vehicle, shattered and emotionally drained. His thoughts were with Kissie. He didn't care less if the police found a ton of cocaine. He would tell them where to shove it. He needed to speak to the Home Office and see what could be done to rescue Kissie from the nightmare in Ukraine.

'You're the goat boy's father, right?' a female voice asked. He turned to see a pretty black woman leaning against one of the concrete columns, which supported the building. Her eyes were bright and intelligent, but there was an air of menace around her.

'The "goat boy"?' Kalu asked, confused.

'Beb,' she said, smiling. 'He was a goat herder, right?'

'He travelled with a Tuareg caravan in the Sahara Desert,' Kalu said. 'He was kidnapped when he was young.' Kalu frowned. 'I'm sorry. Who are you?'

'My name doesn't matter,' she said. 'The goat boy dropped me in deep shit. He was carrying something valuable, but it's gone missing, and I need to know where he would have hidden it.'

'Ah, I see,' Kalu said. 'I think I should call the detective in charge of the investigation.' He took out his phone and scrolled to DS Alfred's number. 'Here it is.' He pressed *call*.

'Drop the phone,' the woman snarled, pulling a knife. It flicked open, the blade as long as the handle, sharp on both sides. She waved it in his face. Kalu stumbled backwards, trying to avoid the stiletto knife.

'Did *you* stab him?' he asked, his ear to the phone. There was no signal in the basement car park. She waved the knife again.

'Put the fucking phone down, or I'll cut you,' she growled.

Kalu glanced at his phone, realising it was useless. He threw it in her face, splitting her lip. She squealed like a wounded animal and stabbed at him. The knife cut his wrist as he tried to deflect it, but she kept coming, stabbing and slashing. He punched her in the cheek, but it didn't slow her. It made her more frantic.

'I need that bag,' she screamed. She stabbed Kalu in the side, below the ribcage. He grabbed her and held her close, tripping as they staggered around. They fell, Kalu on top of her, their eyes locked in battle. Her mouth opened, and she croaked, blood tricked from the corner of her lips. He watched the light in her eyes fade, her pupils narrowed, and the light went out.

CHAPTER 56

Oke & Isime, Monguno

Fanna walked up the stairs to the first floor, looking for Oke. She was shocked when she saw her. Oke was lying on her back, eyes closed, blisters on her cheeks. Oke coughed and turned onto her side, almost choking. She spat congealed blood onto the floor. Isime put a cup of water next to her and Oke sipped from it.

'How long has she been like this?' Fanna asked.

'Since yesterday,' Isime said.

'I'm sorry to hear about your son,' Fanna said.

'Thank you,' Isime said. 'Do you know where they are taking the dead?'

'No,' Fanna said, 'but the Boko men are all sick. They are not coming in for the dead as often. The last who came in looked ill. They could barely lift the bodies. It must be spreading through the ranks,' she said.

'Good,' Oke said.

'They have put us in here, but it hasn't stopped it spreading,' Fanna said, shaking her head. 'Something is going on. I can feel it.'

'General Bassi has done something stupid.' Oke groaned. 'You mark my words, if the other Boko men are getting sick, he has brought whatever caused this back to Monguno and he doesn't know how to control it. The man is stupid and stubborn.'

'I'm worried if they're not coming in for the dead anymore,' Fanna said.

'What are they doing with them when they take them away?' Isime asked.

'Why don't you go and see for yourself?' Oke croaked. 'Are there still guards outside?'

'There were this morning but they've gone and their vehicles have gone too,' Isime said. 'I've been watching them through the window, trying to work out which direction they took Mahid. The last technical went north, but it hasn't come back.' Isime stopped and walked towards the window. 'Can you hear that?' she asked, frowning.

'What is it?' Oke asked, coughing again.

'Engines,' Fanna said. 'Lots of them.'

Isime and Fanna were standing at the window when the first trucks arrived. There were five of them. Boko men dismounted, carrying wooden boards and planks. They headed towards the building with purpose. There was a lot of shouting and arguing going on.

'What are they doing?' Fanna asked.

'They're boarding up the windows,' Isime said, shaking her head. 'Why would they do that?'

They watched with morbid fascination as they were entombed in the building. One of the men began arguing. Some of the others turned on him.

'What is going on?' Oke asked.

'One of the men is saying they shouldn't be doing this,' Isime said. 'He says the school is full of women and children, but the others are saying it is full of the sickness and it has to be contained.'

'They've boarded up the main entrance,' Fanna said. 'Are they going to stop us leaving?'

'No,' Oke said. She coughed and closed her eyes. 'They're going to set fire to the school with us in it.'

CHAPTER 57

Kissie, River Dnipro

Kissie swore at the phone as she dropped it onto the passenger seat. It had been so good to hear her father's voice again, but now she felt lonelier than ever. They had been an emotional crutch for one another since arriving in London. Their loss was immense but shared. His words echoed around her mind. He told her to get off-road and jump the queue by using the fields. The never-ending line of traffic in front of her told her she should. She looked to her right, but the land there was crisscrossed with canals and dams, and she couldn't see any safe way to navigate them without ending up at a dead end. It was like a maze of waterways linked by locks. There was no way through.

When she looked to her left, there were low hedges which led onto agricultural land, and the river was five-hundred yards beyond that. It looked like a meadow waiting to be ploughed, but it ran as far as she could see. The grass was knee deep and there was no visible water to navigate. She couldn't see any obvious obstacles, like ditches or stone walls. Kissie looked at the line of vehicles in front of her. It stretched to the horizon. She checked the mirror, and it was the same story behind her. Her father hadn't been wrong about much in her life, so it would be foolish to disregard his advice now, when she needed it most. She had to do something or sit there like a lamb waiting for the slaughter.

Kissie put the Jeep into first gear and as the vehicle in front crawled away from hers, she had the space to manoeuvre. She steered the Jeep left and accelerated slowly, crunching her way through the sparse hedgerow and onto the meadow. It was bumpy, but more than manageable. She dropped the Jeep into four-wheel-drive and headed south, running parallel with the line of gridlocked traffic, attracting a lot of attention from other drivers. Horns were sounded and fists raised. Some people were laughing, but most were pissed off. The expressions on their faces told the story. The vehicles behind her were clearly impressed with her ingenuity and, to her surprise, several of them tried to follow her. She could see them making their way through the gap the Jeep had made. She smiled as she watched the Toyota which had been directly behind her, trying to navigate its way along the field, followed by a line of others, who were desperate enough to try it. The ground was firm enough for now, but she wondered how those vehicles would cope if the ground became a little bit softer. They had narrow wheels and were overloaded with people and their belongings.

She trundled along for several miles, keeping the Jeep in low gear and engaged in four-wheel-drive. It was eating up the miles with ease, unlike some of the vehicles behind her, which had become bogged down. There was no consideration for one another as the vehicles raced across the field in no order, overtaking each other, like an episode of the *Wacky Races*. Many of them were losing their loads, their cases, and clothing scattered across the fields. Kissie wasn't sure what to make of it. Part of her was glad that there were other human beings in the same situation as her within touching distance, while another part of her could see no empathy between them. The cars bogged down were being overtaken and left to fend for themselves. Consideration for anybody else's plight was absent. It was survival of the fittest as the cars behind her bumped into each other, vying for the best position to follow in her tracks.

Her father had warned her that her biggest threat was not the invading army but the desperate people who were trying to escape from it. She remembered many of their conversations over the years about how the people of Monguno had reacted when the Boko Haram invaded their town. Friends were no longer friends, acquaintances were nothing more than that, it became dog eat dog, and survival of the fittest. It was frightening to see how human nature changed when people were put into dangerous situations; self-preservation overtakes everything else.

She had taken her father's advice and gone off-road in order to overtake the hundreds of people who were waiting in the queue in front of her. Obviously, others had seen that jumping the queue was possible, and then the chaos behind her ensued. She drove parallel to the road for approximately thirty km until she reached the point of the river where the boathouse was situated. She could see it standing tall on the riverbank. It was a big building designed to cater for large groups of students learning to row and sail. The research boat was moored in a different shed at the rear of the building. A narrow access road led down towards the river and into a small car park. She steered the Jeep through the hedgerow and out of the meadow, onto the access road, dropping the vehicle into two-wheel drive, and she headed towards the boathouse. To her dismay, she saw that several of the trailing vehicles were following her, unaware it was a dead end.

Kissie pulled the Jeep to a halt and got out, closing the door and locking the vehicle with the remote. As she walked away, the first of the convoy of following vehicles slid to a halt on the gravel. The driver wound down the window and shouted to her in Ukrainian, but she didn't understand a word of their language. Please and thank you was about the limits of her Ukrainian. She shrugged and shook her head and said that she spoke English. The Ukrainian man spoke quickly and angrily, and she wasn't sure why he was becoming annoyed with her. Kissie pointed back to the main road and told him it would be better if they went back that way, but his English was as good as her Ukrainian. More vehicles pulled into the car park and questions were asked of the driver in the first vehicle. A discussion ensued, which very quickly turned into an argument as the first driver wanted to reverse his vehicle but couldn't do so, because of half a dozen vehicles that were backed up behind him. The drivers were looking confused as they realised there was no more road to follow unless they wanted to swim.

Kissie decided to use their arguments as the distraction she needed to slip away, and she walked around the building to the entrance door. She tapped in the access code and the door clicked open. It was a massive relief. She moved inside and closed the door behind her, slotting two security bolts closed. She leant back against it and closed her eyes, taking a series of deep breaths to calm her nerves. She was feeling less vulnerable having made so much progress without encountering any more disasters. The Jeep had navigated the fields perfectly and the distance between her and Pripyat was now considerable, and that gave her a sense of security for the moment.

When she'd caught her breath, she walked along the corridor and used the access code again to open the kitchen door. Stepping inside, it was spick and span, as it always was. There were six long tables with benches to accommodate visiting students. The river crew were fastidious about keeping it clean and tidy. She opened the fridge and was pleased to see that it was stocked up with bottles of water and cartons of soft drinks. There was a vending machine against the wall, which was stocked with chocolate bars, crisps, nuts, and an assortment of protein snacks. Kissie walked to the far end of the room, where the back door led to the boat shed. It couldn't be seen from outside, neither from the land nor from the river, unless the boat shed doors were open. They were only opened when the boat was leaving or returning. The boat was docked where it always was, tied to iron mooring hoops. It was rocking a little as the river lapped at the hull. As soon as she saw the boat, she knew what she had to do.

It was as if a light bulb had come on in her mind. There were no traffic jams on the river and there were no landmines, and there were no soldiers. There would be nothing between her and Kiev. Kissie went back to the kitchen, and she searched the cupboards, finding some empty carrier bags. She filled them up with water and Coke. Seeing the chocolate bars in the vending machine had triggered hunger pangs. She hadn't eaten for so long her stomach thought her throat had been cut. She patted her pockets but knew she had no coins or notes. She chuckled to herself dryly as she realised, under the circumstances, it really didn't matter. She picked up one of the chairs and smashed the protective glass, feeling like a character in an apocalyptic movie, which, with hindsight, was exactly what she was. She loaded chocolate bars and protein snacks into the bags until they were full. If she couldn't eat them all, others would. She knew the city would be emptied of its food and water supplies rapidly, as people stockpiled.

When she was happy with her supplies, she walked back to the boat shed. As she did, she could hear people banging on the front door. Her heart quickened as she realised what was about to happen. The people who were trying to escape would have followed her to see why she was going inside. When they realised there was food, water, and supplies, the place would be ransacked within minutes, and they would take hers, too. That was the way it worked. The strongest eat, while the weak starve.

Kissie shut the door and bolted it behind her, before unfastening the bow and stern ropes. It would buy her precious minutes if anyone realised where the door led to. She pressed the button which opened the bay doors, stepping onto the bulkhead as quickly as she could. She had piloted the launch several times, and she started the engine. As she navigated the boat quietly onto the huge river, the sound of splintering wood came from inside the boathouse.

It was a straightforward sail to the city and would take two hours or so. Once she reached the docks, it would be a short walk to the British Embassy. Someone inside that building would help her to get away from the war zone and back home. That was the plan. She opened up the engine and took control of the rudder wheel, heading south. For the first time since the invasion, she felt safe and positive.

The engine purred and the sound of water splashing soothed her being. She heard a familiar sound and her soul turned to ice. Kissie turned and looked back. The boathouse exploded, bricks and wood launched a hundred feet into the air. A second missile exploded above the car park and Kissie knew all those people would be dead.

CHAPTER 58

Beb & Heba

Katouh had gambled on finding the Bedouin caravan, and his gamble had paid off, to a degree. The surgeon who lived and travelled with them was a kind and considerate woman and she spent six hours with some of her medically trained companions, and they managed to stem Beb's bleeding. They pumped him full of fluids and brought him back from the brink of death.

Katouh and Heba had tried to stay awake during the operation but hadn't been able to fight the exhaustion, and they slept for a long time. When he awoke, he was summoned to the surgeon's tent, and she explained to him that although they'd done their best and stopped the bleeding, she could not remove the bullet from his chest because it was positioned so close to his heart. She explained to him that unless he had surgery, in a fully equipped hospital, with a skillful cardiac surgeon to hand, his recovery would be temporary, and the bullet would move and tear vital tissue. Katouh had asked her if she had any ideas of how this could be done, because he had none left. He had played his hand and had nothing more to give.

There was a slim chance. Because of the number of migrants trying to cross the desert, the Red Cross had set up a series of first-aid posts in Nigeria, Chad, and on the Libyan border. She knew of one in an abandoned town called Timimoun, which was resupplied on a regular basis by helicopter. The supplies were then distributed by Land

Rovers to the north towards Libya and to the south towards Chad. She told him that if they could reach the town, the Red Cross might be able to fly Beb out of the desert to a hospital where they had a proper operating theatre and surgeons available. It was his only chance, but it could be done. There was no way Beb could be moved by camel. It would kill him, so she sent some of the Bedouin riders out on a reconnaissance mission and two days later they returned, saying that the Red Cross had agreed to send a Land Rover ambulance to recover Beb. They would take him to the first-aid station at Timimoun.

Katouh was both saddened and relieved. He knew that the Red Cross were good people and that they would take Beb and look after him as best as they could, and they would also take his daughter and look after her. It would be a bittersweet moment when the ambulance arrived to take them away, leaving him alone in the desert. There would be no point in him travelling along with them for company, as when the helicopter arrived, there would only be room for the injured man and his daughter.

When the time came, Katouh wanted to say goodbye to Beb face-to-face, but he was unconscious and unresponsive, although his vital signs were strong and it appeared that he was on the mend. He wasn't aware of what was going on. Katouh had to settle for shaking his limp hand and kissing his forehead, promising him that while he was being taken care of in a hospital somewhere, he would be scouring the desert in search of his wife Amira. And when he said goodbye to Heba, she cried, but he held her tightly and whispered in her ear, 'I will find your mother, and I will bring her back to you, Heba,' he said, kissing her cheek. 'On my life, that is my promise to you.'

CHAPTER 59

London

Kalu spent a very uncomfortable night and most of the next day in the holding cells. Being held in police custody on suspicion of murder was no joke. They had let him make one phone call, which was to his solicitor, who had no experience of dealing with criminal cases, but he worked in a practice where some of his colleagues did. He said that he would send the best man for the job as soon as he possibly could. So far that man had not materialised, and Kalu was becoming increasingly frustrated.

The more he thought about the facts of his situation, the worse it looked. The cards were stacked against him, no matter how innocent he was in reality. Sometimes, just looking guilty was enough to make you guilty in the eyes of the law. Reasonable doubt wasn't always reasonable. When the police had arrived at the car park where Suzette had attacked him, he couldn't have looked more guilty than he did. There was a pretty young woman lying on the concrete with a stiletto knife stuck in her chest, which had punctured her heart, and he was standing there covered in her blood.

He had been questioned briefly at the scene and then taken to the accident and emergency department of the closest hospital, escorted by uniformed officers. He had received thirty stitches in total in his hands, arms, and the wound to his abdomen.

Detective Supt Alfred was informed, and Kalu was immediately arrested on suspicion of the murder of Suzette Unganu. Of course, he denied that he had murdered Suzette. It was self-defence. That was as clear as day, in his own mind. However, it wasn't as straightforward looking from an objective point of view. Kalu was certain that he hadn't actually touched the knife with his hands, and that it had been in Suzette's when they fell over. His prints wouldn't be on the murder weapon, which would mean that it wasn't a murder weapon at all. It was an accident. Suzette had attacked him with a knife. They had scuffled, and it had ended badly for her. He didn't feel guilty or responsible in any way that she was dead. It was her own doing. The knife was in her hand when she fell and that was a positive.

He heard footsteps approaching and the metallic sound of the cell door opening. A middle-aged man, greying, in a dark pinstripe suit, stepped into his cell, a narrow smile on his face.

'My name is Gareth Bolton, and I'm going to be representing you at the request of your solicitor,' he said. 'Shall we go to an interview room?'

'Hello,' Kalu said. 'Anything to get me out of this cell.'

They walked through the custody suite and into a cramped little room, which barely had room for the table and four chairs inside.

'Do you want coffee or a cold drink?' Gareth asked.

'Water, please,' Kalu said. His brief went out of the room and came back with two bottles of water. He placed them on the table. 'Thank you,' Kalu said. 'Are you going to get me out of here?'

'Yes. I hope so,' Gareth said, nodding. He took off his suit jacket. 'I want to go over what I know to make sure it's accurate. I'm aware of the background and some of the facts which led to this altercation with the deceased woman, Suzette Unganu. However, what I need from you are the finer details.'

'Like what?' Kalu asked, sipping the water.

'Did you know the woman?'

'No. I'd never seen her before yesterday,' Kalu said emphatically.

'Okay. Good.' Gareth smiled. 'The police have no evidence of a history between you, which is good, and it's very unlikely they would think you attacked her randomly.'

'She was in my car park, where I live,' Kalu said. 'What was she doing there, except waiting for me?' The lawyer shrugged.

'I don't know.'

'Exactly,' Kalu said. 'The woman attacked me. Why am I locked up?'

'Simple. Because a woman has died and it could be a murder,' Gareth said, shrugging. 'This is a serious incident which has to be investigated. There is no doubt that Suzette Unganu is deceased, and she died from a stab wound to the heart.'

'Yes, but—'

'There are no buts here. You fought with her,' Gareth pointed out. 'You are the only suspect.'

'Yes, I understand that,' Kalu said, sighing. 'But I'm innocent.'

'But that is what guilty people say, especially when they're in police custody,' Gareth said, smiling. 'You must understand that there is a process to follow, and it must be followed.' Kalu nodded. 'However, what we need to do is to convince the police that charging you with her murder would be a complete waste of time, resources, and more importantly, money because the evidence doesn't support a murder charge.'

'I've told them I didn't touch the knife,' Kalu said.

'Tell me in your words, what happened?'

'I arrived home, got out of my car, and she was there. She was aggressive, she was threatening, and when I took out my phone to call the police, she took out the knife and attacked me. I've had thirty stitches in my hands and in my side. She was like a crazy woman.'

'What did she say to you?'

'She asked me if I was the father of the "goat boy",' Kalu said, shaking his head. 'Fucking goat boy…'

'Meaning what?'

'She was talking about my son, Beb,' Kalu said. 'He was stabbed to death, and I bet she did it.'

'Let's not share that thought with the police,' Gareth said.

'Why not?' Kalu asked, frowning.

'Because it gives you motive, of course,' Gareth said. Kalu sighed again, frustrated. 'Okay, the fact you didn't actually touch the knife is a bonus and we don't want to muddy the waters with any of the stuff which has been going on at the periphery of this incident,' Gareth said. 'I have been told that your son was stabbed, in what was probably a drug-related incident, but then things become very unclear as I'm also informed that your son wasn't actually your son.' Kalu was about to speak but Gareth held up his hands and gestured for him to let him finish. 'I know it's a complicated story and I don't mean any disrespect to you, but it doesn't matter. What matters is the method of death that Suzette Unganu suffered. She has a knife in her chest and the police want to say that you put it there. Obviously, we're saying you didn't. The fact you didn't touch the knife at all is a bonus. It was her knife – an illegal spring-assisted knife – and she brought it with her, knowing that there would be an altercation of some kind.'

'She called my son goat boy, and she said that he had dropped her in the shit by losing something of value to her and that she needed it.'

'And what did you think she was talking about?'

'I don't know,' Kalu said, shaking his head. 'I can only assume it was something illegal, probably drugs. If they were dealing, I don't know anything about it. Detective Superintendent Alfred thinks I have something to do with it, which is ridiculous.'

'It happens,' Gareth said.

'I am a doctor. I don't sell drugs and if my son was dealing class-As, I don't know anything about it. I didn't even know he wasn't my son until this happened.' Kalu stood up and paced the room. 'I need my mobile returned to me. I need to be able to take calls from my daughter.'

'Your daughter is in Ukraine, I believe?'

'Yes. She was with a research team in Pripyat on the border with Belarus when they invaded. She's trying to get to Kiev, on her own, all alone, in a fucking war zone, and I'm stuck in this cell with my thumb up my arse.'

'They won't part with it,' Gareth shrugged. 'All I can do is get you a new phone and when I get you out of here, I can give it to you.'

'That is no good to me. All my numbers are stored in it. I need my phone and I need it now,' Kalu said, losing his temper. 'I shouldn't be in here. And my daughter is stranded. I spoke to her and tried to reassure her, but we got cut off. My son was stabbed, and my daughter is in terrible danger. Does anybody give a fuck what is going on in my world?'

'If I'm honest with you, Kalu,' Gareth said, shaking his head. 'Nobody gives a fuck what is going on in your world outside of this investigation.'

'Brilliant!'

'That may sound harsh, but it's the truth. It's my job to get you out of here and then you can deal with whatever else you have to do but at this moment in time, you must deal with the job at hand, which is convincing the police that you didn't murder Suzette Unganu.'

Chapter 60

Oke & Isime

Isime watched the Boko men boarding up all the ground-floor windows and doors. They battened thick planks of wood over the fire exits to ensure nobody could escape the building, except from a first-floor window, and that would be brave or stupid. Armed men stood watching their colleagues working, and they all looked ill. Most of the infected in the building were unaware of the danger surrounding them, but the uninfected women and children were fully aware, and panic was spreading through the building. People were running from one end of the school to the other, on both the ground and first floors, looking for a means of escape. One of the older boys was in his early teens, and a fit and agile young lad. He tried to climb out of the first-floor window at the back of the building, to lower himself onto a tree, which was growing nearby. He was spotted, and two of the Boko men raised their weapons and opened fire. The boy was hit multiple times before he crashed into the bushes below. His mother screamed for him to get up, but her son was dead before he hit the ground.

Fanna was sitting as close to Oke as she dared. Her condition was worsening, but despite the panic, she'd managed to remain calm. Oke was as solid as a rock.

'Fanna,' Oke said. 'Listen to me.'

'What is it?'

'My sister is traumatised,' Oke said. 'I need her to be strong for my children.' Fanna shook her head. But the last thing Oke needed was sympathy. 'Don't shake your head at me. I know what I'm saying, and it needs to be said. No one in this school has made a recovery once they show signs of sickness, and it would be arrogant and foolish of me to think I'm going to be any different from those who have died. I'm not leaving this place alive.'

'Shush now. Don't talk like that.'

'I am not going to get better, and my sister will need to take care of my children and herself. I know you have children of your own to look after, but stay together and you will be stronger. Try to get as many of the uninfected out of here before it's too late,' Oke said.

'But how? There doesn't appear to be any way out of the building,' Fanna said, shaking her head.

'There is a way from the ground floor,' Oke said. 'But you must be quick.'

'Tell me where it is,' Fanna said.

'When they built the shower room, they had to put drains in, and the builders had to dig trenches. There was a lot of arguing one day because they'd dug them in the wrong place. They were supposed to go out of the front of the school into an existing drain, but they dug in the wrong direction.' Oke coughed and blood dribbled from her lips. 'They dug the channel through the back of the building by mistake.'

Isime sat down near them. Oke's son, Kareem, sat on her knee. Isime kissed his forehead. The little boy didn't take his eyes from his mother's face. Seeing his mother so sick and not being able to hug her was distressing. He wanted to hold her tightly and not let go.

'You must look after them for me,' Oke said, squeezing her eyes closed. Tears leaked from the corners. 'Promise me you will.'

'Don't say that. You can look after them yourself,' Isime said, wiping her own tears away.

'Don't make me say it again in front of my children,' Oke said. 'Will you look after them for me, sister?'

'Of course, I will,' Isime said, hugging Kareem tightly. 'They are my blood.'

'Oke knows a way out,' Fanna said.

'Do you remember when we used to go around the back of the building and explore the tunnel?' Oke asked. Isime nodded. 'They never filled in the drainage ditch, they just covered it over,' she added. 'It's still there beneath the shower room.'

'Yes. I can remember we thought we were explorers.' Isime smiled through her tears. 'I remember going home and Mother was very angry with us. She put us in the bath and scrubbed us until we were sore.'

'They were running out of time and money, so they just put boards over the ditch and tiled over it. I remember the sound of the floor when we had shoes on. It sounded hollow. The ditch ran out of the school and into the trees. You will be able to take the uninfected along the tunnel beyond where the Boko can see you. The trees will hide you until you reach the edge of town.'

'We should all go now,' Isime said, crying. 'We can get you to a proper doctor.'

'The proper doctors are dead. There are none here anymore,' Oke said, shaking her head and closing her eyes. 'I'm infected and I will only be a danger to you and others if I'm moved. You still have a chance.'

'If they set fire to the school, we can't just leave you to burn to death,' Isime said, shaking her head. Her eyes filled with tears again. 'I am not leaving you here.'

'You have to. We can get the infected who can be moved down the stairs into the shower room,' Oke said. 'I can walk that far, no problem. So can some of the others.'

'Why the shower room?'

'Because of the water. You must turn on all the showers and leave with the children. The water will stop us from burning, although it hardly seems to matter,' Oke said, sighing. 'If I'm honest. I would rather burn than suffer this any longer.'

'That's a good idea, Oke,' Fanna said. 'We could get the children into the trees and hide them and then come back for you. We may be able to find a stretcher to carry you.'

'How are you going to carry me on a stretcher and not become infected?' Oke asked. 'And then what? Are you going to watch me rot and die?' Oke said, coughing. 'Listen to me. I'm dying. Take enough supplies. Then get you and the children out of here.'

'Oke—'

'Shush now. This is hard enough. They're going to burn the building to rid the town of the infected, but that is how stupid they are. It is already too late to stop the spread. That is why the men who are coming to remove the dead are so weak and sick themselves.' Oke coughed, and her face grimaced in pain. 'They are boarding up the school to stop the spread of the sickness when the sickness is already out there. It always was. The epicentre of this outbreak is not this building.'

'What will happen to us?' Isime asked. 'Where can we go? There will never be an escape from these animals.'

'They don't rule the world, Isime,' Oke said, her voice weakening. 'They are here, but my guess is that most of them are infected. This is your opportunity to get as far away as you possibly can. Go far away where there are no Boko men. Go far away from here and live your life, but look after my children, dear sister.'

'I will look after them,' Isime said, weeping openly now. 'And I promise you they will be loved, and I will keep them safe.'

The smell of petrol drifted to them, and they could hear raised voices coming from outside and the crackling of wood burning. The smell of fumes became stronger very quickly, and smoke began to drift over the stairwell and into the first-floor classrooms. Isime went to the window, anxiously looking at what was going on outside. The far end of the building was already on fire, the flames licking up to the upper floors and catching the roof. She could see men stacking piles of wood against the school walls, covering them with petrol, and lighting them with wooden torches.

'They have set it alight!' Isime said, panicking.

'We don't have time to debate this any longer,' Oke said. 'You need to take all the healthy women and children to the shower room and break through the tiles into the drainage ditch.'

'I can't leave you,' Isime said, sobbing.

'I need you to save my children, Isime,' Oke whispered. 'Do as I have asked you. Do your bit, and I will do my mine.'

CHAPTER 61

Marrakesh

Dr Hassan checked on his patient, happy that the operation to remove a bullet from his chest had gone as well as it could have. The young man was a medical anomaly. The fact he was alive at all was completely unexpected and difficult to explain. He was clearly a strong young man with a powerful reason to stay here on Earth a while longer. His determination to survive had got him this far, and he didn't appear to be ready to leave just yet.

The Red Cross had brought him in from the desert, and he had been transferred from one hospital to another before being flown to Marrakesh. It was decided that the operation was too difficult for many to undertake, and Dr Hassan had been singled out as one of the few surgeons who could carry out the procedure successfully. The patient had been in and out of consciousness, sometimes delirious, sometimes appearing to be completely aware of his surroundings, although these episodes of lucidity were short-lived. One thing was for certain, Dr Hassan was convinced that he had seen Beb before, but it was many years ago. When he saw his name, it rang bells in his mind. Dr Hassan was reminded of a catastrophic shift in his own life. He had stored the memories of that traumatic event and kept them covered up, but now they'd come to the fore.

Dr Hassan had been forced to leave his hometown of Monguno many years before. He had known another doctor from the town, and they'd studied at the same university, but not at the same time. His name was Kalu Sammi. He knew Kalu had a son called Beb, as they were friends when they were younger. During a lucid moment, when he asked Beb how he had sustained the gunshot wounds, the patient had told of events from leaving Monguno to escape Boko Haram, heading north with his family, and his father being a doctor. When he mentioned the recent part of his life, he asked for his wife, Amira, and his child, Heba. Hassan had explained that his daughter was downstairs in the creche being cared for by professionals. When Hassan had said he didn't know about his wife, Beb had become so upset that he had to be sedated.

He was now convinced this man was the boy he had known. Beb would need weeks of after-care and Hassan would oversee his treatment personally. There was only one thing more that he could do for him. Hassan was sitting at his desk, searching online for Dr Kalu Sammi.

CHAPTER 62

Kissie, Kiev

As Kissie approached Kiev docks, a police launch approached her at high speed, circling her to see who was on-board. She was expecting twenty-questions, but they made their assessment and decided she wasn't a threat and they roared off towards the port, which was situated on the left bank of the Dnipro. A quick Google search earlier that year had told her the docks were in the Podil area of the city. Three huge cargo cranes towered above the docks, but they were idle. The moorings stretched for several kilometres and were home to a fleet of leisure cruisers and passenger ferries, which were all tied up. The bigger container ships were to the south of the city, which meant Kissie could get to the jetty without any issues with the cruisers or having to avoid bigger boats. There was nothing on the river. Everything was stationary. It looked like the docks were at a standstill. She slowed the boat and aimed for an empty mooring, close to a group of trawlers. A couple of fishermen shouted to her in Ukrainian, but she just waved and smiled. It was the best she could offer. She knew that the embassy was on the edge of the Podil area, in Pecherskyi. She checked her phone where she had the number and address stored in case of emergencies. It was at Nine Desyatynna Street and she brought up the directions.

Kissie tied up the boat and took a laundry sack from the cabin. She filled it with her supplies and climbed off the boat, onto the wharf. It was less than a mile to the embassy and she made good time. The streets were quiet and there was an air of anticipation hanging over the city. A small supermarket had a queue outside, which stretched around the block. There was a run on supplies already. Worried faces watched from the windows of the apartments, which were situated on tree-lined streets which could have belonged in any European capital.

The embassy was a two-storey building with an ornate stone balcony overlooking the street. Huge concrete blocks were painted in blue and gold and positioned at the front of it, preventing a truck bomb from ploughing into the building. As the Russian army poured over the borders, it seemed ISIS paled into insignificance.

There were armed guards at the entrance and as Kissie approached them, they frowned. The colour of skin was a barrier everywhere except when she'd been a child in Africa. She showed them her British passport and explained her situation and they questioned her about where she'd travelled from. They were especially interested that she had seen the fighting, and she was shown inside to a waiting area, which was crammed with people. Men, women, and children occupied every chair, window ledge, and empty bit of floor space. The sound of babies crying was disturbing and irritating in equal measure. She found a wall to lean against and occupied it. On the floor next to her was a woman with two young children. She was visibly upset, and the children were teary and snotty-nosed. She was speaking to someone on her mobile in English. The gist of the conversation was that her husband was Ukrainian and wasn't allowed to leave the country. He was heading north to the frontline, leaving her and their children to find a way back to the UK. Kissie looked around the room and wondered what tales of woe there must be. Each person with their own story. The only men in the room were elderly, testament to Ukraine's determination to defend its borders from Putin's tyranny. Kissie felt the pain and desperation in the room, and it sapped what little strength she had left.

'Kissie Sammi?' a woman in her forties called from a door to her left. The door was dark oak, with framed panels and brass furniture.

Kissie held up her hand. 'Can I have a word with you please?' the woman asked, smiling.

'Yes,' Kissie said, reaching into her bag. She gave the snotty children a Mars Bar and a bottle of water each. The mother mouthed *thank you* as Kissie walked away. She approached the woman who had called her. 'I've only just arrived,' she said apologetically. 'There are so many people here.'

'Yes. It's a bit chaotic. I'm Sarah Marshall, and I work for the ambassador,' she added, stepping back to let her through. 'You have made your way from Pripyat?'

'Yes.'

'Follow me, please.'

Sarah led Kissie through a series of wood-panelled corridors and into an office. There were four men seated around a desk, two in army uniform. Kissie was shown to a seat.

'We've been informed you have travelled from Pripyat,' one of the officers said, without introduction.

'Yes,' Kissie said. 'I was in a research team based around Chernobyl.'

'I'm Charles Jones, ambassador to Ukraine, and these gentlemen are military advisors. Colonel Oaks and Brigadier Marks.'

'Nice to meet you,' Kissie said, wondering why she was talking to such high-powered people about getting a train.

'You said you were part of a research team?' Oaks asked. Kissie nodded. 'Where are the rest of your team?'

'They were all killed at a checkpoint on the Chernobyl ring road.'

'That's terrible,' Sarah said. 'We're sorry for your loss.'

'How were they killed?' Marks asked.

'It was a drone attack,' Kissie said.

'How can you be sure?' Oaks asked, frowning.

'The security team told us the Russians were using drones,' Kissie said.

'Who were your security?'

'Tom was British Army and Brad was a US Navy Seal,' Kissie said. The military men exchanged glances. 'There were two French men, both ex-Foreign Legion.' She paused. 'They were excellent at their job and nice men, too.'

'And they said they were using drones based on what?' Marks asked.

'They found a laser designating gimbal, used for targeting a drone from the ground,' she added. The officers looked shocked. 'It was used to target a pickup truck, which was leading our convoy.'

'Good God. Found it where?' the officer asked, shocked.

'In the woods,' Kissie said. 'They killed the men using it.'

'Can you explain what happened?'

'Yes. We approached a checkpoint, but it was unmanned, or appeared to be,' Kissie explained. 'There was a Jeep parked nearby, so one of our security team, Frank, got out of the pickup and went to the sentry box to open the barrier and he was fired at from the woods. The rest of the team got out and engaged the attackers. They were attacked by Russian sympathisers,' Kissie said. 'There was a firefight, and our security killed them. They found the Ukrainian security guards who had been manning the checkpoint, bound and executed in a ditch.'

'How did they identify their attackers as sympathisers?'

'They were wearing combats but not uniforms and their IDs were Ukrainian. One of them had the laser targeting gimbal and Brad, who was the navy seal, said it was the latest technology being used by US special forces in tandem with drones.'

'Did he say what type of gimbal it was?' the officer asked, as if she was stupid. 'It's a lot to ask you to recall that.'

'Yes. It was a GS205-XRZ, US special forces were trialling it last year,' Kissie said. They looked shocked. 'I remember things,' Kissie added.

'You do indeed,' the officer said. 'Say that again, please,' he asked, writing it down as she spoke.

'GS205-XRZ,' Kissie repeated. 'It was white and looked like a speed camera with four lenses.'

'Four lenses,' he repeated, writing it down. The men exchanged glances and looked suitably impressed. 'What is it you were doing there?' the civilian man asked.

'I'm a nuclear biologist, studying the effects of reactor four's meltdown on the environment,' Kissie said, half-smiling. She knew what they were thinking. Black, female, and smart. The condescending glances had vanished.

'And after this engagement, a drone strike killed your friends?'

'There were three actually,' Kissie said. 'I wasn't sure why we had been attacked at the time, but with hindsight, the pickup had a cache of weapons in the flatbed, and we had armed men and women in every vehicle. From an observer's perspective, we could have been a unit of militia, trying to take the checkpoint.'

'Yes, you're right,' the officer said. 'Tell me about the three strikes.'

'The first hit the pickup directly,' Kissie said. 'I was frightened and wet my pants, so I was behind a tree when the second explosion happened. That was an airburst, a hundred metres above the convoy. It showered the area with razor-sharp metal cassettes. Thousands of them. That was followed by an incendiary device. It exploded, and I stayed down for a few minutes. When I looked, the vehicles had been decimated. There were no bodies. There was literally nothing left.'

'How did you get here?' Jones asked.

'I took the Jeep,' Kissie said. 'The road south to Kiev was jammed, so I took a research boat and came down the river.' Kissie explained. 'A drone took out the boathouse not long after I left. There were two missiles. One hit the building, the second was another airburst over the car park, where there were about a dozen vehicles.'

'This is vital information,' Sarah said. The men nodded. 'I assume you're trying to get out of the country?' Kissie nodded. 'We need you to sit down with some of our colleagues in the UK and tell them everything you have told us. It will be fed back to the Ukrainians and could be very useful to them,' she added. 'I'm leaving here in an hour, and you'll be with me. We're taking a military helicopter to Warsaw and then a jet to Stanstead. You'll be debriefed in London when we arrive. It won't take more than a few hours and then you can be on your way, and we'll make sure you get home.'

Kissie nodded and felt drained. She needed to tell her father she was on her way home. She dialled his number, but it was turned off.

****

Katouh found his father's caravan after weeks of trekking through the Sahara. Bedouin nomads had seen them days before and pointed him in the right direction. When he'd approached, the elders of the tribe had welcomed him with caution. The Tuareg have a caste system and despite their differences of opinion, Katouh was still the son of a chief, born from the ruling caste. His father was very poorly, and the elders were concerned for his life. They hadn't sought professional help for his gunshot wounds. When he heard of his son's arrival, Ali demanded he be put in chains and dragged behind a camel until he died. Of course, no one had the appetite for such barbarity and Katouh asked to see his father.

Katouh had sat next to him and spoke calmly and in a gentle voice about what a dreadful chief he had been and how his people would celebrate his passing. His reign would be remembered only for its sadness and unfairness and lack of empathy for anyone but himself. Ali had been furious and insisted that when he recovered, Katouh would be executed, and he would marry Amira. Katouh squeezed his father's nostrils between his finger and thumb hard and placed his other hand over his vile mouth. His father had struggled for a few minutes, but he was weakened by infection and blood loss, and he suffocated quickly.

When Katouh left his tent and announced his father's passing, the elders met immediately, and announced his son and heir as their new chief. Katouh told them he would be away for a while but would return to take his charge.

CHAPTER 63

Kalu

Kalu was at the limit of his patience. He had been interviewed and released without charge. His solicitor had advised him to answer all their questions but not to connect his son with Suzette Unganu or speculate about why he was stabbed. Fifteen minutes after the interview, he was out with a new phone in his pocket. He was dropped off at home by Gareth, and he rushed inside to back-up his data onto his new mobile. He needed to get Kissie's number. There had been no contact since he was arrested and she could be anywhere by now, even dead. He was feeling incredibly emotional and needed to hear her voice.

Kalu went to Beb's room and looked inside. There wasn't too much mess following the police search, and they hadn't left fingerprint dust everywhere. There had been no point in dusting for prints. They had found no evidence of drugs or drug trafficking.

He went to the living room and noticed the light flashing on his landline. Only the hospital called him on that phone. He pressed play, to hear a doctor had left a message about one of the children they were treating at Great Ormond Street. She had passed away the previous night. He poured himself a Scotch and sipped it as he listened to the message again. The parents were such lovely people. He really liked them, and his heart sank for them. Cancer doesn't give a fuck how nice you are. It is ruthless and relentless, coming back just when you think it's fucked off. The next message was his hygienist, confirming a dental appointment. He was going to run a shower when the landline rang.

'Hello, Kalu speaking,' he said.

'Dad, it's me,' Kissie said. 'Listen, I don't have long. I've been trying your mobile, but it's off.'

I've been arrested for murder, he thought. 'It's broken. I have a new one and I'm transferring the number. I was about to message you on my new one,' he mumbled. 'It's so good to hear your voice. Tell me you're in Kiev.'

'No,' Kissie said. 'I'm at Stansted Airport.'

'What?' Kalu said, automatically looking at his watch. 'How on Earth did you get there?'

'It's a long story, but they're taking me to a secret location in London to debrief me,' Kissie said. 'And then they will bring me home.'

'Who will?' Kalu asked. 'Debrief you about what?'

'A laser designating gimbal,' Kissie said.

'Oh, that,' Kalu said, chuckling. 'What are you talking about?'

'I saw some stuff which might be useful to the Ukrainians.'

'I see. Are you hurt?'

'No, Dad,' she said. 'I needed to hear your voice. I have to go. There're police officers here waiting for me. I'll see you later. Love you.'

'I love you too,' Kalu said. He closed his eyes and prayed. 'Thank you,' he whispered.

He placed the phone back on its cradle and it rang immediately. Kalu stared at it and hesitated before picking it up.

'Kalu speaking,' he answered, filling up his Scotch.

'Kalu Sammi?' the voice said.

'Yes. Who is this?'

'Dr Hassan Omar,' he said. 'From Monguno,' he added.

'Hassan?' Kalu said, shocked. 'Wow. How long has it been?'

'Nearly twenty years,' Hassan said.

'Where are you?' Kalu asked. 'You sound like you're making an international call.'

'I'm in Marrakesh.'

'This is amazing,' Kalu said. 'I often wondered what happened to you.'

'You were easier to find than I expected,' Hassan said. 'Look, Kalu, I have some very shocking news for you. I think you should sit down.'

'What?' Kalu said, confused. The hairs on his neck bristled. He sensed something earth-shattering coming. 'What is it?'

'The Red Cross brought a man in with gunshot wounds to the chest and we had to operate, but I managed to speak to him before we took him down,' Hassan said. Kalu couldn't speak. 'His name is Beb Sammi, and he's from Monguno.'

Silence.

'Kalu?'

Silence.

'I knew it was your son as soon as I saw his name.'

'Have you got a picture of him?' Kalu asked cautiously. He couldn't accept the news. It could not be Beb. Beb died in the desert, and someone took his identity.

'Give me your mobile number,' Hassan said. Kalu read it from the paperwork he had. 'I've sent it.'

Kalu felt his phone vibrate and opened the message. He scrolled to the image. Tears streamed from his eyes, and he cried out. It was Beb.

CHAPTER 64

Oke & Isime

Oke held tightly to the banister as she made her way downstairs. She was supporting another lady, who was as sick as she was. They weren't concerned about coming into contact with each other. It was too late for them to avoid the sickness. She could hear the sound of tiles being smashed and water running. The smoke was billowing up the stairwell to the ceiling, black and acrid, and a roaring sound was coming from the other end of the building. Screaming echoed down the hallways. Some were not able to escape the flames without help, and not all the able-bodied people were keen on touching the infected. Some were left where they lay. Oke tried to block it out. They couldn't be helped now. That opportunity had been missed.

Human nature at its best, she thought.

When they reached the shower room, she could see children being lowered into the drainage ditch beneath it. Isime and Fanna were organising the evacuation and there were only a handful of uninfected remaining. Oke saw her children clinging to each other. Her heart broke when Kareem tried to run to her, but the others pulled him back.

'Stay there, son,' Oke said. 'You mustn't touch Mummy. I'm not well,' she said. 'Go with Aunt Isime and I'll catch-up soon.'

'I want to stay with you, Mum!' Kareem shouted. Isime picked him up and lowered him, kicking and screaming, into the tunnel. 'No, I want my mum!'

'I'll see you soon, Kareem,' Oke lied. 'Be good for Aunty Isime.'

'No, I want my mum!'

She could hear him crying until the last of the children were lowered. Her daughter, Rida, was hysterical and waved at her mother, knowing she wasn't going to see her again. She wasn't stupid. The eldest, Najma, blew a kiss. 'I love you, Mum,' she cried as Fanna lowered her down.

'And I love you, Najma,' Oke said. 'Go and live a better life than I have,' she whispered into the smoke. Isime stared, not wanting to go. Oke nodded and smiled. 'Go, Isime. Go and look after my children and live your life,' she said, blowing a kiss. 'I love you, sister.' Isime broke down as she disappeared into the ditch. 'I will look over you all with our mother and father,' she said, closing her eyes. 'Goodbye and God bless you all.'

Isime led the children along the tunnel, stooping as they went. It was longer than she remembered. Twenty minutes later, she could see the light.

The escapees gathered in the trees and looked back at the burning school. It was an inferno burning from end to end. The children wept, and the adults comforted them as much as they could. Isime held Oke's babies, and they sobbed uncontrollably. There was a loud crack and the sound of wood splintering, and the roof collapsed inside. The building folded in on itself as the first floor collapsed into the ground floor and flames spiralled skyward. Isime held her breath, knowing Oke was gone.

CHAPTER 65

Beb sipped water from a straw. He felt like he'd been run over by a bus. The time between being shot, and the present was just a haze. There were memories there, which couldn't be true. He'd seen his mother talking to Oke, telling her off for being dirty from playing in the tunnels beneath their old school. Oke wasn't sad. She was happy to see her mother, and he was happy to see both of them. It felt like forever since he had seen them. His life as a boy, surrounded by females, had been such a happy one. No boy could have been loved more than he had been. He tried to walk to them, and he called to them, but he couldn't reach them, and they didn't hear him. Then smoke came from everywhere and he could feel fire on his skin. Flames flickered between him and them, driving him back, and then they were gone.

'Oke!' he called again, but she wasn't there. It wasn't a dream. It felt like a memory, yet it couldn't be.

Dr Hassan walked into the room, smiling. He was always smiling. There was an aura around him, which glowed but couldn't be seen. He was a good man and a good doctor.

'Morning, Beb,' he said. 'How are you feeling?'

'Like I have a hole in my chest,' Beb said.

'Had,' Hassan said. 'You *had* a hole in your chest, but I fixed it, so cheer up.'

'I am as cheerful as I can be in this hospital,' Beb said, smiling. 'The food is terrible.'

'You've only eaten twice,' Hassan said, frowning.

'Both times were terrible,' Beb said. 'Put me back on a drip.'

'Don't be so ungrateful,' Hassan said, checking his stats.

'Can I see Heba?' Beb asked.

'Would that cheer you up?'

'Always.'

'She's not in the creche today,' Hassan said.

'Why not?'

'She's been busy telling someone all about her adventures getting here,' Hassan said.

'She's a proper little chatterbox,' Beb said. 'Who is she chatting to?'

'Her mother,' Hassan said.

'What?' Beb whispered.

He went to the door and opened it, stepping back to allow Amira to step inside, holding Heba. Beb thought his heart was going to burst. His lips trembled, and he reached out with his good arm. Amira came to him, and they embraced, Heba between them. They stayed that way, without words, for a very long time.

CHAPTER 66

Monguno

Isime watched the school burn, unable to move her eyes from the flames. Black smoke spiralled skyward like a giant mushroom. Even the children had stopped wailing as the group of survivors watched in terror from the trees. Suddenly, gunfire broke the night and the sound of diesel engines drifted to them. Isime watched tanks and armoured vehicles approaching the school along the access road. She watched as heavy machineguns felled the Boko men like a bowling ball scattering ninepins. Some of them returned fire, but their bullets were no match for the armour. Within minutes, the Boko men were wiped out.

'Who are they?' someone asked.

'They're United Nations troops,' Fanna said. 'See the UN on the side of the vehicle.'

'What are they doing here?'

'I don't know, but I can hazard a guess,' Fanna said. 'Whatever General Bassi has done, it's affected other places, not just Monguno. The government must have asked for help from the international community.'

'The troops have Hazmat suits on,' Isime said. 'The sickness must have spread to other places, and they've come to help us.'

'Help us!' a voice called from the darkness.

'Who is that?'

'I don't know,' Fanna said. 'Where are you?'

'In this tunnel, bring us water. We're choking.'

'Oke?' Isime grabbed two water bottles and ran towards the entrance of the tunnel. 'Oke, is that you?'

'Yes, I'm here, sister,' Oke said, coughing.

'We thought you were dead,' Isime said, crying. 'I saw the school collapse.'

'I was waiting to die, and Mother came to me,' Oke said. Isime sobbed. 'She told me I could go into the tunnel and get dirty. She told me to get into the tunnel and everything would be okay.'

'The UN troops have killed the Boko,' Isime said. 'They have Hazmat suits on, sister. They've come to help us!'

EPILOGUE

Three Weeks Later

Kalu and Kissie were standing at the graveside as the coffin was lowered. Damilola Kanye was being buried under his true name. They hugged each other, emotionally confused, burying a man who had been an impostor in their home and in their hearts.

Seeing Beb again had been one of the most traumatic experiences imaginable. There had been tears of sadness and tears of joy and a million questions to ask and answer. Meeting his wife and daughter was the icing on the emotional cake. They were so beautiful; Kissie couldn't stop kissing them and as the days passed, it was as if they'd never been apart. Her love for Beb had been natural, but for Damilola, she'd felt different. Now she knew why.

Kalu had explained to his son why they'd left him behind. It was simply because they thought he was dead and buried in the never-ending dunes. When he told him about his return from the dead and the gold coin, Beb had cried a river and asked to see a picture of the man who had claimed to be him. When he saw the photograph, he identified him as Damilola Kanye, the son of his mother's cousin. And the brutal truth became clear. He hadn't been attacked by pirates or rogue Bedouin from the Blue Mountains. He had been attacked by his only friend, who dumped him in a hole in the sand and left him for dead. It all clicked into place for him.

Beb had described how his life had been when he was sold to the Tuareg. He woke up every day thinking that his parents would come for him that day. There was no doubt in his mind that they were looking for him and one day they would find him and take him with them. For years, he believed that and then one day, he knew they weren't coming. He said it was the saddest moment of his life, realising his family were either dead or had moved on without him. They had left him in the desert alone.

Listening to him talk about those days was soul-destroying for Kalu, to think that his son had been alive and desperate for him to rescue him, praying each day that he would come. Beb felt no malice or regret because he met Amira in the desert. They planned to join Kalu and Kissie in London, but the visa process was slow and complicated, but their days of being nomads were over.

Kalu and Kissie said goodbye to Damilola the best way they could. There were such mixed emotions. He had been Beb for so many years, but now he was the man who had tried to kill Beb, to steal his life. He had succeeded in stealing some of theirs too, and that was impossible to forgive. Kalu felt love for his son and granddaughter like he had never felt before. He spoke to Beb every day and hounded the Home Office daily for updates on their immigration status. The separation anxiety was intense, and he couldn't shake it. He needed them to be there with him and Kissie. Their family had been through so much loss and pain, it was difficult to handle the absolute joy of being reunited without feeling its fragility. Life could take them away from them again in the blink of an eye. Nothing in this life was certain, especially tomorrows.

When they got home that night, they ate a little but didn't have much of an appetite. Kissie had been surfing the internet when a news story about Nigeria caught her eye. It mentioned Monguno. She read the article, and it led to others. Kalu was reading a report for work when he heard a bloodcurdling scream.

'Father!' Kissie screamed. 'Oh my God, come here!' She covered her face with her hands. 'Look at this!'

'What is it?' Kalu asked, panicking. He ran to her and looked at her laptop. It was a newsreel from Monguno. It took him a moment to compute what he was looking at.

'The United Nations sent troops into Nigeria,' Kissie said, shaking her head.

'I saw it this morning,' Kalu said. 'They're accusing general Bassi of acquiring a novichok agent from the Soviets?'

'Yes, and the idiot doesn't know how to store it or deploy it, so hundreds were infected, and thousands displaced from their villages and towns,' Kissie said excitedly. She was distressed and jabbering. 'Look at this…'

Kissie replayed the article she'd watched. The reporter was inside a hospital somewhere in the north of the country. Then it skipped to footage of some of the patients. Kalu was focused on the journalist.

'Look!' Kissie said. She pointed to a patient in the background. The woman was sitting up in bed. The skin on her face looked patchy and burnt. Kalu looked and took off his glasses. He wiped them and put them back on.

'Can't you see?'

He looked at the woman again.

'Look at the woman next to the bed,' Kissie said, almost hysterical. 'Oh my God, can't you see it?'

Kalu looked again. First at the patient, then at her visitor. He looked at Kissie and shook his head.

'That can't be,' Kalu said. 'That fucking cannot be…' His voice trailed to a whisper. 'They are the image of your mother,' he said. 'How can this be?'

'That is Oke and that is Isime!' Kissie screamed. 'That is them, Father. As sure as I'm sitting here, it's them!'

They both stared at the screen in shock. He held Kissie to his chest and felt her sobbing. Kalu felt tears spilling from his eyes as he looked at his daughters and he knew he had to go to find them.

'We must go there, Kissie,' Kalu said. 'We must go back to Monguno and find your sisters.'

****

Jet Unganu was standing at the graveside, watching her niece being put into a hole in the ground. She was heartbroken. Her death had been so unavoidable. There was no need for her to try to go it alone. She could have had anything she wanted. Money was no object. It never had been. The death of her mother had hit them hard, and Jet tried to step into her shoes and be a mother to Suzette. She had fucked it up and it hurt. The funeral was grim and forgettable. She didn't see the faces around her or hear their condolences. It was a blur. She took out her phone and opened a text message. It was a photograph of Dr Kalu Sammi. She nodded and typed her reply.

I want him dead. Him and anyone related to him. Kill them all.

When?

ASAP

She put the phone away. Her asset was a true professional, and she was good at her job.

The Sammi family was in grave danger once again.